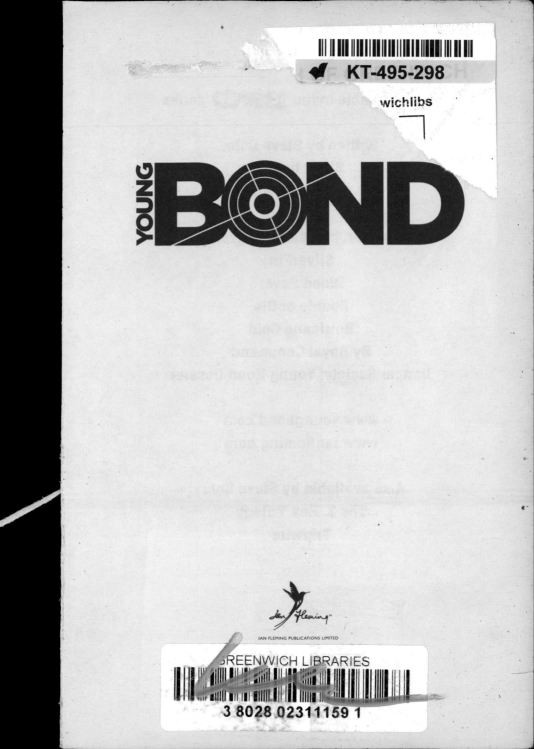

Also available in the YOUNG **BOND** series

Written by Steve Cole:
Shoot to Kill
Heads You Die

Written by Charlie Higson:
SilverFin
Blood Fever
Double or Die
Hurricane Gold
By Royal Command
Danger Society: Young Bond Dossier

www.youngbond.com
www.ianfleming.com

Also available by Steve Cole:
The Z. Rex Trilogy
Tripwire

STRIKE LIGHTNING

STEVE COLE

RED FOX

For Amy

RED FOX

UK | USA | Canada | Ireland | Australia
India | New Zealand | South Africa

Red Fox is part of the Penguin Random House group of companies
whose addresses can be found at global.penguinrandomhouse.com.

www.penguin.co.uk
www.puffin.co.uk
www.ladybird.co.uk

Penguin
Random House
UK

First published 2016

001

Set in Bembo Schoolbook by Jouve (UK), Milton Keynes
Printed in Great Britain by Clays Ltd, St Ives plc

A CIP catalogue record for this book is available from the British Library

ISBN: 978–1–782–95242–8

All correspondence to:
Red Fox
Penguin Random House Children's
80 Strand, London WC2R 0RL

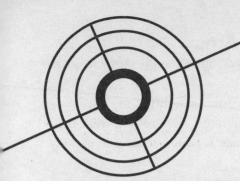

Prologue
The Dead Land

Another day, another game of war. Duncan squeezed through the tiny gap in the fence and pushed past the DANGER sign. The other boys would never expect him to go into the Dead Land, but then, that was the secret of victory: take bold actions to surprise your enemy.

'*Duncan, you're the German sniper and we're the British soldiers hunting you down.*' As ever, the older kids made him the enemy, the target. That was the only reason they let him bunk off school with them. '*You get a ten-minute start, then we're coming after you to blow you to bits.*' And when they found him, they would really let him have it with the stones they threw for 'bullets' – by the handful for machine guns, or one at a time for carefully aimed revolvers. Either way, it hurt like hell.

Not this time, thought Duncan. This time he would sneak up behind them and throw his stones first, 'shoot' them in the back and win some respect for once; not just for his victory, but for braving the Dead Land, and at only thirteen years of age!

The place was full of stories: strange lights in the sky overhead . . . fields full of dead animals . . . a rotting stink that carried clear across the Highlands . . . ghost soldiers marching through the woods at night . . .

Duncan moved as silently as he could through the wild landscape. Rocks of every shape and size peeped through the shrubs and trees, and the towering Binean, the 'Mountain of Birds', reared its lofty head above everything. He could hear no birdsong now, despite the fair summer weather. Once, this land had been part of a general's estate and well-tended, but that general had never returned from the Great War. No gamekeepers watched the woods now, of that Duncan was certain – there were no pheasants or partridge, no vermin boards, no snares for stoats or weasels. Fifty yards in from the fence, the weeping birches with their pendulous branches and waving ringlets had given way to bare mud and the sharp charcoal scratch of skeletal trees.

It seemed that the Dead Land was so named with good reason.

Duncan felt spooked in the unnatural stillness. It was as if the soil had been poisoned and the landscape with it; birds and animals stayed away, as if they sensed that this place meant danger.

Maybe once, Duncan told himself. *There's nothing here now.*

He soon realized that cutting through the fringes of the Dead Land was impossible; the wood was too dense. The branches and brambles grabbed at his limbs, scoring them with scratches. He could either turn back, or he could go deeper into this unknown territory before trying to cut round behind his schoolmates.

Duncan pictured possible triumph – his stones bouncing off the backs of the boys' heads; new respect on their faces. He pushed on for several minutes, his progress marked by the snap of brittle branches.

But when he stopped, sore and sweating, the sounds of struggle continued behind him.

Chilled to the bone, Duncan heard the crash of trampled undergrowth. It sounded like a small army advancing quickly through the dead wood. And beneath it, a noise that sounded out of place in the still forest: a hissing, whirring, bubbling noise that Duncan couldn't place.

'The ghost soldiers . . .' he breathed.

Terrified now, Duncan hurled himself forward, branches striking and snapping against his body. Stealth was unnecessary – whatever pursued him was making an unholy racket. And now, to Duncan's ears, it sounded not like a group of soldiers, but like one enormous mechanical giant, moving at a relentless clockwork pace.

Duncan charged into a fence, climbed it automatically. The rusted barbed wire at the top snagged on his clothing as he tipped over onto the other side. Teeth gritted, he scrambled up and ran on through a field of long grass, the stalks blackened and browned, poisoned with a chemical tang. *The stories are true,* he realized, tears stinging his eyes, bloody hands clasped together in fervent prayer. *Everything's dead here. Please, let me get out. Please.*

He dropped down onto the bed of dry grass, and listened. The unearthly crashing of the thing in the woods was fainter now. It was moving away, and in the quiet of its passing Duncan could hear the distant babble of a stream. He heaved a sigh of relief, but as he did so, he realized just how much he was hurting. The barbed wire had cut him badly, and his shirt was soaked with blood.

Gritting his teeth, Duncan got up and stumbled on towards the sound of the stream. How deep inside the Dead Land was he now? *You'll find a way back*, he told himself as a brook came curling into sight. *Water first. Drink. Bathe these cuts. Water.*

But the water here ran dark and smelled foul, its surface oily. Duncan didn't dare touch the stuff, let alone taste it.

He jumped across to the far bank and waded through the desiccated brush towards what looked like the mouth of a ravine. *I have to get out of here.* Huge blocks of stone blocked his way; debris from a rock fall, most likely. Perhaps if he climbed up one, he would be able to spy the best path out of here.

Before he could even try, he heard a thud of compressed air, the sizzling rush of a projectile. Then Duncan was hurled to the ground in a storm of rock and dust. He curled up, eyes closed, his breath coming in rapid gasps, as stone chips rained down.

A strong, commanding voice, thickened by a lisp, emerged from the explosion's last echoes. 'The BR-12 mortar fires a special high-explosive projectile, *Generalleutnant*.' It was coming from the other side of the rocks. 'You see, the shell uses a tiny rocket motor to "bounce" off the ground of the target area. Fragmentation thus occurs in mid-air, causing far greater damage . . .'

As the dust cleared, Duncan made out a group of figures standing in the ravine. A tall, suited, weatherbeaten man was surveying the damage to the boulder, while waiting beside him . . .

Duncan shivered as he took in the hunched apparition, still speaking about the mortar like a proud parent. Despite the warmth of the day, the man wore a heavy black cloak. A hood hid his features, and he gripped a cane with a gloved hand. Two large men hovered behind as if ready to catch him should he fall.

'It is a most satisfactory weapon, Mr Blade. If a little conventional.' The suited man spoke stilted English; he must be the Generalleutnant, a German officer, Duncan thought. What was he doing here in the middle of the Scottish countryside? 'The minimum order, now – remind me . . . ?'

'Shall we say thirty thousand?'

Duncan closed his eyes . . . 30,000 mortars? These were not ghosts of war. These men were preparing for one, by the sound of it; here, in the heart of the Dead Land.

'First, tell me . . .' the German replied. 'This clever projectile of yours – it is enough to destroy the Steel Shadow?'

'It would barely scratch it.' The hunched man wheezed with laughter. 'We are committed to pushing the Steel Shadow technology to its limits. When my operator returns from the speed trial, Generalleutnant, you may fire the mortar point blank and see how it fares for yourself.'

Still crouching on the stony ground, Duncan looked round suddenly. Was that his imagination, or . . . ?

No. That was the same crashing noise, all right; he heard the heavy splash as whatever it was strode across the dark brook, the rumble and wheeze of strange engines. The thing he'd heard before was on its way here, ready to be tested further.

Panicking, Duncan broke cover and ran as fast as his aching legs could manage.

'*Schiessen Sie den Eindringling!*'

Gunfire followed the officer's bellow, and bullets whined and ricocheted all around. *They're going to kill me!* Duncan raced to his left, away from the ravine. He had to find a way to circle back round to the fence, to get clear, to find the others. They'd never believe what had happened here. *There really was a German sniper, and he had a mortar, and there was a—*

Skidding to a stop, Duncan realized that the hissing, bubbling *thing* was somewhere to his right, approaching through a swathe of forest. He glimpsed metal gleaming through dead branches.

Faster. Go faster. Duncan swiped at the dense undergrowth ahead of him with bloodied hands, forcing his way through the wild tangle on a haphazard course. Finally, lungs burning, he emerged into an open field. Hope flared: further woodland fringed the far side, offering good cover, and he ran for it, barely registering a toppled signpost close by. If he could only hide out in the undergrowth and evade whatever was coming after—

The blast engulfed him in a roar of fire and heat, hurling him into the air. Duncan landed on his back, shocked and blood-soaked, eyes drawn to the faded letters on the sign: KEEP OUT! MINEFIELD.

For a moment his biggest fear was that the noise of the explosion would lead his pursuers straight to him. Duncan made to get up, but nothing happened. He stared uncomprehending at the rubble of flesh about him. Shock and adrenalin must be sparing him the pain.

But nothing could save him from the lumbering, hissing *thing* fast approaching through the smoke. Its bulky shadow fell over him, and finally an agonized scream tore from Duncan's throat.

The ghostly echoes rang out across the ravine.

'*Was ist los?*' The German *Generalleutnant* looked troubled. 'Blade, that intruder . . .'

'Damned local children.' Hunched and muttering, Blade pulled back his hood to reveal hawkish features in a warped, deformed face. 'They hear the stories of our testing ground and make dares to come here. Little fools.'

'A most regrettable incident. What will you do?'

'Regrettable, yes, but we can't allow it to hinder our work. We must dispose of the body where it won't be found . . .' Blade snorted. 'And then build a higher fence.'

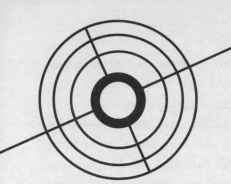

1
Whatever Life Throws at You

James Bond hurtled through the air, caught a glimpse of the high beamed ceiling – and then his back hit the wooden floor with a crash that echoed around the gymnasium. He'd barely managed to utter a groan before his opponent pounced on his chest, a knee digging in either side of his torso, hands reaching for his collar.

If he gets me in a neck lock now, James thought, *I'm finished*. He brought up both arms inside his attacker's to break the grip on his collar and bucked his hips, twisting to his right. With no arms to anchor him, his opponent fell to the floor, but quickly rolled over and jumped back onto his feet. James rose with him, threw a punch, landed a glancing blow to his jaw.

'Barely felt that.' His panting opponent grinned, cheeks as fiery as his thick, curly hair. 'Losing your touch, Bond?'

'You'll be finding it, Stephenson.' Hoping to unnerve him,

James stepped in as if to execute a move, but Marcus Stephenson dodged out of reach and then feinted forward. The boys were locked together in frantic struggle for a grip.

One hand on his opponent's lapel, the other grasping his elbow, James pulled Marcus towards him, lifting at the same time to put him off balance. But Marcus landed a punch of his own to James's chin, and sent him reeling back. At the same time he launched a counter-attack, the *Uchi mata*, using his leg as a lever to whip James round over his hip.

In the split-second before he crashed to the ground, James knew that the fall would be a bad one. His head hit the floor and he gasped as he saw sparks. Gingerly he reached up to his thick black hair, prodded his skull. Intact, it seemed! Well, then, get up. To give in was not an option.

Giving in was never an option.

'Had enough yet?' Marcus enquired.

Slowly James rolled onto his side; dust motes milled about him in the rays of winter sun that lanced through the tall windows. He pushed his palms against the floor, willing the pain away. The fight, he knew, could only be won through focus and concentration.

Marcus waited for him to get up. Then the contest began again. James found himself stepping forward, back, feinting now to the right, now to the left. His fingers found fleeting purchase on Marcus's jacket, but then dizziness overwhelmed him and he lost his grip.

Then a hand reached for his sleeve. Shaking off the fog caused by the fall, James suddenly had an inkling of the sequence of events to come. Marcus's foot flicked to one side, ready to hook around James's and topple him once more.

James waited until the last second, and suddenly twisted through 180 degrees, reaching for Marcus's left bicep and wrist. His fingers closed on sinew; then, ducking forward, he tipped the whole weight of his opponent over his back like a seesaw. With a shout, Marcus tumbled through the air and crashed down flat on his back.

My turn, James thought. He sat astride his opponent, crossing his arms at the elbows and holding his jacket by the collar, then squeezing his forearms inwards, putting pressure on either side of Marcus's neck. Marcus writhed away from him, groaned and strained . . .

Finally he tapped twice on the floor.

James let go and jumped up, panting for breath, elated. 'How was that?'

'You swine!' Marcus grinned up at him and offered his hand to shake. 'I hadn't expected you to try *Kata Juji-jime*.'

'Always happy to try it. Just don't ask me to spell it.' James clasped his hand and helped him up. 'You're not hurt?'

'M-m-merely his pride!' Perched on a heap of crashmats at the side of the Fettes gymnasium, Perry Mandeville clapped. 'Considering the two of you are friends, that was a fierce contest. At least, it looked that way to the layman.' He reclined as if to emphasize his status.

'The lay*about*, you mean.' James pushed his hand through his sweat-soaked hair, but a stubborn comma of black fell back down across his forehead. 'We didn't invite you along just to observe, Mandeville. If we're to get a proper judo club up and running, we'll need recruits.'

'And to order up more *gi* for our members.' Marcus, a gangly boy of seventeen, pulled at James's old, torn judo jacket with a wicked grin; it was one of his he'd now out-grown. 'Victory was yours, but it was hardly stylish!'

'I'll sweet-talk Matron into running me up another,' James said, 'and let Perry have this *gi* when he joins us.'

'I think not, old thing.' Perry smiled. 'I'm a thrill-seeker. I live for the risk of falling on m-my backside – not the certainty of it.'

'Judo's better exercise than herding sheep into your head-master's study,' Marcus teased. 'I still can't believe you did that, Mandeville. That could only ever end *baaa*-dly.'

'Ho ho ho. Bring up m-m-my criminal record, why don't you. Haven't I suffered enough – sent down from Eton and forced to dwell here among the likes of you?' Perry jumped up and took up a fencing stance. 'Had I m-my trusty foil, honour would be satisfied, I assure you.'

'Oh, would it?' Marcus raised an eyebrow. 'You really must like to live dangerously.'

'Is there any other way?' Perry flashed a smile at James. 'Just ask m-my good friend here. I taught him all he knows.'

James scoffed fondly at the claim. Perry really had been a good friend back at Eton; he was also a founder member of the school's 'Danger Society', a clandestine refuge for pupils wishing to rebel against authority. James had taken up membership without hesitation. Although some of his adventures since had made sneaking out of dorms for an illicit cigarette seem tame, he now looked back with fondness at a more innocent time.

I sound like a veteran home from the Great War, James realized.

'Now, listen, fellows, now that you've got your precious Japanese grapples over with . . .' Perry lowered his voice, and beckoned James and Marcus closer. 'I'm sure we're all grateful to George and M-M-Marina for getting hitched on a Thursday, and it means we are duty-bound not to squander this precious free time . . .'

James smiled. Prince George, HRH the Duke of Kent, was to marry his second cousin, HRH Princess Marina of Greece, and by command of the King, every school in the land had been granted a holiday on 29 November. It was usually on Saturdays that the Head dispensed a shilling to each child in turn, so that on Sundays the tuck shop was besieged by a gigantic scrum of customers desperate for Bourbon and Café Noir biscuits. But in honour of the royal wedding he had coughed up the funds that morning, so that pupils could celebrate in the bustling city of Edinburgh – at approved destinations, at least.

'So what's it to be?' asked James. 'Do we really want to go to the Kings Cinema on Home Street and watch some whole-some motion picture as the masters wish?'

Perry smiled. 'I say we sneak off to the Coliseum on West Fountainbridge and watch the new Tarzan feature.'

'With Johnny Weissmuller as Tarzan? I still can't quite believe I met him back in the summer.'

'You never did, Bond!' Marcus exclaimed. 'How on earth . . . ?'

'There was a party in Los Angeles . . .' James trailed off as a chill ran down his spine; better his time in Hollywood stayed swept under the carpet of his consciousness. 'Really it was only a glimpse.'

'So m-m-modest!' Perry slapped him on the back. 'Since you're a close, personal friend of the star, James, you'll want to support his work. I've read there's a positively epic conflict with jungle natives in the first reel . . .'

'I'm in,' James declared.

'We'll stand out a mile in our up-town togs. If we're caught . . .' Marcus rubbed his hands briskly through his curly red hair. 'Ah, well. Man cannot live by good, clean physical exercise and pioneering scientific research alone, eh?'

'Spoken like a true philosopher.' Perry jumped up. 'Now, who can stump up threepence for my admission, hmm? I lost my tuck m-m-money to a boy who's far too good at cards, and now I'm stony broke.'

'Of course you did,' James said.

'Let it be noted,' Marcus announced, 'that a friend in need is a real pest.'

2
Following Orders

It was close to midday when James, Perry and Marcus left the gymnasium to get togged up, ready for their excursion. With no afternoon school and his muscles stretched by his judo exertions, James felt content. It was an unusual feeling, and had sneaked up on him.

'You've come on well in the sport, Bond,' Marcus told him. 'Perhaps at Christmas break you should have some proper lessons . . . try for a belt.'

James thought of his aunt's country cottage. 'I'm not sure they've even heard of judo in Pett Bottom. Perhaps if I came to stay with Mandeville in London . . .'

'Like last year?' Perry grinned. 'That would liven the hols up no end.'

The end of term was in sight, and James marvelled at the fact; he still vividly remembered his first weeks at Fettes, and the crushing conviction that they would last for ever. The sense of bewilderment, the minute-by-minute timetable, the familiar, miserable lack of privacy. But just now, he and his friends could please themselves.

'Meet you on the drive in twenty minutes?' James called as Perry hared off towards his own boarding house, Carrington. James belonged to Glencorse, thrown in with fifty other boys with only a tiny cubicle to call his own. Knowing your place was essential, while 'side' – or airs and graces – was the worst vice; the house prefects who ran the show under the house-master were more than ready to thrash it out of you. Marcus, in the lower sixth, was one of those prefects, and one of the kindest. He lived up to the house motto, *Numquam Onus* – nothing is too much trouble. When they'd discovered a shared enthusiasm for judo – Marcus was a blue belt and James eager to learn – a friendship was soon forged.

James got changed in his little cubicle on the first floor. On the partition wall were three pegs: one held the tails for Sunday best, one his overcoat and the third his Cadet Corps uniform. His regular school uniform was folded neatly on the table by the window: a suit of closely woven herringbone tweed in black and grey, a flannel shirt, black tie and a stiff collar, rounded in the old-fashioned style his grandfather might've worn – only prefects were allowed to wear pointed collars.

It wasn't just the collars that lacked a point; as a 'new man' starting at the school, James had found himself heir to ancient routines and traditions, just like at Eton. At seven a.m., the plump, unwelcome figure of Watson, the houseman, battered on cubicle doors and rang his bell. There followed the rush for the obligatory cold shower and then the swift struggle, still damp, into uniform.

By 7.20 James was swilling cocoa with the throng, and at 7.25 the bell for early school began to ring. James took his place in the tide of boys surging up the green, wooded slopes from Glencorse to the magnificent school building set in sprawling grounds. Built to be noticed, with its towers and turrets, gargoyles and gilded ironwork, the school looked (and often felt) like some vast fairy-tale dungeon.

As autumn edged into winter, it was only the cold that kept James awake through the dull, dusty half-hour of early school each day – that and the smell of breakfast drifting through the building. Chapel was a chance for quiet thought and anticipation of the meal to come: hot chocolate and bread rolls spread with butter and sugar.

Morning school followed. Classics – ancient Greek and Roman literature – dominated the curriculum, and James hated it. Why couldn't they study something they might actually find useful? Marcus, who had a deep interest in physics and biology, told him that one master had tried to ban science from the modern curriculum because 'an absorption with science interferes with Latin verse composition'.

James found the sciences interesting, but his tutor was a remote, eccentric ogre: Dr Randolph Whittaker, also known as Captain Hook. The nickname was an obvious one, since Whittaker's right hand had been blown off in the war, and his tyrannical nature endeared him to none. Sweeping in from shores unknown – and with plenty of money, judging by the Rolls-Royce he drove – he'd arrived in September with the aim of raising scientific standards. Whittaker was a true genius, it was said. Withdrawn and aloof, he was rarely glimpsed about the school outside lessons. James wondered where he'd taught before: he seemed bemused and revolted by his pupils, and in class would mete out punishments for everything from 'gross obliviousness', to 'ignorance of the use of the domestic pocket handkerchief'. Every lesson, he looked as if he wanted to be somewhere else. James sympathized.

Fettes was also very much a rugger school. After lunch, the games for the day were posted on the blackboard outside the hall, and pandemonium ensued in the fight to see name, position and colour. James endured, rather than enjoyed, rugby; team sports weren't for him – he preferred to do his own thing. So while sometimes called upon to play in the House Belows for less gifted players, more often than not his name was not on the list. There was an option to play squash, or to swap racquet for palm in a game of fives, but James preferred the traditional cross-country runs – the Third Miler or, shorter and less satisfying, the Quarry Circle.

Afternoon school started at four o'clock, and tea was at six. Prep was followed by House prayers and, finally, supper, with quantities of proper Scottish porridge ladled out by old 'Ho' Cooper, the housemaster, before bed in his little room, its door standing wide, the window left open its regulation foot, listening to the hooting of night birds and the forbidden whispers of younger boys in the dormitory, dying out to snores or silence, ready to start the cycle all over again the next day.

James donned his striped trousers, morning coat, top hat and umbrella, and climbed down the stairs to join Marcus, who'd changed ahead of him, umbrella and top hat at the ready. With his red curls poking out from under the stern black brim, he achieved an unlikely comic air instead of the desired suave swagger.

Identically dressed, Perry was waiting for them by the red railings at the end of the school drive, and the three boys set off together.

'Here's a welcome change of routine,' Perry declared. 'Like having two Sundays in the week.'

'And two occasions to wear Sunday best,' Marcus added a little ruefully. 'Hoorah.'

James shrugged. Having worn a similar outfit at Eton, he was used to the sort of stares he and his schoolmates attracted when out 'up-town'. He was just glad to escape the confines of the school for the busy streets of Edinburgh, vibrant with the throaty song of traffic and the chatter of the crowds. How different from the quiet hamlet of Pett Bottom, where his aunt Charmian lived: his home for these last years since his parents had died. But was it really a home? Given that he boarded at school for so much of the year, given his trips away, James sometimes felt as if he had lost his roots as well as his parents. A restlessness chewed away inside him, a need for adventure. Sometimes it seemed that only with danger biting at his heels did he ever feel at home.

Stop thinking so damned hard, James told himself. Self-analysis was a waste of time. *You are who you are.* And right now, James Bond was out with two friends, tasting freedom. It was a chilly day, though the sun blazed boldly over the dark splendour of the streets, and James breathed deeply of the crisp air. However you felt about life, the moment at hand was all you ever had.

Marcus strolled between James and Perry, a half-head taller than either. 'You know, leavers throw their top hats and umbrellas into Inverleith Pond,' he told them. 'That'll be me, come 1936!'

James smiled at the thought of battering his brolly to death before hurling it into the dark water. 'Lucky you,' he said. 'We're stuck here till the thirties' bitter end.'

Perry nodded. 'Wonder what the world will be like then?'

'From what I've been hearing on my crystal set about the Nazis building up their forces, the army will be camping outside the school gates to enlist the lot of you.' Marcus shook his head. 'Herr Hitler has made no secret of his ambitions for taking land from the Slavic peoples. It will lead to war in the end, I'm sure of it.'

'A bit of adventure at last,' Perry quipped.

'I think I'd sooner follow a soldier into battle than a teacher into Classics,' James said ruefully. 'At least you're making a difference there.'

'It is sweet and honourable to die for one's country, eh?' Marcus muttered. 'As the poet said: the old lie.'

'It's not a lie,' James argued, 'if you believe the fight is worth it.'

'The politicians tell you it's worth it, but the families of the soldiers who're never coming home . . . what would they tell you?' Marcus pushed his hands into his pockets as they turned left into Coates Crescent, with its smart townhouses. People were stringing Union Jack bunting from the trees in the well-kept communal gardens, ready for the wedding celebrations. 'Wouldn't you rather stay here in this green and pleasant land than rot in the corner of the poet's forgotten field?'

'Of course I would,' James agreed. 'But I couldn't let others fight for my freedom and not go myself.'

'There are many ways to serve one's country,' Marcus

said with a frown. 'I've been told I won't be called up because I'll be serving in a reserved profession.'

'Hark at you!' said Perry. 'Thought that was m–m–mostly farmers or coalminers.'

'A scientific position,' Marcus told him. 'I've been promised work in research and development for the electronics industry when I leave Fettes.'

'Well done!' James said, and meant it. 'Is that through the careers fair?'

'Er, no, not exactly . . .' Marcus hesitated for a moment. 'It's through Dr Whittaker.'

James raised an eyebrow. 'You're helping Captain Hook?'

'Aha!' Perry tapped his nose smartly. 'Fettes' m–miserable m–master of m–m–mystery. Come on, tell all!'

'I've just helped him once or twice,' Marcus said vaguely, and James sensed that he was keen to deflect any interest. 'You know, with this and that.'

Perry smirked. 'I suppose it's hard to wire a plug when you've only the one hand.'

'That's beneath you, Mandeville.' Looking cross, Marcus turned onto Canning Street. 'Whittaker lost that hand saving an injured soldier at the Battle of Neuve Chapelle. He's a good man, for all his temper.'

'I have information.' Perry was unrepentant. 'Arbuthnot – you know Arbuthnot, from Carrington, in the lower fifth? A few weeks back he m–made an error transcribing algebra and Hook sent him to the Head's office to be caned. Arbuthnot was waiting outside and heard the Head through the door, complaining to somebody on the telephone about old Hook, wanting him gone. When Arbuthnot went in, and said that Hook had sent him, the Head barely marked him.'

Marcus snorted. 'Arbuthnot's full of it.'

James was inclined to agree. 'Who would the Head have been talking to? Surely hiring and firing is down to him.'

'There's something odd about him, I tell you,' Perry insisted. 'I overheard the porters groaning about having to clear out the trunk room before term started so Hook could set up his secret laboratory.'

'All the way up there?' James wondered. The trunk room was at the very top of a tower in the centre of the building, where the boarders' cases were usually stowed during term time. 'What's wrong with the school labs?'

'Antiquated.' Marcus's cheeks had reddened. 'Whittaker has his own equipment. I'm helping him with . . . a project. A sort of demonstration.'

'Of black m-m-magic?' Perry was about to go on, but he suddenly stopped dead and grabbed hold of Marcus's arm. 'There we were, speaking of the devil, and you've gone and bloody summoned him up!'

James stopped too, struck by the sight of a handsome motorcar, a Rolls-Royce 20/25 limousine in midnight blue, that had pulled up at the kerb. The chauffeur was invisible – the watery sunlight was reflecting off the windscreen – but there was no mistaking the tall, scrawny man emerging from the back seat.

'Captain Hook in person,' James murmured, heart sinking.

Dr Randolph Whittaker looked like some emaciated Victorian patriarch: his white face contrasted with his hair, eyebrows and side-whiskers, which were as deep a black as his coat and trousers. His right hand was artificial – enamelled wood with metal springs tipped with leather for fingers. The only relief from the monochrome came from the heavy gold chain across his waistcoat.

He strode up to the little group, and James prepared himself for the inevitable roasting: he, Perry and Marcus had strayed off the route to the approved cinema, and Whittaker would exact a price. This would mean the slipper or the cane back at Fettes this evening . . .

But Whittaker ignored James and Perry completely. His anger was directed at Marcus alone. 'We've been driving all around Edinburgh looking for you, you irresponsible little idiot. If you signed up for the cinema, as the porter told me, why aren't you on the specified route, hmm?' His voice was high and nasal. 'Your circuit board was completed incorrectly, boy, and here you stand, revoltingly oblivious. It must be made ready as quickly as possible.'

James swapped awkward looks with Perry, waiting for Whittaker's wrath to fall. But it seemed that this was a private drama between the master and Marcus.

'Sir, the Head said we could take the day off because of the wedding, so I thought I was free to—'

'You think we're *playing* at this? We're behind schedule. The storm is forecast to break tonight and we must carry out the instructions of our . . . our sponsor.'

Marcus looked pale. 'But, sir, I thought the risks—?'

Whittaker held up his hook of a hand. 'When weighed against the greater good . . .' He realized he was attracting looks from passers-by and stared around imperiously. 'Well? It is my misfortune to have to educate these nauseating miscreants. Get in the car, Stephenson. There's much to be done before the storm breaks.'

Marcus didn't argue. Ashen-faced, he hurried over to the waiting Rolls-Royce and got in the back. Without a backward glance at James or Perry, Whittaker turned, stalked after him and folded his bony body into the motorcar.

'I can't believe our luck!' Perry said as he and James hurried away. 'Let's scarper before old Hook comes back for us.'

James glanced back. As the dark blue Rolls swung out into the traffic, he glimpsed a young, fair-haired figure at the wheel — another pupil, pressganged into helping the old tyrant?

'*Much to be done before the storm breaks* . . .' James murmured. 'I wonder what, exactly?'

He watched the Rolls until it was out of sight.

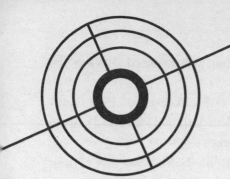

3

Breaking Storm

James and Perry made it to the cinema in time for *Tarzan and His Mate*. But despite the promised flesh and fighting, James hardly took in a scene. His mind kept returning to the mystery of Marcus and Whittaker, and the secret lab up in the trunk room. What was supposed to happen when the promised storm lashed at its gables? What had Marcus got himself into . . . ? James didn't like Whittaker, or the way he treated his pupils.

When the film ended and people rose from their seats, James leaned over to Perry. 'Whittaker ignored us; we didn't matter to him. But this project clearly does.'

'A lot m-m-more than the lessons he teaches,' Perry agreed; it seemed that he'd been mulling over the encounter as well. 'Stephenson said he was helping him with a science demonstration.'

'*Helping* him? More like a soldier obeying orders.' James

25

pursed his lips. 'And demonstrating what, exactly? What's so vital? What requires a storm?'

'Perhaps old Hook's doing a Frankenstein?' Perry suggested. 'Trying to bring his hand back to life! Dark and stormy night, blast of lightning, the works . . .'

'He's up to something, all right. Something Stephenson can't say no to.' James grinned. 'To polish off the day's holiday, Mandeville . . . how hard do you suppose it would be to get up to the trunk room and spy on Whittaker's lab after lights out? Purely for argument's sake.'

'Profoundly difficult, I imagine.' Perry smiled back. 'But, pure or otherwise, no argument from m-me.'

Laying plans with Perry for the evening's subterfuge on the walk back to Fettes, James felt his heart beat more quickly. After spending a quiet term, his days stubbornly normal, the urge to take risks was now surging through his veins. Moreover, he was genuinely fond of Marcus, and knew that if he was keeping quiet about his work with Whittaker, there was a good reason for it. James would take that on trust from any friend. Perhaps Marcus would tell him more at tea time; share some insights into the rigours of slaving for the old monster.

That evening James looked around the common room expectantly as his fellow boarders swapped stories of how they'd spent their day's holiday. But Marcus didn't appear. He was still absent come bed time.

James felt uneasy. Spying on a friend seemed a lousy thing to do; but spying on a miserable devil like Whittaker, whom even the Head wanted rid of, had a definite appeal. And if Whittaker really *did* have some secret hold over Marcus, maybe it was worth finding out more so they could help their friend if it came to it.

Before lights out James decided to ask 'Ho' Cooper, the housemaster at Glencorse, where Marcus might be at this late hour.

'Don't trouble yourself about young Stephenson, Bond.' Unlike most of the masters, Cooper was a handsome man; with his strong features and broad brow, he was like some ancient Greek statue made flesh. 'To have become so essential to Dr Whittaker's project, the boy must be applying all he has learned here at Fettes in fine fashion. You can be proud of him.'

'But for Dr Whittaker to hunt Stephenson down like that on a public holiday,' James persisted. 'I was just concerned—'

'Now, now! He is serving the school, and through the school, his fellow man.' Cooper smiled in kind dismissal. '*Numquam Onus*, eh, Bond? More than just the house motto: words to live by.'

'Nothing is too much trouble,' James murmured as he rose to go. 'I'm sure you're right, sir.'

And it won't be too much trouble to spy on Whittaker's private lab in the old trunk room, James thought, now feeling fully justified. *No trouble at all.*

James waited in his hard, narrow bed for quiet to descend on Glencorse – or for Marcus to return so he could abort the mission. He'd agreed with Perry to rendezvous at ten-thirty in the stand of trees behind the school.

Ten o'clock came, heralded by distant thunder. James heard the faint whine and wheeze of an illicit crystal set, breaking down radio waves into words and static. He thought he caught the harsh rant of Adolf Hitler, Germany's leader, and recalled Marcus's words that morning. Apparently anti-war, and yet obeying Whittaker's orders like a fine young soldier.

The words gave way to ragtime music. Those boys listening in would be for it, if caught.

As will I be, James thought as he dressed soundlessly and crossed to the open window, leaning out and shivering in the night breeze. It was a ten-foot drop down past Cooper's study window to the bushes below – the most hazardous part of the exit. If he made a noise, Cooper would be onto him and the expedition would end in disgrace and the cane before he could even begin to brave Whittaker's wrath.

There was no sense in fretting. James swung himself out of the window and dropped like a cat, landing on all fours in a rustle of vegetation. He held still, teeth gritted as the impact worked its way up through his wrists and ankles, and the thunder sounded – almost overhead now. The study window curtain didn't move, so James extricated himself and ran across the slope into the cover of the trees.

He had to circle round the school to reach Perry, keeping to the darkest shadows. The wind was rising with the coming storm, and with each reckless step James could feel himself casting off the effects of routine and learning by rote, and coming to life.

As his eyes grew accustomed to the moon-grey gloom, James spied Perry lurking like a dark, hunched beast in the shrubbery facing the coal store, as agreed.

'*Ave, Caesar!*' Perry whispered as James approached. '*M-m-morituri te salutant!*'*

* Those who are about to die salute you!

28

James smiled back. 'Don't salute me while you're climbing up that chimneystack, for God's sake, or you really will wind up dead. And with the storm building, well . . .'

'All adds to the fun.' Perry seemed absolutely serious. 'Besides, the trunk room's on the fifth floor, as high as you can go – the only way to see inside is from the top of the chimney.'

'How will you get up there?' James wondered.

'You know the towers at either end at the front of the building? There's a window in each that gives access to the flat roof. It's used by m-m-maintenance when they need to run a flag up the flagpoles – or by the upper sixth School-house lot when they need a smoke. From there, you simply shin up a ten-foot chimney and balance on top.'

'Perhaps I should have a go,' James mused, 'and you try inside.'

'Hands off my glory, James. I've been planning this stunt pretty m-m-m-much since I got here,' Perry said, grinning. 'The oldest boys guard that patch jealously. I always m-m-meant to climb the chimney with bottles of beer in my pocket and call to them from up there – you know, impress them.'

'Let me guess – you always drank the beer before the critical moment?'

'How well you know me, James.' The wind was blustering, shaking the branches and making the leaves rustle loudly. 'Now, we shouldn't delay. I'm the eyes on the window, you're the ear at the door. At this time of night the m-m-masters will be in their studies, but there will be servants and housemaids abroad. Tread carefully.'

James nodded. 'And you hold on tight.' As he checked his watch, the first spots of rain started to fall. 'I make it ten-thirty. Join you back here in ninety minutes' time – and if either of us can't make it, we try again every half-hour from then on.'

'Very well.' Perry raised his hand in swift salute, drew a deep breath and stole away into the darkness.

James looked across at the wooden trapdoors that led to the coal cellars. He ran over and lifted one, then lowered himself inside, feeling for the coal slope with his feet. Upon contact, he dropped down and closed the door after him. He heard the patter of rain against the oak, and a furtive scurry in the blackness. *Rats*, he realized.

Cautiously James headed towards the dim light shining through from the passage. Somewhere behind him he heard the rush and whisper of a cistern. Down here, too, he was close to the underfloor tunnels for the steam and hot-water channels leading from the boilers, and there were clunks and clangs as the pipes protested.

James moved along the passage, making for the steps that led up to the ground floor. A sudden scraping on stone alerted him to the presence of someone in the wine cellar ahead on his right. He pressed himself flat against the wall and held his breath as a servant came out with a bottle of red wine, pre- sumably for one of the tutors. The man didn't look back, and once his footsteps had faded, silence returned. James strode along the corridor, past the boot room, heart banging in his chest.

At last he was climbing the narrow stairs and then moving silently along the passageways. He thought of Perry attempting his hazardous climb and shook his head. *We're madmen, the both of us.*

Or perhaps just too curious for our own good.

Thunder cracked and rumbled again. The windows he passed rattled in their frames in the gusting wind. James used the noise for cover as he climbed a spiral staircase, past the second floor and up to the third, his nerves on edge. As he sneaked through Schoolhouse – the boarding house based in the main building – he was glad of the storm; he imagined masters and staff staring through their windows, waiting for the sudden flash to fork across the skies.

Finally James reached the spiral staircase that would take him up to the fourth floor, past the staff quarters, and up to the trunk room on the fifth. If just one servant was to come down those steps and catch him on the prowl after lights out . . .

But there was no one about. As he reached the next landing, James saw a metal barrier set in front of the stairway, and a printed sign that read, NO ADMITTANCE. Suddenly he became aware of a strange atmosphere. He stopped and listened. A deep, heavily charged whine hummed from the floor above.

Lightning sparked at the dark window. In the sudden flash, James felt horribly conspicuous. He vaulted the barrier, landed like a cat and hurried up the winding steps, heart pounding . . .

There it was, ahead of him: the door to the trunk room. Storm clouds massed at the window, but he could see a small crate and some lengths of wood stacked to the left of the entrance – leftover materials from the makeshift lab's construction, James supposed, and a blessing should he need to hide. He crouched down, put his eye to the keyhole – and found it blocked. No easy glimpses of the interior, then. Instead, James pressed his right ear to the door. The oak was thick and solid, but he could feel a thrumming in the floorboards underfoot. It was as if some huge generator was running hell for leather . . . and something else: a curious sound James couldn't place; a kind of bubbling, steaming, hissing noise.

Minutes passed. Now and then he caught Whittaker's voice: he sounded excited, but it was hard to decipher words. He knew that he also had to listen out for anyone coming up behind. An acrid smell reached his nostrils; it put him in mind of riding the dodgem cars at fairgrounds. Thunder punched through the air again, making him jump.

Suddenly Whittaker's voice came clearly – though intermittently – through the door, interrupted by the loud grinding of machinery: '. . . strike the conductor . . . God knows why we have to . . . must be running. Stephenson?'

Marcus is in there. James held his breath and pushed his ear closer to the door. 'Safeguards switched in.'

A muttered instruction from Whittaker, then James thought he heard another voice replying. It sounded like a girl, but James couldn't hear any more as—

'Professor!' Marcus sounded urgent. 'What about the secondary systems?'

'Prime assault manoeuvre three,' came the female voice, calm and assured. 'The incoming energy must be expended.'

'But the systems—'

'Damn it, boy,' Whittaker shouted. '*Now—!*'

Whatever else he said was lost in a terrific peal of thunder. The crashes rolled accusingly across the sky as the storm reached its climax. James could feel the hairs on the back of his neck standing on end.

Then the lightning flashed through the leaded glass windows, filling the staircase with white brilliance. James held rigid as a bloodcurdling scream went up. *Marcus*.

4
Lightning Strikes Twice

'Stephenson!' James banged on the door to the trunk room, forgetting his subterfuge, heedless of the consequences. He had to reach his friend and get him out of there.

But the sound was lost amongst the raised voices (Whittaker's and the girl's), the rumble of machinery and the powerful thrum vibrating through the lab. James felt helpless; he kicked the door in frustration. 'What's happening in there?'

The hum wavered, then began to fade. 'We weren't sufficiently prepared . . .' Whittaker's voice was lost amid a clatter that sounded like heavy clamps being released, and James only caught the end of his sentence: '. . . knows what blade will do.'

Blade? What was happening in there? James banged on the door again. 'Hello?'

'Go away!' Whittaker shouted from inside. 'Everything is in order here.'

James persisted. 'I heard a scream.'

'No,' he snapped. 'You heard my equipment. The lightning struck the conducting mast outside and overloaded the secondary generator. I cried out because I received an electric shock while uncoupling the power supply.' He paused. 'Who is it?'

'It's . . .' James hesitated. Whittaker would have his guts for garters. 'I'm fetching the Head right now.'

'Your illustrious headmaster knows better than to interfere with my business. Now, be gone!'

James burned with the dismissal. He checked his watch; it was almost half-past eleven. *Perry. If he saw what happened, we can tell the Head together, and hang the consequences.*

Steeling himself, James hurried back down the staircase, retracing his steps to the cellar. The rain drummed hard against the windows, helping to mask the creak of old doors and floorboards.

At last, pushing up on the heavy wooden hatch over the coalhole, James peered out into the night, wary of anyone who might have been roused by the unearthly noises coming from the top of the school. Then the trapdoor was hefted open from above. James flinched, held up a hand to shield his eyes as the rain hit his face, and found his wrist grabbed by—

'For God's sake, James, get out of there and under cover.' Dripping wet, Perry reached for James's other hand and helped him to scramble out.

Heart pounding, James got to his feet and shut the trapdoor, then followed Perry back under the trees. Pale moonlight was now shining intermittently through the storm clouds.

'What the hell happened up there?' he breathed. 'Marcus was screaming.'

'I thought I heard something, but I couldn't see anything clearly.' Perry's voice was hushed, and James got the feeling that this wasn't just because he didn't want to be overheard. 'There was this m-m-m-metal rod coming out through the trunk-room window. Proper cornucopia of wires and whizz-bangs at its base – I could barely see past it. There was steam in there too. It was like a bloody train pulling away. But I saw Whittaker – and a girl, I think.'

'I heard her too, whoever she is.'

'And I saw Stephenson through the smoke. He was in a cage.'

'Locked up, you mean?'

'Whittaker *called* it a cage. It looked a bit like the radiator grille from an automobile . . . I glimpsed Stephenson flailing about, and this cage thing . . . I swear it m-m-moved with him.'

James felt a chill travel down his spine. 'What happened next?'

'After the lightning struck, the lights went out.' Perry looked apologetic. 'Thought the place would soon be swarming with m-masters – thought I'd best come down and look for you.'

James straightened up. 'It ought to be swarming with masters. We should go to the Head.'

'Admit to being out and caught up in it all? We'll be crucified!' Perry considered. 'You know, perhaps we're overreacting. Stephenson could be staggering back to Glencorse right now. Glowing in the dark, but otherwise well.'

'I don't know . . . But Whittaker will surely call a doctor to have him checked over.' James nodded slowly. Whatever Marcus had been put through, he was strong and fit. 'Let's hide out and keep watch on the school drive.'

Perry hugged himself, shivering. 'Filthy night for spying.'

James nodded. 'Filthy occupation.'

Moving as stealthily as they could over sodden grass and through wet undergrowth, James and Perry worked their way round to the front of the school. A light still burned dimly in the trunk room's blackened windows. The wind blew, and James had to clench his teeth to stop them from chattering. The minutes went slowly by, stretching into long hours. No motorcars appeared on the drive; there was no movement at all. The school building stood silent and solid in the storm.

'How long do we wait out here?' Perry murmured beside James, stamping his feet into the mulch. 'All night?'

'I hope it won't come to that.' James looked sideways at him. 'You can sneak off back to bed, if you like. I wouldn't blame you.'

'Enough excitement for one night, eh?' Perry said ruefully. 'Well, I don't suppose I'll ever dry out again, so I'll linger a little longer.'

'Wait . . .' said James. Distant lightning escaped the scudding clouds and showed . . . *something*, a good way off in the grounds to the east. He caught only a glimpse of unnatural, awkward movement: a large, hunched figure, quickly lost to the darkness as clouds covered the moon again, leaving only a chill in his spine. 'Someone's out there, Perry.'

'What?' Perry peered over James's shoulder. 'I don't see anything.'

'Someone huge, making for the golf course.' James was already setting off in pursuit. 'He might've been carrying something on his back . . .'

'Such as?' Perry started after him. 'Bond?'

James didn't answer. He just ran towards whatever it was he'd seen, hugging the treeline for as long as possible. The sinister oversized *thing* had disappeared; beyond the golf course there lay acres of dense deciduous woodland, before the dour grey houses of the Old Town beyond.

Perry caught up with him. 'Whatever you saw, you can't track it in these conditions—'

'It's time we went for help.' James turned to look at him, wiping the sodden lock of hair from his forehead. 'Get your housemaster to raise a search party. Say we know that Stephenson was helping Whittaker – and that something serious has happened to him.'

Perry met his gaze for a few moments, troubled. Then he nodded, turned and headed into the night.

James took off in the other direction, hoping to catch a glimpse of the figure again. As the wind drove the rain into his face like tiny icy daggers, he heard something up ahead: a low, mechanical grinding noise. And was that a light bobbing in the darkness? It was gone in a moment, extinguished by the night.

Head down, James broke into a stumbling run across the golf course towards the light he'd glimpsed. His heart almost stopped as he startled a hare and sent it running for cover. Cursing, James was about to run on when he saw it leap over something on the ground.

It looked like a body, laid out on its front.

The wind seemed to drop a little as James approached, almost in a trance, fearing what he might find but still praying that he was wrong. He crouched beside the body, flinching at the stench of charred meat, and saw that the back of the head was a mass of blisters and singed curls.

'Marcus . . .' James whispered. He looked around, but whatever the boy had been carrying, it wasn't here. 'Marcus?'

Marcus stirred, turning his raw, burned head to look at him. James saw his ruined face.

'Ruskie,' Marcus hissed suddenly.

'What?' James stared down helplessly, shivering. 'A Russian, you mean? What happened to you?'

'Not ready for Ruskie.' Marcus's arm convulsed suddenly. 'Twenty . . .'

'Twenty what?' James looked around, wishing he hadn't sent Perry away. He tried to cradle his friend's head. 'Look, you're excelling at the dying-man bit, muttering your vital last words, but you needn't bother. You're not going to die, Marcus — you hear me? Help's coming.'

'No time.' Marcus licked froth from his bleeding lips, his eyes rolling back in blackened sockets as his left arm convulsed again. 'Not ready . . .'

'Stay with me, Marcus.' James leaned in. 'Marcus?' He heard movement behind and began to turn round. 'Perry, is that—?'

Something cold and wet was sprayed in his face — a mist, cloying and vile.

James wondered what he'd inhaled, even as he collapsed onto the ground.

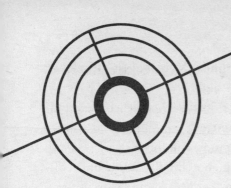

5

In the Dark

Consciousness returned suddenly. His body felt stiff and sore and he could hardly move. *Where am I?* James wondered. Scraps of memory flitted ghostlike through his mind but he couldn't hold onto them.

Slowly he opened his eyes, and a young woman came sharply into focus, her face pale, her hair close-cropped, gold-blonde. She was a beauty, with classic Nordic looks: grey eyes, the lids stencilled with black kohl; teeth, as she grinned, as sharp as her cheekbones. James could smell the cool, sweet odour of lily of the valley.

'You're awake, then, Bond.' The girl's voice was low and the foreign accent seemed somehow familiar. 'Do you remember anything from last night?'

James took in his surroundings: a narrow bed with starched sheets, the familiar cream walls and high ceilings – though this wasn't Glencorse. 'Where am I?'

'You're in the school sanatorium. You had an accident. The groundsman found you last night.'

'Last night . . . Accident . . . ?' James's head throbbed and his mouth was dry. 'Are you a nurse?'

'I am Miss Axmann. But you may call me Herta.'

'Wait.' James tried to get up, but his shoulders hurt; his body wouldn't respond. 'Marcus . . . My friend, Marcus Stephenson, was hurt. We were out in the grounds—'

'You were lucky. To be struck by lightning—'

'Lightning?'

'Last night your friend was out on the golf course when he was struck by lightning. You must've been with him. The two of you, out in the night, playing a prank of some sort, I suppose . . .' There was regret in Herta's eyes. 'I'm afraid Marcus Stephenson is dead.'

'No.' James turned his head as if to shake the words back out of his ears. Pain stabbed into him, and memories slipped through. 'No, I remember . . . He wasn't struck by lightning. It wasn't like that—'

'You're lucky you weren't killed too, Bond.' She stared at him with cool grey eyes. 'You so easily could've been.'

'I'm telling you, it wasn't like that.' James took hold of her wrist. 'Listen. Marcus was in the trunk room with Whittaker . . .'

Herta's smooth forehead grew lined with concern. 'I'm sorry?'

'He was helping with an experiment . . .' James stared up at her. 'Wait. Your voice . . . I've heard you before . . .'

'Oh, dear. You're growing distressed.' She looked sadly down at him. 'I must give you a further sedative, Bond, while we decide what to do about these troubling memories.'

42

'What?' James gasped as he felt a needle scratch his arm. 'Please, Nurse . . .'

'I'm not a nurse, I'm a scientist.'

Her smile was the last thing James saw as the blackness closed in.

'You did hear my voice in the trunk room, James,' she said quietly, stroking his forehead. 'I've come to work with Dr Whittaker, you see.'

James couldn't tell how much time had passed when he felt a pressure on his neck, cold and metallic. His mind was full of darkness, but he could hear voices close by, garbled and indistinct.

'Something to convince the doctors . . .'

James tried to open his eyes, but then a great pulse of energy surged through his body. He arched his back, convulsing, a scream trapped on the edge of his lips as he was thrown into darkness again.

He was lost in that void for a long time. He had hazy recollections of thermometers being pushed into his mouth, of being helped to the bathroom, of a fine mist, its sickly scent mingling with lily of the valley . . . Then, finally, something softer, warmer; something he recognized. Lavender and dusty books. A smell of home amid the disinfectant of the school sanatorium.

'Aunt Charmian?' James opened his eyes. 'Is that you?'

'James.' Charmian stood up and brushed down her trouser suit; she looked relieved. Her bobbed brown hair was in disarray, and the bags under her eyes showed how little sleep she'd had. 'Oh, thank God. You know, you've been drifting in and out of consciousness for over three days!'

James was appalled. 'As long as that?'

'I've come to take you home, when you're well enough.' She squeezed his hand. 'We'll take the train and get you better in time for Christmas.'

James hardly heard her: his mind was struggling with half-remembered fragments. 'What . . . what happened?'

'A blast of lightning is an unpredictable phenomenon, but no lasting damage is expected. The doctors are optimistic.' Charmian's smile didn't extend to her grey eyes. 'It could have been so much worse, James.'

'Lightning?' He let his head fall back against the pillow. 'I . . . I don't remember . . .'

'But you gave a statement to the police.'

'Police?'

'Given the terrible tragedy you've just lived through, the Headmaster feels you've suffered enough. You won't be disciplined further,' Charmian said quietly. 'Oh, James. All this for the sake of some silly schoolboy prank—'

'What?' James fought to keep his voice down. 'Aunt Charmian, some of the details are a bit fuzzy, but . . . This master, Dr Whittaker – he was working on some project and was using Marcus to help him—'

'The Headmaster explained it all to me, James.' Charmian looked uncomfortable, and placed her hand on his. 'Marcus was assisting Dr Whittaker; he was due to start an apprenticeship at a research and development centre for a weapons manufacturer at The Hague, in the Netherlands . . .'

'Weapons?' James queried. He remembered their ill-fated expedition into Edinburgh: Marcus had talked of being spared military call-up in order to work in a reserved profession. In times of war, he supposed, the development of better ways to kill was the most important profession of all. 'I don't . . . You say I made a statement?'

'I read it. Marcus was working late, and when he'd finished, you and he met up in the school grounds to celebrate the holiday with a prank of some sort. He'd taken a lightning rod from the trunk room, was trying to fix it in a tree—'

'No.'

'According to your account—'

'I don't remember telling the police anything.' James screwed up his eyes, concentrating. 'I'm sure that Marcus was already hurt when I found him. It was something Whittaker had done to him. He . . . he was talking about a demonstration; about Russians . . .'

'Your signature was on the police report, James,' Charmian said gently. 'You were standing beside Marcus when he was struck by lightning. The shock that killed him injured you too.'

'But there *was* no lightning then! Earlier, yes, but—'

'The Headmaster showed me photographs of the scene: a tree close by was struck and scorched, and . . .' Charmian sounded awkward. 'I know how upsetting this must be for you, but I read the coroner's report. Your friend Marcus's body showed damage to the central nervous system and burns in Lichtenberg figures: all characteristic of a lightning strike. The coroner recorded a verdict of Death by Misadventure.'

James licked his dry lips. 'They told you a lot, didn't they?'

'Well, I demanded to know what had happened. They said it was important that you get some proper home rest. Didn't sound like you, James, so naturally—'

45

'All this happened while I was asleep?'

'I believe the Headmaster urged swift action to save the school embarrassment.'

'From stories like mine?' James pushed himself up onto his elbows and winced as he was overcome by nausea. 'Aunt Charmian, I think Whittaker was using that promise of a job to force Marcus to work late that night in the trunk room. Something involving the storm . . . I went there in secret because I was worried about him. I heard him scream. This girl, Miss Axmann – Herta – she knows—'

'James, it's quite understandable that you're confused,' Charmian said. 'Try not to tax yourself. We'll be going home as soon as you're fit to travel.'

'I can't.' He gripped her hand. 'Maybe Marcus *did* receive a massive electric shock – but it happened in Whittaker's lab. I found him in the grounds. He was still alive, but in a bad way . . .' He slumped back against the pillow, willing the memories to return. 'I'm telling you, Aunt Charmian, Marcus spoke to me about not being ready for Ruskies, or something. Then . . . I blacked out.' He gritted his teeth. 'If I was hit by lightning, why aren't I burned?'

'Lightning's not always around long enough to cause much skin damage. But there's a burn mark on your shoulder, and Matron said you'd complained of numbness in your arms, stiff muscles—'

'But Marcus and I were never up in any tree with a lightning rod,' James insisted. 'I know it. Just ask Perry!'

'Perry Mandeville? He's been asking after you, wondering what happened.'

'He knows what happened!' James had to force himself not to shout. 'Something's going on here. A conspiracy.'

'Organized by the Russians?' Charmian said gently. 'James, survivors of a lightning strike often find themselves feeling confused for a while, or with memory problems . . .'

James stared at her, his whole body trembling. 'You really don't believe me, do you?'

'I'm sure that once you're back in Pett Bottom—'

'Why is the Headmaster pushing all this evidence at you?'

Before Charmian could respond, Matron, a formidable woman with a complexion and figure like an unbaked cob loaf, bustled into the room. 'Now, now, James. Calm down, if you please.'

'What happened to Herta?' he demanded. 'I remember her visiting me.'

'Dr Whittaker's German friend, you mean? He asked her to keep an eye on you. You know, after it happened.'

'I woke up and she injected me with something.'

'Just a sedative.' Matron clucked and fussed around his bed, smoothing the blanket and tucking in the sheets. 'Now, see here, James, you're not in the debating society now.' She eyed Charmian pointedly. 'You're here for quiet.'

'Matron's right, of course.' Charmian looked awkward. 'You've been through such an ordeal. You must try to rest.' Stepping forward to interrupt Matron's circuit of the bed, she patted him briskly on the shoulder. 'I'll come back and see you tomorrow. I'm staying in town until you're ready to go, so if there's anything you need from the world beyond these walls, you must let me know.'

'I'm sure I'll think of something.' James forced a smile for Charmian as she turned to leave, but his heart felt heavy. *Marcus's death is being covered up, and I've been made a part of it. Whatever happened to me out in the grounds was no lightning strike.*

Matron finished her ministrations and left the room. Wearily James sank back onto his pillow. What was the truth? Herta had smiled down as if butter wouldn't melt between those perfect pink lips, but she must have done something to leave him bed-bound for days, with gaps in his recall . . .

He closed his eyes. A flash of memory emerged from the dark – of metal pressure on his shoulder. *Something to convince the doctors . . .*

James jerked as if a shock had gone through him, eyes snapping open, heart pounding.

There was a quiet knock at the window. He looked round in alarm – only to see Perry waving surreptitiously through the glass.

With a glance at the closed door, James struggled weakly out of bed and over to the window, opening it as quietly as he could. Perry quickly climbed over the frame and into the sick room.

James gripped him by the hand – not only in greeting but to hold himself steady. 'Good to see you.'

'You too, old thing. God, you look rough. Forgive my not entering through the sickhouse door, but currently you're more prisoner than patient. Off limits.'

'Prisoner?' James said, frowning. 'My aunt Charmian was allowed in . . .' He trailed off. 'Perhaps they hoped she'd convince me that this guff about a lightning strike is true.'

'She believes that Stephenson was killed by a prank you

put him up to?' Perry grimaced. 'The Head announced as much at assembly. Said it happened after Marcus'd finished working with Whittaker. Afraid your name is m-m-mud around the school, Bond.'

'And what about yours?' James's look hardened. 'You know what happened; you heard the screams up there in the trunk room – but you haven't said anything?'

'Think about it, James. This whole story you're m-m-mixed up in . . . some powerful people m-must have invented it. If I backed you up, they'd only do to m-m-me what they've done to you. But while I'm at large . . .'

Reluctantly, James saw the logic of what he'd said. 'Well, how did you come to *remain* at large? I left you to get help.'

'I was running off to m-my House when I saw the groundsman out with a torch, trudging off in the direction you'd taken. Tailed him at a distance. He headed straight for Stephenson, as if he knew where to look.'

'How could he have, though?' James wondered. 'It was a filthy night.'

'Don't know.' Perry shrugged. 'Anyway, in the dark I didn't realize you were there too. Just assumed you'd m-made yourself scarce once the cavalry had come. So I did the same – got back to my bedroom without waking anybody. Thought it best to play dumb . . . If m-my poor parents have to find me yet another school after only two terms . . .'

'I understand.' James climbed stiffly back into bed. 'But that's about the only thing I *do* understand.'

Quickly James told Perry what he could recall about finding Marcus, and then the version of the story that Charmian had been given.

'So they want you safely away in Pett Bottom, eh?' Perry mused. 'Out of sight and out of mind.'

'Herta did something to me,' James said. 'My memory's not clear, but perhaps it's clearer than they'd like it to be. That's why they've got Charmian up here to cart me off home in disgrace.' He craned his stiff neck round to look at the small burn mark on his shoulder. 'This could've been made by an electrode. They could easily have given me an electric shock.'

'Extreme m-measures,' Perry noted.

'Suggests they have something extreme to hide,' James agreed. 'Herta . . . she's meant to be working for Whittaker. But who is Whittaker working for? He told me, "Your illustrious headmaster knows better than to interfere with my business." *Your* headmaster, not *our*.'

'As if old Hook was nothing to do with the school at all, eh?' Perry nodded. 'And this girl, Herta . . . It's no secret she's working with him. They say she's replaced Stephenson.'

'But she was there in the trunk room with him, I'm sure of it.' Another spark of memory came back to James. 'Whittaker's chauffeur in the Rolls. The last time we saw Stephenson . . .'

'Could've been her,' Perry agreed. 'But in God's name, why is this happening?'

James looked at him. 'That's what we've got to find out.'

6

A Twisted Blade

James spent a broken night tossing and turning. His pulse was racing, his mind racing faster, dipping in and out of blackness. Violent pins and needles in his arms kept tugging him awake.

The next morning Matron seemed disappointed with his progress. 'You have an important visitor coming this afternoon.' She shook the thermometer forcefully. 'We need you bright for that, don't we?'

'Who?' James grunted.

'An *international businessman*.' She was clearly impressed. 'A friend of the Headmaster's. You'll see.'

'Why would he want to see me?'

'I believe he knew Marcus Stephenson . . .' Matron said as she bustled out.

James dozed until it was time for a lunch of scrambled eggs on hot buttered toast. He chose not to take the white tablets

Matron presented with his cup of cocoa. He didn't quite believe that they were only simple painkillers, so he crushed them to a powder and obscured the debris in the dark foam in the bottom of the mug.

At two o'clock sharp he was woken by a rap on the door. 'Yes?' he called uncertainly.

The man who entered was dressed in a thick black cloak and carried a gold-topped cane. He was perhaps in his late thirties, James thought, but he walked like an old man, slowly and deliberately, one shoulder hunched forward. His face was somehow twisted: the nose long and aquiline, the chin broad, the brows bunched under a high forehead. James could feel the ferocity in the lopsided grey eyes, an implacable will – and instinctively shifted back against his pillow. A burly grey-haired man in a chauffeur's uniform followed him into James's room, hovering uncertainly.

'Thank you, Carrel, you may wait in the corner.' The man with the twisted face spoke without turning round; the chauffeur duly retreated. 'I'm sorry to disturb you in your convalescence, Bond. My name is Hepworth Maximilian Blade.' Although he spoke with a lisp, his voice was deep and strong. 'I am Managing Director of Blade-Rise Industries, an electronics research company with headquarters in London and The Hague. Your friend Marcus Stephenson was going to work for me upon leaving Fettes.'

James nodded slowly. 'Dr Whittaker was training him with work on his . . . special project.'

'Indeed. I wished to afford you my condolences. While I have lost a most promising apprentice, you have lost a good friend.'

'Yes.' James had a feeling that he was being tested. 'I . . . I'm not sure I'll ever forgive myself for my part in his death.'

'Come, Bond. It was a tragic accident, that is all. Prank can turn to tragedy so quickly, and in ways no one can foresee.'

Not trusting himself to speak, James simply nodded and offered his hand, but Blade eyed it as he might a poisonous snake, and Carrel, the chauffeur, shook his head from across the room. In an accent that sounded Dutch he said, 'Mr Blade can't be touched.'

'I take my life in my hands each time I rise from my bed, and must avoid all unnecessary risks.' Thin lips parted to reveal pink gums as Blade spoke, though his jaws hardly moved. 'You see, I have a medical condition identified in dusty medical textbooks as *Fibrodysplasia ossificans progressiva* – more colloquially known as Stone Man Syndrome.' Perhaps seeing that James was none the wiser, he continued: 'The soft tissues of my body – my muscles, tendons and ligaments – are hardening irreversibly into abnormal outgrowths of bone. The process cannot be controlled or arrested. In the end it will leave me a prisoner inside my own body, as a second, deformed skeleton grows over that which I was born with. I will perhaps starve as my jaws seal shut, or suffocate as new bone growth constricts my lungs. In any case, the many doctors I consult are certain that I shall be dead by the time I reach forty. I have perhaps four or five years left to live.'

'I'm sorry,' James said.

'A redundant attitude. Knowing that my early death is inescapable has meant I've used my time wisely.' No emotion showed on Blade's face – James wondered if it even could – but those eyes flicked to and fro, never resting, blazing with the terrible fire of a man held captive by his own body. 'I could never attend a normal school such as this, so my parents brought me tutors, and I learned. Most of all, I studied the language of science and technology that translates into the tools with which we can change and shape the world around us.' Blade leaned forward on his gold-topped cane. 'I have pushed technology to its limits in order to extend my empire and enhance my life – so that I, in turn, may enhance the lives of others.' He straightened, and Carrel stepped forward as if ready to catch him. 'Perhaps if I'd been born twenty years from now, a cure for my condition might be found. But wishing things were different is the refuge of the weak-minded. The strong take change into their own hands. We must make the most of our talents *while we can* . . . and take any and all opportunities to create a better future.'

Mention of the future brought a recollection from the past into James's mind. 'My father worked for Vickers Armaments. I remember he mentioned Blade-Rise as a competitor. Your company makes weapons, doesn't it?'

'Ah. And you wonder how war can create a better future?' Blade's thin lips stretched in what might have been a rueful smile. 'You are aware, perhaps, of the Treaty of Versailles, which was signed at the end of the Great War? Its terms prevented Germany from re-arming. And yet today, Herr Hitler, leader of the Nazis, is poised to build an air force and preparing to expand his army, in defiance of those terms. He speaks of needing to take "living space" from other nations – by force, if needs be.' He tapped his cane sharply on the polished floor. 'The shadow of war is falling across the whole world, and to ignore that would be a grievous error. For war is won by the nation best equipped to fight it, while peace depends on a suitable deterrent. And the creation of weapons – thanks to the large budget that it is afforded – allows technology to progress, for the benefit of all.'

'Was Marcus working with Dr Whittaker on a new weapon for you, here at Fettes?' Refusing to be intimidated, James met the man's blazing stare. 'Something that can harness the power of lightning?'

'Lightning? If this is a joke, boy, I fear it is in very poor taste.' Blade's eyes went on boring into James's own. 'Quite apart from the impossibility of predicting just where and when lightning will strike, the high-voltage energy is too great to be collected and stored.'

'Perhaps for the moment,' James pressed, 'but in the future—?'

'I am an architect of the future. I suppose, when you try to picture a future world, you see flying automobiles, a robot butler in every home, and whole cities powered by lightning?' Blade gave his twisted smile. 'Alas, I fear you will be disappointed. The future will see the creation of smaller electronic components that work with greater efficiency. Companies such as Blade-Rise will change the world with more streamlined and powerful machines; mass-production will be made possible with automated assembly lines . . .'

'So what *was* Marcus working on?' James asked bluntly.

Blade paused. 'The answer is really rather dull. Whittaker's pet project, in his spare time while he teaches here, is to find a new way of creating electronic circuits. The process eliminates complex, error-prone wiring by hand. Instead, one sprays molten metal through a stencil onto an insulated surface to create an electrical path.'

'You mean . . .' James tried to get his head around this. 'Instead of connecting brass wires onto a board with rivets, you simply *spray* the wiring onto it?'

'Quicker and simpler all round. It could be of use for certain machines we make.' Blade inclined his head and upper body. 'Alas, it would be of little use as a weapon.'

'Dr Whittaker told Marcus that the storm was important to testing this project. Why? Will work on this circuit continue with another pupil—?'

'The work is now complete.' Impatience, or anger perhaps, pulled at Blade's brows. 'The results will be analysed.'

The result is that Marcus is dead, James thought. 'Thank you, sir . . . for answering my questions.'

'Not at all.' Blade turned his face towards the window. 'I understand you'll soon be going home with your aunt to recuperate in more pleasant surroundings.'

'People seem to think that's best for me,' James said carefully.

'Oh, it is, Bond. Indubitably.' Blade leaned forward, his lips peeled back again in an attempt at a smile. 'Allow me to give you some advice. Don't dwell on the past. You have a future, and that is a precious gift. Don't squander it.'

'I fully intend to make the most of my time, sir,' James replied.

Blade's eyes were studying him closely. 'Quite.' Stiffly, awkwardly, he turned to Carrel, who stepped forward to assist. 'Goodbye, Bond.'

'Goodbye, sir,' James muttered.

Carrel held the door open for Blade, then followed him out and let it shut behind them. On the back of the door, an old Cadet Corps uniform hung from a hanger.

I've been told I won't be called up, Marcus had said. Now he was dead, all choice and potential taken from him.

Not destined to fight.

'But *I* am,' James whispered.

In the quiet and solitude of the san, James mused on the hobbling figure of Hepworth Maximilian Blade. He brooded over all he knew and what he might do to confirm his suspicions.

When Perry sneaked back in after school, James was feeling better and more alert than he had in some time. He quickly filled him in on his visitor.

'I've heard of Blade-Rise,' said Perry. 'My aunt and uncle have a holiday home in Scheveningen, just outside The Hague, and not a visit goes by without Uncle George boring someone to death about the way old Blade is buying up all the land to build his factories.'

James nodded. 'Why should a man like Blade risk his health to travel here and check up on me? I wonder.'

'He m-m-must be m-meeting old Hook to check over this circuit whatsit,' Perry suggested. 'Stephenson wasn't m-m-meant to die . . . I suppose Blade wanted to be sure you're toeing the line about the lightning.'

'And that I'll soon be heading home for peace and quiet,' James added. 'Well, they can forget that.'

Perry looked askance at him. 'But your aunt . . . ?'

'She'll listen,' James insisted. 'Marcus was killed – perhaps not on purpose, but that's what happened. His inquest will say he died in a schoolboy prank – because of me.'

'Picked the wrong person,' said Perry with a smile, 'didn't they?'

'They damn well did,' James agreed. 'And somehow I'm going to find out what really happened. Blade was right when he told me the strong take things into their own hands.'

7

Confrontation

The next day Matron finally gave James a clean bill of health – or at least, one that was only moderately soiled. Charmian was informed, and came straight over from her rooms at the Sheep Heid Inn at Duddingston to collect him. James suggested they take a walk in the grounds together.

Fettes was quiet, with tutors and pupils taken up with morning school. The day was cold and grey as the year tightened its belt, ready for winter. Even Whittaker's Rolls-Royce, its bodywork spotless, could barely muster a shine. Three large, grey, unmarked trucks had the Rolls surrounded, and scaffolding had gone up around the trunk room's tall turret, with workmen scurrying up and down like sailors in ship's rigging. The windows had been taken out so that machinery could be removed on a joist and winched down.

'That's where it happened.' James felt a pang of anger. 'That's where Marcus was helping Whittaker.'

'They're clearing everything out,' Charmian observed. 'And now it's your turn to do the same for that dismal cubicle of yours.'

'Aunt Charmian, I want to stay.' James stopped and turned to look at her. 'Please, will you let me see out the term with my friends?'

She looked at him doubtfully. 'You really want to stay after all that's happened?'

'I may have made mistakes,' James said carefully, 'but I'd sooner not run away from them. Now that I'm fit again, I'd dearly love to stay.'

'Dearly love to stay . . . at school?' Charmian looked at him for a moment, then smiled warmly. 'James Bond, you never fail to surprise me – or to impress me.' She linked arms with him. 'I'll tell the Head of my decision to let you stay on. And I'll be seeing you again in a matter of weeks anyway.'

James nodded, giving her his best smile, though inside his mood was darkening like the sky. *A matter of weeks . . . to find out what's going on around here.*

The next day, James climbed the pupils' staircase to the chemistry classroom. It was early; the school timetable had brought him crashing back to cold showers and a rumbling stomach as he readied himself for morning class. But for once, James was certain he'd have no trouble staying awake. His heart was beating hard: an encounter with Whittaker was on the cards, a chance to learn more of his connection to Blade-Rise Industries.

The Head had seemed pleased that James wanted to stay; had summoned him to his office for a brief lecture. 'We are none of us privy to God's great pattern, Bond,' he said fiercely. 'We cannot know why Stephenson was taken from us. But we must all do our Christian duty – and yours is to forgive yourself. To dedicate yourself to your moral wellbeing, and to the general good of the school.'

And to getting answers, James added privately. *And – yes, why not admit it? – revenge.*

The pungent atmosphere of the chemistry room greeted James as he stepped inside, hoping to be first into class. Whittaker was already present, his tall frame bent over his desk beside the window, studying a flat piece of Bakelite board the size of a cigarette pack which was covered in trails of silver paint. The other side of the board bristled with small components, connected by soldered wires pushed through tiny holes in the metal.

'Excuse me, sir,' James said, remembering Blade's explanation of the previous day. 'Is that an electronic circuit board?'

Whittaker looked up sharply, his hook raised. 'It's none of your damned business what it is, boy.'

James tried not to react. 'Yesterday Mr Blade mentioned that's what you and Stephenson were working on.'

'The work's complete,' Whittaker said. 'Stephenson had a good mind – I could teach *him*, unlike the rank and file of this place . . .' He looked James up and down disdainfully. 'Emphasis on the *rank*. Sit down, Bond. It's your first day back, but if you think I'll spare you the rod, think again. I know all about the trouble you've caused. For God's sake, and for your own, speak only when spoken to.'

As the classroom began to fill with pupils, Whittaker carefully picked up his piece of board and placed it in his briefcase.

'Sorry, sir.' James headed towards his seat. He could feel the eyes of his classmates upon him, and ignored them as best he could, waiting for the lesson to start. But Whittaker was still staring out of the window, his face drawn.

A minute later, Herta breezed in with a sheaf of papers, her lily-of-the-valley scent freshening the air. James's heart jumped, but for different reasons from those of the other boys; they straightened in their seats and stared at her – the only girl in the school. However, she looked only at James, winking, then grinning at him as she placed the papers on Whittaker's desk. James could feel the glares of the other boys on him.

'I have some figures I'd like you to check,' Herta announced, as if she were in charge and Whittaker her assistant.

Whittaker looked up at her. 'Would you indeed?'

'For inclusion in tonight's report.'

'Very well. If you'll excuse me now . . . I must attempt to bend what passes for the minds of my charges towards science.'

'Of course.' As she headed for the door, Herta gave James another smile. Some of the other boys muttered angrily, and James felt a ruler poke him in the back.

'That's enough.' Whittaker took a deep breath and exhaled again. 'Now, can anyone tell me how to go about calculating the trajectory of an artillery shell based on weight, velocity and angle of the barrel? Well?'

A boy called Hazel put up his hand. 'Split the initial velocity into two different axes, speed and direction, using trigonometry . . .'

James put up his hand too, and Whittaker glanced over. 'Speaking of shells, sir, is it true that Germany are re-arming?'

'Of course it's true. And if war should break out again, you'll find that the means and method of battle will not be as they were twenty years ago.'

'I understand that many of the artillerymen used guess-work when firing infantry guns,' James went on. 'They needed high-angle fire to try and hit the trenches and low-angle fire to engage bunkers.'

'You . . . *understand*?' Whittaker turned a murderous stare on him. 'What do you *understand*, exactly, you pampered boy? You *understand* the fear of living in those trenches, night after night, the noise of the shells all around you? You *understand* the losing of a limb, I suppose; the pain, the horror of looking down at a stump where once you—' He closed his eyes and bit his lip, his voice shaky. 'An acquaintance with the facts, Bond, is not the same as *understanding* it.'

James felt his cheeks burn. He hadn't expected such a violent reaction. And Whittaker wasn't through with him yet; he grabbed a book off his desk and flicked through the pages.

'Ah, yes. This is the chemical composition of mustard gas, as used on the battlefields of the Great War: $(Cl\text{-}CH_2CH_2)_2S$.' He advanced on James, a vein throbbing at his temple. 'There. Do you *understand* mustard gas now, Bond? Do you *understand* the pain as your skin blisters and burns, as your respiratory system starts to melt, as the ulcers form on your eyes?'

'No, sir,' James said quietly. 'I didn't mean—'

'You'll copy out the Depretz method of synthesizing mustard agent by adding ethylene to sulphur dichloride five hundred times, Bond, and hand it to me by lunch time.' Whittaker slammed the book down on James's desk. 'Do you understand *that*?'

James looked into the dark, bulging eyes that must have seen so much; eyes that had watched the dying Marcus as he screamed.

'You'll get what you asked for,' James said. 'Sir.'

On his second day back in the cut and thrust of school life, James was considered fit enough to tackle the Quarry Circle – three miles through wooded hillsides. It felt good to exercise properly, to focus on his breathing, his steps, his pace. It was something over which he had full control.

The countryside seemed to have changed in the few days he'd been confined to bed. The fiery autumn-red trees had been stripped bare by a westerly wind, and now stood silent in the *haar*, or sea fog, that had drifted in off the Forth. James shivered as he ran, his white shorts, shirt and jersey spattered, his brown stockings soaked, his running shoes caked in mud.

All at once he heard someone coming up behind him; someone who was sprinting . . . But why, with so far to go before the finish—?

The answer came painfully as James was rugby-tackled and brought crashing down onto the wet ground. He gasped and tried to raise his head, but now his attacker was sitting on his back, holding him by the hair and grinding his face down into the mud. He squirmed and writhed – until someone else grabbed his arms, pinning them down so he couldn't lever himself up. He tried to shout, but the wet mud blocked his mouth and nose. He almost gagged on the foul taste. The pressure on the back of his head increased, forcing his face into the earth. He was suffocating.

How far will they go? he wondered. Had Whittaker set

64

this up? Herta? James suddenly let himself go limp, feigning unconsciousness, hoping that his attackers would slacken their hold. He tried not to react as they pulled his hair, lifting his head out of the muck, but the next moment a kick in the ribs made him gasp with pain; wet mud oozed out of his mouth as he rolled onto his back.

Panting for breath, James wiped his eyes and saw four sixth-form boys standing over him in a circle. He'd noticed them around school; they were housemates of Marcus, and 'Mods' – like him, they'd chosen to study sciences over the Classics.

'There he is.' The tallest and burliest, a Scottish lad called Dockerill, sneered down at him. 'The little cretin who got Stephenson killed.'

'That's not true.' Panting for breath, James glared up at him. 'I had nothing to do with—'

'Liar.' A shorter boy – James didn't know his name – kicked him in the ribs again.

He rolled with the blow, but cried out as if badly hurt. Outnumbering him four to one, his attackers must be feeling cocky; let them grow even more complacent, thinking their target weak. 'I'm telling you . . . I had nothing to do with it.'

'You were thrown out of Eton, weren't you?' said one of the others – a blond, snub-nosed boy called Ibbotson. 'What happened – did you get someone killed there too?'

'Stephenson was with Whittaker that night . . .' James said slowly. 'I found him in the grounds – he was hurt—'

'You still sticking to that fairy story?' Dockerill came closer. 'That lightning really did something to your head, didn't it? But don't worry . . . I reckon we can knock some sense into it.'

'Reckon we can,' said the boy behind him.

Pushing himself up on his elbows, James quickly glanced around, assessing his options. He could hear no other runners coming through the fog; perhaps another of this little gang was redirecting people away.

Dockerill and his friends closed in around him. One of the boys raised a foot, ready to bring it down on James's skull . . .

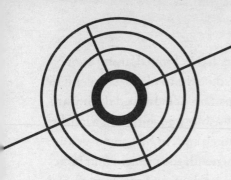

8
Allies and Enemies

James grabbed a handful of thick mud and hurled it at Dockerill and Ibbotson; the slimy spray caught them both in the face. As they recoiled, he launched himself into a backward roll, kicking his attacker in the stomach with both feet. The boy doubled up and fell back with a cry.

The fourth member of Dockerill's hunting party came at James with a snapped-off branch which he swung like a club. James dodged backwards and it whistled past his face. Then he flattened his hand and brought it down on the boy's wrist in a chopping motion. With a shout, the boy let go of the branch, and James dropped him with an uppercut to the chin that sent him sprawling.

With an angry snarl, Dockerill came in next. *You're the one to beat*, James thought. *The ringleader.* He turned and ran out of the clearing as if put to flight, and Dockerill gave chase. James had a plan, but its success depended on split-second timing.

He made for a low-hanging branch that looked strong enough to support his weight, then slowed down to allow Dockerill to catch up. All at once James jumped up and gripped the branch with both hands; his momentum allowed him to swing his whole body up and over the branch in a tight gymnastic arc. Dockerill skidded to a stop just beneath the branch, and James swung both feet down into his back, knocking him to the ground.

Now it was James who had his knee jammed up against Dockerill's spine, pushing his head down into the mud. For a moment he just wanted to strike hard at the other boy – to take out his frustration and grief. But he realized that Dockerill must have attacked him for much the same reasons.

He bent forward and hissed in Dockerill's ear: 'I didn't get Stephenson killed. But try this again and I'll have a damn good go at you.'

Ibbotson and the others were crashing through the trees towards him. James scrambled up and ran on through the misty woods, adrenalin ebbing, its aftertaste clinging to the back of his throat. He ran on until he reached the school grounds – by now he was feeling weak, his head pounding. *I'm pushing myself too hard, too soon*, he realized, and slowed his pace. There was a hut up ahead, and he leaned against it, panting for breath, trying to will away the dizziness . . .

James froze as a tall figure loomed up out of the mist in front of him. It was a man in a rumpled grey overcoat, bald and wrinkled, his eyes narrowed as if trying to see past the bulbous nose that dominated his face. 'Och,' he said, 'not you again.'

James suddenly realized where he was. 'You're the

groundsman,' he said, relieved. 'You found Stephenson and me. I might have died too if you hadn't—'

'You damned fool. Think I wanted to come across bodies like that in the middle of the night?' The man's voice softened as he saw James swaying on his feet. 'You don't look right, lad. I suppose you'd best come in for a moment. Don't want to have to pick you up off the lawn again.'

The hut, lit by a paraffin lamp, smelled of earth and tobacco smoke. The groundsman's belongings looked as battered and timeworn as their owner. There was an old hat-stand leaning under the weight of capes and coats; pots and gardening tools; a wireless set; and an ancient chair. Keys of all sizes hung from hooks on the wall, and there was an anti-quated key-cutting machine on the workbench in the corner, with a handful of blank keys scattered about.

'You look like you could use a nip of this.' The groundsman poured whisky into a grubby glass and passed it over.

James sipped politely, then grimaced. The taste was peaty, but the warmth it brought was welcome. 'How did you know Marcus and I were out there, in the dark, so late?' he asked.

'I got called on the *telephone*' – the man spoke as if the device was dangerous, and not to be trusted – 'in my cottage. A girl, if you please, and at that time! One of the maids, I suppose, up to no good; she thought she'd seen two boys struck by lightning . . .'

James decided it was pointless to argue that this 'maid' was lying. 'Well, I'd love to thank her. Do you know who she was?'

'Not a clue.' The groundsman snorted and shook his head. 'She sounded foreign. German. She's got better eyes than me, wherever she's from; I saw no lightning then. Found no trace of a strike, either.'

James leaned forward. 'Did you tell the police that?'

'Aye, course.' The old man looked defensive. 'What d'you take me for, lad? I suppose they must've talked to the maid themselves . . .'

'I don't know of any foreign maids,' James thought aloud. 'But could it have been Miss Axmann – the girl who helps Dr Whittaker?'

'I wouldn't know.' Another snort, this time of derision. 'That man, Whittaker . . . A proper barmpot. The hours he had me kitting out that old workshop behind the school to his satisfaction, all on top of my normal duties . . . And for what? Man's taken leave of his senses.'

'Why?'

The groundsman frowned; it was as if he'd just realized he was gossiping with a pupil. 'Come on, now, lad. If you're feeling better, best be on your way. And see you stay inside at night.'

'Of course,' James agreed. *And it's what's inside that workshop you fixed up for Whittaker I'd like to see.* 'Thanks.'

He left the hut, and jogged off towards Glencorse to join the rest of the boys for showers.

Later that afternoon, James went out into the grounds again. He remembered seeing a larger hut behind the main school building – that must be the workshop the groundsman had mentioned. He soon found it among the trees – a single-storey brick building. The windows were blacked out, and he saw that the door was padlocked shut. What was kept in there?

As he stepped away from the door, he thought he caught movement in a window of the main school building, up on the third floor; a watching figure, which quickly stepped back out of sight.

Feeling uneasy, James returned to his cubicle.

After brooding all night, he decided to return to the grounds-man's hut. The old man had admitted he'd seen no lightning; a fact that the police had apparently ignored. If James could somehow persuade him to make a further statement that tied in with his own; and if he could only find the key to the workshop . . .

At breakfast James grabbed his bread and butter, then slipped away into the grounds, sprinting for the hut. But when he got there, he discovered that it was locked. Peering through the grimy windows, he saw that the hat-stand now stood empty. The chair was gone.

Then he noticed a blank envelope pinned to the wood beneath the window. He tore it open and pulled out a single sheet of writing paper. Two words had been typed in the middle:

Predictable, Bond

James felt a chill run down his spine. *If someone did see me at the workshop*, he reasoned, *they could take a pretty good guess at who must've told me about it.*

He ran back and pushed his way through the heavy wooden door into the school reception. The woman at the front desk turned flinty eyes on him.

'The groundsman,' James panted. 'I . . . I have an urgent message.'

'Mr Peters left us first thing this morning,' she said.

'Left?' James frowned. 'But I saw him yesterday, and . . . It's important I get hold of him.'

'Why?' A second after asking this she shook her head, as if the answer could be of no interest to her in any case. 'I can't say when he'll be back. Compassionate leave. A death in the family. All very sudden.'

James felt cold. 'Yes. Very sudden . . .'

All at once he noticed Herta looking down at him from the minstrel's gallery above the hall. Her chin was thrust out as she smiled at him, then turned and disappeared into the shadows of the landing.

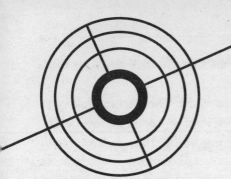

9

Investigation

The nights shortened, the days grew colder, and finally the Christmas holidays came round. At 7.55 p.m. on 19 December 1934 James and Perry were due to catch the sleeper train to London. From there they would continue their journey onward to Canterbury station – to be met by Charmian, who would drive them the last few miles to Pett Bottom.

That had been the plan.

Instead, James and Perry were now heading in the opposite direction in a stolen Rolls-Royce, making for a tiny hamlet in Stirling. In the frosty distance they could see the Trossachs, smooth-ridged shields of moonlit rock guarding the horizon.

'What a way to kick off the holidays, eh, James!' Perry remarked from the passenger seat.

James didn't bother to reply. He checked that the riding-control lever above the steering wheel was still set to maximum, for the most comfortable ride at the highest speed, and again mulled over the events that had led them to this point.

His shoulders ached as he gripped the wheel – largely from catching up on all the schoolwork he'd missed. The low desks and wooden chairs were so uncomfortable that the so-called 'Fettes stoop' was the result.

Frustrating though it was, James had taken pains to keep to the school rules. It was the only way to quell the suspicions of those watching him. Herta was undoubtedly the prime mover in this impromptu spy ring, and her tactics were effective: she recruited different boys to her cause at different times, either with bribes or charm, with the result that James was never quite sure who was watching him when.

But behind the smokescreen of playing the model pupil, James had managed to conduct his own investigations. Perry was able to move around unobserved; he gathered good intelligence, and had a ball into the bargain.

'Whittaker's room is located on the third floor, Bond,' Perry told him after they had 'bumped into each other' behind the rifle range. 'I've tried the handle a few times – it's always locked. As for Herta, well – now they've shipped out m-most of the lab equipment, she's been installed up in the trunk room, out of the way. There are porters on patrol on the staircase. They think it very improper that only old Hook's allowed up there.'

'I doubt whether it's romance on his mind,' James had answered. 'Their secret project – the project Stephenson died for – goes on . . .'

And who else might die in its name? The question was never far from James's thoughts.

Herta usually sat apart in the dining hall, her cool stare on

James as he ate in silence. The eyes of the boys flicked about her like flies over ripe fruit, while the masters regarded her with disapproval. Herta seemed oblivious to it all, however, her face impassive.

One evening James had stopped at her table on the way out. 'Why are you here?' he asked quietly.

Her smile seemed painted on the porcelain, doll-like face. 'I am eating, James.'

'I mean, how did you come to work with Dr Whittaker? Did Mr Blade sponsor you?'

'I'm not working for Blade-Rise. You could say I'm here on loan.' Herta rose from the table, arching her slender eyebrows. 'You ask a lot of questions, James. That's healthy for an enquiring mind. But really, you should know when to stop.'

James watched her go. 'Don't count on it,' he muttered. The veiled threats, the hints of conspiracy . . . they only strengthened his resolve to find answers.

Several times over the next few days, hoping that Herta's spies were engaged in their own affairs, James slipped up to Whittaker's room when he knew the man was teaching. He'd already broken into the empty groundsman's hut and helped himself to some blank keys. James blackened the blade of one of them on the sputtering flame of a candle lantern on the staircase up to the third floor, then worked it into the warded lock on Whittaker's door. As he tried to rotate the blank key, he met with resistance; when he pulled it out, the ward had left a mark in the soot, showing him where he needed to file the next notch in order to overcome the lock. Over the course of four illicit visits, the skeleton key took shape. But James was always aware of scrutiny.

After the fourth foray he found Herta sitting at his place in the library. 'Where have you been, Bond?' she asked. 'I found your prep abandoned. I was worried.'

Through gritted teeth, James answered, 'I went to see Matron for some aspirin. I don't need supervision.'

'But you've been through so much. And your head hurts – you say so yourself.' She beckoned to a tall, stocky boy waiting by a window. 'I've asked Hazel here to keep an eye on you.'

James stared at Hazel, a prefect at Glencorse and full-back for the Fettes first XV. 'There's no need.'

'If the lady wishes it, so let it be.' Hazel patted him on the shoulder with a patronizing smile. '*Numquam Onus*, Bond, remember? Nothing is too much—'

'Trouble ahead, James!' Perry's voice brought James back to the present; a truck had appeared round the corner of the narrow lane. James braked quickly and mounted the grass verge to allow the other vehicle past. The truck's horn blared and it rumbled past into the night.

'Well!' Perry was grinning as he perched on the edge of the smooth leather passenger seat. 'That was a near thing!'

James said nothing. As he accelerated away, he noticed that the engine was pinking: he knew he'd been pushing the car too fast. He checked the thermostat on the dashboard, made sure the radiator shutters were operating correctly, then changed into a lower gear and pushed the throttle in a little. If the car overheated now, and they got stuck in the middle of nowhere . . .

'I hope your hunch pays off,' Perry announced.

James shot him a glance. 'So it's *my* hunch now, is it?'

'If you're wrong, certainly.'

James smiled. Perry had invested a lot of time into their mission; and a lot of time face down on the only crashmat at Fettes that hadn't been requisitioned, as they continued the fine traditions of the fledgling judo club, talking as they fought.

'I forced the padlock on that workshop, James,' Perry had said. 'You wondered where the crashm-mats had gone? Well, m-m-most of them are in there, along with those great cushions that m-maharajahs sit on. The walls are piled up with sandbags – that's why you can't see through the windows. There's a path cleared between the door and some seating, and all the edges of the furniture have been covered with sponge and chamois. Strangest thing I ever saw . . .'

'A meeting place for someone fragile?' James remembered how the chauffeur had lingered behind his visitor in the san, as if ready to catch him should he fall. 'Sounds like it's been converted into a safe meeting place for Mr Blade.'

'During the war, field headquarters used sandbags to soundproof the place against spies.'

'So Blade's been having secret meetings at Fettes . . . And for old Hook to put the groundsman to so much trouble, he must have met him there often . . .'

Since then, James had kept an eye out, watching for Blade's return.

Three days ago he'd been staring at the endless Latin of the *Remedia Amores* and hoping Ovid had rotted in the Underworld when, through the library window, he'd heard the smooth growl of a powerful V8 engine. Peering out, he saw a futuristic-looking automobile moving slowly along the drive, and whistled at the beauty of the shining silver machine: it was styled in sweeping aerodynamic lines, from the sleek, sloping bonnet to the huge clamshell boot. It was heading towards the stables and workshops behind the main building. In the centre of the curved bonnet was a red disc that confirmed the marque to James.

'A Tatra 77,' he heard an older boy say as the motorcar approached. 'That's the freak's car!'

One guess who they're talking about. So! Another meeting with Blade was about to begin. Whittaker would be summoned; Herta too, perhaps.

Which meant that Whittaker's room on the third floor would be empty. James knew he would never have a better opportunity to search it. *After so many attempts, my key must be filed correctly by now.*

He waited fifteen minutes, until he was sure Whittaker would have made his way to the soundproofed outbuilding. There was no sign of Herta's gang of spies, so James left his Latin prep, went through the library doors to the spiral staircase, climbing quickly to the gloomy third floor. He crept along the passage, wincing with each squeak of a floorboard. If a master caught him up here . . .

Whittaker's door was locked, of course. Heart thumping, James pushed the well-filed key into the lock, and turned it first fiercely, then gently, then—

The lock finally gave. Letting out a breath, James turned the doorknob and slipped inside.

The room was a mess and reeked of pipe tobacco. Oak-panelled, filled with threadbare Victorian furniture, it could barely have changed since the turn of the century. James crossed to the little desk that was buried underneath scraps of paper covered with abstruse equations and diagrams that made no more sense than Ovid had.

On the table beside the heavy Bakelite telephone lay a notepad, and that looked more promising. A page had been roughly torn off the top; James saw that the pen nib had left impressions in the sheet beneath, and carefully tore the paper out. He folded it and put it in his trouser pocket.

What else? A calendar on the wall showed a futurist landscape at odds with the Victorian furniture, with a red cross through *20 December*, the day after term ended. *What happens then?* James wondered, turning his attentions to the drawers and cupboards. He was hoping for draft notes for a doctored police report – or anything that might shed light on what had been going on in the trunk room. But while he searched methodically, he found nothing, save for the keys to Whittaker's Rolls. He was tempted to take them out of spite, but if Whittaker realized that someone had been in his room, he wouldn't need to look far for a suspect.

Feeling frustrated, James withdrew. He'd barely turned his homemade key in the lock and started along the passage when Hazel appeared, blocking his way.

'What do you think you're doing, Bond?' The boy folded his arms across his chest. 'You know Miss Axmann wants me to watch out for furtive or eccentric behaviour . . . I'd say you qualify for both.'

James swore to himself. How long had Hazel been there? How much had he seen? 'I was just calling on Dr Whittaker to apologize for being so difficult.' He palmed the key to conceal it. 'There's really no need to follow me everywhere.'

'You'd rather we turned a blind eye?' Hazel looked amused

as he came up to James. 'It'll cost you, Bond. How much do you have?'

'Just get out of my way.'

Hazel put a heavy hand on James's sore shoulder, setting his nerves jangling. 'How much?'

As temper overcame caution, James slid the key out beyond his knuckles and punched Hazel in the ribs. The boy turned white, spluttered and sank to his knees.

'About *that* much,' James hissed, and marched past him.

Half an hour later, back in his study, James had gently shaded in soft pencil over the paper he'd taken from Whittaker's room, revealing the words imprinted there:

Demonstration – H Operator
Stay Thornhill 182

James remembered the sense of achievement as he stared at the ghost of the words. *H Operator* – H for Herta, perhaps? And *Thornhill 182* . . . Could that be an address? Or perhaps part of a telephone number?

That night he'd called the local switchboard operator from Cooper's study while the housemaster was with the Head. The operator said there was no listed number that matched those digits, but at least confirmed that there were two *Thornhill*s in Scotland, one in Dumfriesshire and one up in Stirling. James and Perry had met in the library to look up both places on a map.

'First up . . .' Perry ran his finger along a narrow trail heading through steep gradients. 'To the north-west, around fifty miles from here: a village named Thornhill.'

'And look what's next to it.' James felt the hairs on the back of his neck stand up as he brought his finger down beside Perry's. 'Ruskie. It was nothing to do with any Russian – it's a *place*.'

Perry gasped in realization. '*That's* what Stephenson was trying to tell you with his dying words?'

'A demonstration *in* Ruskie . . . or between there and Thornhill . . .' James nodded, excitement growing. 'That red cross on the twentieth on Whittaker's calendar – it could mark the date of that demonstration.'

'You said Stephenson didn't think they were ready for it, didn't you?'

'Yes. Perhaps that's why Blade had to come visiting – to chivvy them along . . .'

'Could be. But what does the 182 m-mean?' Perry closed the map book with a dusty slap. 'Perhaps old Hook was calculating how m-m-many lives you have!'

The next morning James had been sent to the Headmaster's study to discuss his 'unprovoked assault' on Hazel outside Whittaker's room.

'Every consideration has been afforded you, Bond, given the loss of your friend, but your behaviour simply goes too far.' The Headmaster picked up his wooden cane from beside his desk. 'I sincerely hope, now that Dr Whittaker has departed Fettes, you can go back to—'

James's heart thumped. 'He's left, sir?'

'Mr Blade's chauffeur collected Whittaker and Miss Axmann yesterday. They've both left and will not be back. If you keep up this behaviour, Bond, nor will you.'

'But I saw his car outside—'

'That's enough of your impudence, Bond,' the Head barked. Then his voice softened. 'I respect your dedication to your studies; how you've chosen to work instead of convalescing. And I can appreciate your preoccupation with Dr Whittaker's secretive work with Stephenson. Be assured that he is leaving the country directly. His car was hired, I understand, and I dare say he has made arrangements for its collection.' He looked troubled as he flexed the cane in his hands. 'We can all put this business behind us now, Bond. Hold out your palm . . .'

Whittaker's gone. James could hardly take it in. Yesterday was 18 December – could that account for the '18' in *182*? And the '2' could refer to Whittaker and Herta – their abrupt departure must have been planned all along . . . *Or am I trying to find patterns where none exist?*

James flinched as the Head's cane sliced down and bit into his palm once – twice – three times . . .

With his quarry gone and no evidence remaining of the trunk-room experiments, and with the term ending on a sermon that encouraged the spread of goodwill to all men, James had been faced with a stark choice. Go home, move on, try to forget . . . Or steal Whittaker's splendid car – risking certain expulsion – and take Perry with him on a road trip to Ruskie to learn the truth of things.

So, after swiping the keys from behind the desk in reception, they'd snuck into the Rolls under cover of darkness, deciphered the correct sequence of levers and controls to start her up, then driven away unchallenged and elated, justifying their theft as the logical next step in their quest for truth.

But as James reflected on the events that had brought them

from the stern cloisters of Fettes out into this wild Highland landscape, the enormity of what they were attempting was beginning to sink in.

'It would be funny if we ran into old Hook himself on one of these roads, eh?' Perry chuckled. '*You forgot your automobile!* we could tell him. *Just dropping it back to you!*'

'He and Herta must be busy preparing for Red-Cross-on-the-Calendar Day tomorrow,' said James. 'The demonstration of whatever they've been creating for Blade-Rise – with Marcus's help. We're finally going to find out whatever the hell it is.'

The words sounded feeble now. *The truth at all costs*, James had been telling himself, throughout this long journey. *Justice for Marcus*. But there was more to his motives, he knew. He'd left Eton under a cloud with scant silver linings, bound to silence by the Official Secrets Act, his life packaged up and redirected by powerful men for the good of his country. He'd accepted that, and his adventures in Los Angeles and Cuba had reminded him that you could choose how to live your life – and, by embracing a cause, the manner of your death. But now, faceless forces had sought to turn manslaughter into misadventure, and he was damned if he would meekly go along with that too.

As they crossed the coniferous flanks of the Menteith Hills, the Rolls was running on the last fumes in its eighteen-gallon tank; they circled the area, hoping to find evidence of some major human trespass. But it was dark, and the area vast. Deep down, James didn't expect to find a thing.

And that was when he saw it.

10

Night of Discovery

James stopped the car halfway down the hill, and pulled on the handbrake as Perry reached over to switch off the headlights. Great ripples and flashes of blue-white light were illuminating the tree-clad valley.

'What in the name of God . . . ?' Perry stared. 'What's causing that?'

They both knew the only way to find out. James flicked the headlights back on and depressed the handbrake, setting the Rolls roaring off into the night. 'If that's Whittaker and friends, there must be an access road leading to this demonstration,' he reasoned. 'It must have taken several trucks to clear out the trunk room.'

'And they m-must be setting up near a building to use the power supply,' Perry agreed.

James steered them back through Ruskie and headed for Thornhill, excitement thrumming through his veins. Several rutted muddy paths led off from the main road; James slowed to scrutinize them for signs of heavy tyre-treads or flattened vegetation – any evidence of recent activity.

There was nothing. Not a sign. He stared at the fuel gauge. How much petrol was left in the tank now?

'James?' Perry grabbed his arm so hard it caused the car to swerve.

'What the hell—?' James braked hard.

'Back up. Look!'

James slammed the gearstick left and up into reverse, sending the car rolling back along the deserted road until the signpost was lit by the glare of the headlamps. Through the shadows cast by the spindly branches in front he read:

THORNHILL ABBEY

PRIVATE PROPERTY

NO TRESPASSERS

'*This* is the Thornhill he meant,' James breathed. 'Must be named after the village.' Further down the long drive he could see a grey truck blocking the way. 'We've found it. This is the place.'

'So m-m-move along before we're spotted right outside in Whittaker's m-motorcar!' Perry urged him.

James quickly pulled away. 'We'll dump the car and double back on foot,' he said.

He parked the Rolls at the edge of a muddy field behind a hedgerow so it couldn't be seen from the road. There was a torch in the glove compartment, and he took it, along with the heavy starter handle from the toolbox as a possible weapon. He wished he had his pistol, Queensmarsh, with him, but he'd left it at Aunt Charmian's. Starting afresh – that had been the idea . . . Yet here he was again, rushing headlong into danger, and he recognized that it was a truer homecoming than a visit to Pett Bottom could ever be.

James locked the doors and dropped the key, threaded on a long silver chain, into his pocket. The Ever Ready torch was reassuringly heavy in his left hand as he led Perry back along the road; both were still dressed in their school suits and coats, collars turned up against the freezing drizzle.

'The grounds must go on for miles,' James whispered. 'We're sure to find a way in somewhere.'

'To where the action is,' Perry agreed.

They struggled through the brambles beside the road and in amongst the conifers, with their damp, Christmassy smell. Plenty of cover if they needed to hide. But then James's torch beam found a wire fence that had to be eight feet tall. It looked like copper wire, with barbed wire coiled behind it.

'Quite a climb,' Perry remarked. 'You'd think they didn't want visitors.'

'Of any kind,' James added, holding the torch still as it illuminated an owl, lying dead and twisted between the two sets of wire. Moving the beam downwards, he picked out black junction boxes joining the wires to the fence posts. 'It's electrified. Must be quite a current.'

'Oh, m-m-marvellous.' Shivering in the cold, Perry swore. 'D'you think it stretches round the whole area?'

James considered. 'I think we may have to risk the main drive for a way to get past that problem.'

Switching off the torch as they neared the sign, James ran

lightly down the driveway in the pale light of the clouded moon, approaching the parked lorry. Its bulk blocked his view of the drive beyond, but it was the wooded area to the right that mattered.

'If we climb up onto the roof,' James said, 'we should be able to reach the branches of that tree and use them to swing ourselves over the fence.'

'Inspired by *Tarzan and His M-M-Mate*, I suppose! I only hope you don't yodel as you swing through the trees.'

James ignored him, putting one foot on the running board and using the oversized wing mirror to swing himself round onto the bonnet of the lorry. From there he reached up with frozen hands to the cold, rain-slick metal roof and hauled himself up as quietly as he could.

Perry followed him, and then said, 'I'll go first.'

Lying flat on the roof, James watched his progress: the wet bough swayed but held his weight. Perry went hand over hand into the shadows, swung himself over the deadly fence, making steadily for the trunk. The clacking and rustling he made as he went sounded loud enough to wake the dead.

But compared to the gunshot, it was nothing.

James looked up sharply and stared out into the dark. A sentry dressed in charcoal uniform stood perhaps twenty feet further down the drive, rifle aimed up at the tree – at Perry. Had he been hit? James wondered.

Heart hammering, he lowered himself back down onto the road as quickly as he could – as the sentry fired again.

Prising a large stone out of the ground beside the drive, James edged round the side of the lorry and hurled his missile as far as he could. It sailed past the sentry, landing somewhere behind him, further along the drive. The man turned round and moved off to investigate.

Immediately James broke cover and ran like hell towards him. *I'm unarmed*, he thought, *and I'm facing down a professional sentry*. His footsteps seemed so loud, the distance to cover so great; it felt as if he was running in slow motion. He reached into his pocket.

The sentry turned, saw James and brought up his gun.

At the same time, driving himself onwards, James yanked the ignition key and its chain out of his pocket and threw it at the fence to his right. There was a bright flash of sparks as the chain touched the wires and the circuit shorted. The guard wasn't prepared: blinded by the sudden glare, he fired his rifle. Fired and missed.

James kept on running, bore down on his target, then tried to knock the gun out of the man's grip. No good: the sentry held onto it, turning as he did so, presenting the back of his neck; James raised his hand, flattened it and brought it down in a judo strike onto the top of his spine.

With a shout, the guard threw back his head and dropped the rifle. But the blow wasn't enough to fell him, and he swung round, his hand closing round James's throat.

Gasping, James punched the side of the man's face to break his grip. At the same time he twisted his whole body and threw the man over in a somersault. The guard's head struck the hard driveway. He didn't get up again.

Crouching, James felt for a pulse, found it, and then looked around for further movement. How many guards were posted? he wondered. Others might have heard those shots and be on their way to investigate right now.

He dragged the sentry back towards his starting point. 'Perry?' he hissed.

"That was bloody close,' came the shaky response from the other side of the fence. 'Is that guard out of action?'

'Hopefully for a while.' James carried on dragging the man back towards the lorry. 'Are you fit to keep going?'

'We've come this far . . .'

The vehicle was locked, so James rolled the body underneath it, out of sight. Then he climbed back up onto the roof and threw himself into the branches, scrambling over the barrier and swiftly shinning down the tree trunk to where Perry stood waiting.

'No one shot at you,' came his friend's mock complaint. 'Where's the fairness in that?'

'Life's not fair,' James replied as a crackling, thrumming sound started up. The air seemed to fill with static, and the night sky flickered white-blue through the branches. Then the blackness of the wooded night returned, thicker than ever.

Death's not fair, either.

'Come on.' Switching on the torch, James led the way through the woods in the direction of the unearthly light. The hairs on his arms and the back of his neck stood up – and not only with cold. It was the same feeling he'd had back at Fettes, the night Marcus had died. There was an electric energy in the wintry night air. James's instincts warned him away, but the old determination to see things through was impossible to ignore.

Progress was slow; it seemed as if woodland had sprung up wherever there was soil. There were clouds overhead screening the moon, and the night was silent now; no hoot or scurry could be heard.

James felt a moment's relief when he saw clear space up ahead. Then he saw the rusted metal sign that stood before it, warning in faded capitals, KEEP OUT: MINEFIELD.

Perry groaned softly. 'What on earth . . . ?'

'Blade-Rise makes weapons,' James murmured. 'I suppose they've got to test them somewhere. So they buy up some remote Scottish countryside that they can blow to bits unobserved. We'll just have to go round.'

'And if we've m-missed a different sign, warning us of worse horrors . . . ?'

'We'll go slowly,' James suggested.

Midnight drew close and the temperature dropped further. James's back was slick with cold sweat as he struggled through bramble and scrub. After what felt like an age, he stopped dead at the sound of a heavy vehicle approaching.

'M-must be a road ahead,' Perry hissed.

James threw himself back into the undergrowth as stark white headlights lit the space around him. A lorry was coming, a heavy-duty six-wheeler with tall metal sides. Gears crunched and shifted as wheels churned through the mud.

'Follow in its tracks and we'll know the way is safe,' said Perry. 'With any luck it's headed for where the action is.'

James looked at him. 'Why follow when we can take a ride?'

'Reckless' – Perry gave a half-smile – 'but practical.'

They waited for the lorry to pass by. Luckily its rear lights were filthy and gave little illumination. James jumped out as soon as it had passed, praying he'd not been seen by the driver in his wing mirror. Stumbling through the thick mud, he leaped for the running board at the back, fingers latching onto a heavy-duty ramp – for loading and unloading – that was folded up against the rear doors. He slipped twice, struggled to keep his balance – and saw that Perry was falling behind as the lorry accelerated away.

He stretched out his arm. Perry ran faster, trying not to lose his footing. If he was so much as glimpsed by the driver . . . James stretched out his hand as far as he could; at last his fingers brushed against Perry's and he managed to grab hold of them. For a few feet he was actually towing Perry through the mire.

'Finally,' Perry gasped, beaming as he got a foothold and clung on beside James. 'Close one, eh?'

'Close enough,' James agreed. He prayed no one was inside the lorry, then remembered that the walls were solid metal with no ventilation – for carrying cargo, not passengers.

'Roofwards?' Perry nodded to the folded ramp. 'Stepping stone.'

With James to support him, he placed a foot on top of the ramp and clambered up onto the roof. James reached up and took Perry's offered hand as he climbed up behind him.

Now they were lying flat on their fronts in the middle of the roof, slipping all over the place as the lorry climbed up the bumpy track. Strangely, James found his thoughts turning to Charmian. By now she must be wondering where on earth he was, calling the school, thinking about the police . . .

Unless Whittaker's car is found, James reflected, *no one will ever imagine we're here.*

Finally the track levelled out. *We're a good way up*, James realized, staring around at wooded peaks and the silvered bulk of the Trossachs. The lorry came to a stop close to the lip of a vast floodlit ravine. *So much light . . .* James raised his head cautiously and saw below him the ruins of the old abbey; the whole area was a hive of activity. Two huge carbon arc searchlights, each as tall as two men and maybe sixty inches across, illuminated the scene – surely the source of the blue-white light they'd seen from afar. They crackled with energy from an unseen generator.

People – technicians or soldiers? – were crawling all over the area like termites on a mound. James saw that a great concrete bunker had been built into the abbey. *Like a hide, for observing,* he supposed. *So why has the driver come all the way up here?*

As if to oblige him with an answer, the cab doors opened on either side of the lorry, and the driver and his mate got out. They went round to the back, let down the ramp and swung open the huge insulated doors. James held every muscle rigid, barely daring to breathe as the men moved about inside, manoeuvring something heavy into position.

A loud noise rang out across the ravine. '*Shadow to position.*' It echoed wildly with cracks of static, the words repeated as they bounced off the bare rocks. '*Shadow – take up your position, please.*'

Even distorted through the loudspeaker, the voice was instantly recognizable. 'Whittaker,' James whispered.

Perry nodded. 'Who's he talked into taking over from M-M-Marcus?'

'Whoever it is must be mad if they—' James broke off as the men reappeared, wheeling out a large mortar. They set up the two-man weapon at the edge of the cliff. Then one of the men fetched a smaller tripod and began to set up a movie camera.

James's nerves jangled. *Recording the demonstration from different angles . . .*

'*Stand clear.*' Whittaker again, his voice loud and rasping. '*Final charge. Activate.*'

James felt the static in the air, as if a storm was about to break. *Giving power to something,* was James's best guess. *The same thing Marcus was caught inside . . . ?* Then he saw some kind of machine moving through the ravine with a speed that belied its considerable size. James realized that it was taller than a human, and bulkier. But as he squinted against the dazzling spotlights, he saw that this wasn't just a machine. Someone was actually strapped inside a kind of armoured cage.

'That's what I saw,' Perry hissed. 'Through the window of the trunk room – with M–M–Marcus inside.'

Whoever it was wore a dark protective helmet and a gas mask, which obscured their features. The arms and upper body were encased in silver bindings, lashed to the heavy metal frame. The legs disappeared into a complex set of splints, rods and callipers, like a skeleton reimagined in steel; the enormous metal feet left deep impressions in the wet earth. The legs powered along, rising and falling, while some kind of steam-powered generator chuffed and bubbled away on the figure's back. The overall effect was of a medieval knight recreated with 1930s technology, hooked up to steam power and electronics.

'That sound . . .' James shivered. 'I glimpsed that thing, or something like it, carrying Marcus out into the grounds. That's what it is they've been building – and what they're here to test out.'

Another, lower voice echoed across the ravine. '*Turn ten degrees clockwise . . . then five paces left into final target position, Miss Axmann.*'

'What the——?' James stared, transfixed by the eerie scene in front of him. 'Herta's in that thing!'

11
The Girl in the Iron Suit

She followed Whittaker's command; she was secured within the clanking robotic suit, yet pulled it along as if it weighed nothing.

The suit stopped as Herta stayed still, like a metal statue.

'*Target position attained*,' barked the voice. '*Assault sections one and two – signal readiness.*'

James watched as a crimson flare flew high into the freezing night. An identical flare went up from the other side of the ravine, burning against the dark sky. The flickering whir of the film camera had started up.

Perry stared. 'Is this all spectacle for a m–m–motion picture?'

'Whoever watches these scenes won't be sitting in the back row of the Coliseum,' James muttered, his words lost in the fiery punch of the mortar as it launched its grenade. The vapour trail sounded like nails scraping down a blackboard.

A further grenade jumped from the other side of the ravine, and then—

A roiling, brilliant firestorm engulfed Herta and her mechanical suit. The shock wave was enough to rock the lorry. James stared in wonder as flames gave way to thick black smoke . . . and almost swore out loud as the metal suit came clanking out of the conflagration. A huge metal arm swept up, and blooms of machine-gun fire burst out of its end.

'Built-in weapons,' James whispered.

Ripples of applause sounded across the ravine as Herta's machine headed steadily towards a solid block of what looked like concrete. The other arm rose up, then chopped down, reducing the slab to rubble in a single blow.

She was still moving round when another familiar voice lisped from the loudspeakers. *'This is Blade.'* The sounds of celebration quickly faded. *'May I remind all present that the controller unit is far from fully tested; we have very little time left to input new data. So let us proceed to the next assault exercise. Miss Axmann, reset all systems, then prime assault manoeuvre three . . .'*

James was already cold, but now, as the words echoed in the eerie atmosphere, it seemed to permeate through to his bones. He remembered the voices he'd heard from behind the trunk-room door: *Prime assault manoeuvre three . . . Damn it, boy! Now—!*

And then Marcus's scream . . . James would never forget it.

As if in mocking memory, a siren sent up an electronic howl across the valley. It died away, and Blade's voice came again. *'Intruders sighted near main entrance. Possible breach of perimeter fence. Likely local children again, but take no chances. Units B and C, full search. Live ammunition.'*

Perry looked horrified. 'We'll never get out of here now!'

'Live ammo . . .' James felt sick. 'Wait. Perhaps we can *ride* out?'

'On top of this thing, skidding and lurching down the hill?' Perry said; he looked pale. 'We'll be thrown off!'

'I mean *inside*. Safely hidden away. The doors are still open . . .'

'All right.' Perry started to inch his way along the soaking wet roof.

James gripped his wrist. 'But shouldn't we stay and watch what else—?'

'For God's sake, no!' Perry was adamant. 'We've seen enough.'

James hesitated. Then, checking that the men were still by the edge of the ravine, he followed Perry towards the rear of the lorry, swinging himself into the cold, dark interior and landing with a hollow clang. *Too loud?* James tensed, his hand on the crank handle tucked inside his coat. But no one came looking.

Cold, wet and aching, he took out the torch and switched it on. The lorry had only a few crates left inside it. Perry emerged from behind the largest and pulled James back, out of sight of the doors.

'So, now we know, don't we?' he said shortly. 'The reason for the lies and the secrecy. M–Marcus died helping Whittaker develop that thing out there.'

'Imagine a battalion of soldiers in those things, taking the enemy by surprise. Britannia really *will* rule the waves. Any waves she wants.' James scowled. 'But they still sacrificed

99

Marcus to their war machine and made him a fool instead of a hero. It's not damn well fair.'

'Why use Fettes to build a secret weapon, for heaven's sake?' wondered Perry. 'Blade-Rise m-must have its own workshops and research centres—'

'And no end of spies who'd know just where they are,' James broke in. 'What if something like this is so secret it needs to be built in pieces, in deep cover . . .'

Perry considered. 'You mean, Blade arranges to get his genius friend Whittaker installed in a Classics-oriented school like Fettes for a term or two, working on this project in secret . . .'

'He might be using a dozen schools around the country . . . around the *world*, for all we know.'

'Hell, James.' Perry pushed out his bottom lip. 'So it seems that the lightning-strike baloney, and hanging poor M-Marcus out to dry, comes down to the best interests of national security. We should have left all this well alone . . .'

Maybe. James felt hollow. The red-hot flame of his fury had gone out and left behind a mingled ash of emotions. He had pushed and pushed, and finally found the truth; and it had proved to be ghastly and unfair and ruthless. He hated it, but at least he understood it.

'You know, if we're caught,' said Perry quietly, 'we could be shot as spies.'

James summoned up the ghost of a smile. 'Let's not get caught, then,' he said.

As the sound of crashes and gunfire carried from the ravine, James and Perry lifted another crate and placed it on top of the one they'd used to hide behind. Then they pushed it up against the side wall, leaving a small cramped space for them to hunker down inside. James's plan was simple: once the demonstration was over, the lorry would surely head back to civilization – a factory depot, a workshop, even a petrol station. The doors opened from the inside as well as from outside, so as soon as they stopped somewhere, he and Perry could jump out and run for it . . . start the holidays in a more sensible fashion, have their luggage sent on from Fettes, enjoy the festive break with clearer consciences . . .

That was the plan, nurtured hopefully over long hours. The lorry was duly reloaded with the mortar and film camera, and driven slowly back down the steep hillside. They waited for their chance. The lorry stopped, and the doors were opened, but James could still hear the rumble of the great carbon arc lamps. They hadn't gone far. And now more things were being loaded up. Huge crates, many of which were stacked up to the roof all around James and Perry's hiding space. The lorry was filled swiftly and economically; several boxes were secured to the wall by a rope mesh.

Then they heard the clank of chains and the snap of a padlock on the other side of the doors. James's heart plummeted. *Locked in.*

'How do we get out now?' Perry whispered.

'We'll get our chance,' James insisted, trying to stay calm while wedged into the small dark space. When the lorry pulled away again, his watch read ten past one in the morning. Over an hour went by – they must be leaving Ruskie far behind – and then, through the insulated walls, they were aware of the low boom and hoot of foghorns, along with the cry of questing gulls.

Perry stirred from fitful sleep. 'Where are we? The coast?'

'A port . . .' James felt his heart sink. The lorry was trundling forward, down a slope. It kept stopping and starting. Now they could feel a reverberation beneath them: large engines thrumming through the dark space. 'I think we're being loaded onto a ship.'

'A cargo ship?' Perry swore. 'We could be travelling to the other side of the world, James! The trip could take days. We could die of thirst, or starve—!'

'Or suffocate,' James snapped. 'So save your breath.' Already the air seemed stale. *What do we do?* he wondered, hugging himself in the darkness.

What the hell do we do now?

12

Brought Down Low

After travelling for ten hours, James's stomach felt scoured out, both with nerves and hunger pains. Perry lay listlessly on a box. The dying torchlight had shown no details on any of the crates; no clues as to their final destination.

'You awake?' James murmured.

'I sleep no m–more!' came the mournful reply. 'Damned uncomfortable beds in this hotel. I shall complain.'

'I was just thinking about Whittaker's calendar . . . that red cross marking the twentieth.'

'Oaf. I was thinking about a fine Christmas dinner around a hearty fire.'

'I was wrong,' James went on. 'The cross didn't mark the date of the demonstration at all. It marked the date for setting sail.'

'Eighteen . . . two.' Perry recalled the numbers James had

retrieved. 'Old Hook and Herta left Fettes with Blade on the eighteenth – two days ago.'

'So there were two days and nights of tests at Thornhill Abbey . . .' James nodded. 'That makes sense.'

'M-m-marvellous, isn't it?' said Perry. 'The way a puzzle becomes clear when you're trapped inside it.'

James had forced the back doors open a crack, pushing against the chains that held them, so at least they could breathe and, with careful aiming, pee. That hadn't helped the smell of the air outside – thick stuff that already reeked of salt and diesel. They were at sea in a darkened hold, together with other unmarked trucks. James's watch told him it was gone eleven in the morning, but down in the hold it felt like unending night.

How much longer will we be trapped in here, like animals? he wondered.

'All things pass,' James muttered, trying to calm himself. He thought of the injuries he'd suffered over the years, the times when it felt as if he'd never heal; and yet here he was, still strong and ready for whatever the future might bring. He thought of the raw need he'd felt for his parents in the months after they'd died, and how they'd been buried at the back of his mind till he chose to revive them. He thought of the girls he'd known, the friends he'd made, and all the lessons and sermons so dull it seemed they'd never end. Yes, all things passed: love; longing; childhood. James wanted to wring full value from each moment that was his.

'We should try to open some of these crates,' he announced. 'Perhaps there's something inside we can use to get the doors open.'

Perry yawned. 'A rocket launcher perhaps?'

'Something that can cut through the chain . . .' James tried using the starting handle on the lid of the nearest crate and managed to prise one end up. Then the sonorous blast of a foghorn shook through the hold. 'What's that for?'

Perry was back on his feet. 'M-might signal we're nearing our berth.'

James listened. The note of the ship's engines lowered, heightening his anticipation. 'We're slowing. Better get those doors shut again. We could be moving out soon.'

Perry hurried to oblige, tugging on the handles, rattling the chains. 'I wonder where the hell we are . . . We drove for a couple of hours, then they loaded us aboard . . .'

'Eight hours or so by sea from Scotland,' James added. 'Could be the south of England, or else Europe. Ireland, even.'

There was a loud clang from outside that made them freeze.

'What was that?' Perry murmured.

James put his ear to one of the rear doors. Footsteps rang out on the metal floor, coming closer. 'Hide,' he hissed, switching off the torch. Perry made for the back, but James grabbed him, pulled him aside. 'Near the doors. Perhaps we can slip out . . .' He heaved at the crates, making a little space behind one of them – as the chains outside clanged against the doors, and someone wrestled them out through the handles. James pushed in beside Perry in the confined space – and the doors opened.

Herta climbed inside. She was dressed in a full-length blue woollen coat and black cotton trousers. Her hair was tucked under a black cloche hat. But even in the low light James could see that her eyes looked like they'd been blacked, the delicate skin bruised and swollen. She had a slim silver torch that cast a white beam about the interior in a narrow arc.

James felt pins and needles prickle at his calves, felt the first spasms of cramp. He bit his lip. There was no way he and Perry could get out through the open doors without Herta spotting them. Should they surrender now, admit what had happened?

No. She and Whittaker had simply allowed Marcus to die and dumped his body. How far would they go now to protect their secret?

As he looked at the blonde girl, James felt sudden fear. Dying for your country could be right and proper, sure enough . . . but never like this.

Herta unhooked the rope mesh, searching for a particular box. She had clearly found it, because now she pulled a jemmy from inside her coat and prised off the lid. James watched from the shadows as she reached in and drew out a bundle wrapped in cotton wadding and white cloth, opening it carefully, like a child at Christmas. Finally, as the last of the wadding fell away, she pulled out a circuit board. It looked like the one Whittaker had been working on in the chemistry lab—

'What are you doing?'

James's heart almost stopped. Whittaker stood in the opening at the back of the lorry. Luckily it was Herta who held his baleful gaze.

'Dr Whittaker,' she said quietly. 'I did not hear you.'

'I said, what are you doing?' He stepped into the lorry and

took the circuit board from her with his good hand. 'The controller unit is not to be handled.'

She studied him with dark eyes, arms folded across her chest. 'Grünner requires me to deliver the primary controller unit to his embassy upon arrival. He wishes to be sure—'

'Grünner can go to hell.'

James frowned at Perry. *Who's Grünner?*

'The film footage of last night's trials has been processed overnight,' Whittaker continued. 'He can pore over that to his heart's content, and listen to your adventures at the Steel Shadow's controls . . . but he will get nothing else until full payment and conditions of delivery are finalized, as agreed with Blade.' He picked up the wadding with his hook and held it up to her. 'Wrap it up again, Herta.'

She shrugged, her eyes glittering in the torchlight. 'I should warn you, Grünner will not be pleased.'

'Perhaps you might remind him of the Steel Shadow's value on the open market were it to go to auction. We're talking millions.' Whittaker stooped and placed his metal hook against her shoulder. 'We have tolerated your input into this project on sufferance, a condition of the terms of sale. We have allowed you to test the Shadow yourself in order to report back to your superior. However, to overreach yourself at this stage of the game would be most . . . unfortunate.'

What the hell is going on here? As Herta put the rewrapped circuit board back in the crate, James found he was holding every muscle tensed, his body ready for fight or flight. He caught a furtive movement from Perry, beside him. Outside the lorry, from across the hold, they heard a clang and a clatter. Whittaker and Herta both jumped and spun round to look.

James realized that Perry had taken the crank handle from where he had set it down and lobbed it out through the opening.

'Hello?' In an instant Herta had moved over to the doorway; she was standing almost next to James. 'Who's there?' she called.

He tried to shrink down further behind the crate. *If she looks to her left now* . . .

But Herta's focus was on the possible intruder. She stepped outside, training her torch into the darkness, and Whittaker followed. 'I'll guard the door to the deck,' he said. 'Stop anyone getting out.'

As they moved away from the lorry, the white torch beam played over the floor and around the walls like a phantom. Perry tapped James's arm and crawled out as silently as he could, making for the open doorway.

But James hesitated. It sounded as if this primary controller thing was key to the whole project – the Steel Shadow couldn't function properly without it. Boldly he moved deeper inside the lorry, towards the open crate. Heart pounding, he reached inside and groped around for the circuit board. *Got it!* He held it tight to his chest, then followed Perry out, dropped down flat against the wet oily floor and wriggled underneath the lorry beside his friend.

'Did you have to stop them talking just then?' he breathed. 'I wanted to hear more.'

'What – wait till they'd finished and locked us in again?' Perry shook his head. 'Know when to stop, old boy.'

'At least I got hold of that controller unit they were talking about,' James breathed.

'You did?'

He nodded. *Perhaps it's something we can barter with Blade for the truth about all this.* But hiding out on the floor of the hold, the idea of ever having any influence, any power at all, seemed ridiculous to James. He and Perry might be out of the lorry, but they were far from out of the woods.

We don't even know where the woods are.

Suddenly Herta spoke again: 'No one here. Must have been something falling down.' She tucked the torch into her belt and returned to the lorry to secure the doors with the chain and padlock.

Whittaker joined her. 'Carrel is driving us straight to the Hotel des Indes for a celebratory luncheon ahead of the party there tomorrow night.' He sighed as they turned to head for the exit. 'If your precious Grünner would only deign to see us today, this whole business would be over.'

'He is unavoidably detained—'

The door leading out of the hold closed on the conversation.

Shakily, James pulled himself out from under the lorry and took deep breaths of fetid air. 'I wasn't sure we were going to get out of that one.'

'Personally, I had every faith.' Perry crawled out and smiled wonkily at James. 'And now I know where we are.'

'Lying in our own pee?'

'Please, James. It's obvious when you think about it.' Perry was milking the moment. 'The Hotel des Indes is the m-m-most glamorous hotel in The Hague.'

'And Blade-Rise has its headquarters there. I assumed that Blade was making that soldier-suit thing for the British. But what if he's not? He told me about the extent to which the Nazis were re-arming . . .' James looked at Perry. 'What if he's selling *them* the Steel Shadow?'

'What?' Perry said, shaking his head. 'Grünner sounds German, but what does that prove? He m-m-might be a Dutch businessman and Herta his partner. Maybe it's a private sale.'

'Perhaps.' James looked down at the circuit board in his hands. 'Whatever the case, I'm not sure how well his mechanical marvel will work without *this*.'

Perry raised an eyebrow. 'I don't know, James. Perhaps you should put the thing back . . . let these people do what they want with their precious weapons.'

'I suppose that would be the wise thing to do,' James said, and outside a ship's foghorn boomed as if passing judgement. 'But this isn't only about Marcus now. We can't let Blade get away with it – and remember, no one knows we're here. No one will realize we have this thing – provided we can get off the boat without the drivers seeing us as they return to their trucks. Let's get a feel for the layout of this hold – and the way out.'

James walked over to the door, the one by which Whittaker and Herta had left. 'Assuming we really *are* nearing The Hague, can we stay in Sheveningen with your relatives, d'you think?'

'If they've gone away for Christmas as they usually do, we can make ourselves at home. This is *Den Haag*, James, I can feel it in my bones,' Perry assured him. 'I'm sure it is . . . Certain!'

★   ★   ★

Soon afterwards James and Perry were crouching out of sight on deck; their view of the coast came in snatches through the smoke: it was long, flat and stretched out for miles.

Perry looked sheepish. 'Of course, it could be Rotterdam.'

'Rotterdam?'

'Put it another way . . . it *is* Rotterdam. But that's not so very far from The Hague. Perhaps forty minutes on the train.'

One more obstacle, James brooded as their ship ploughed through a wide stretch of water, as grey as the sky above, that led inland. There were countless smaller waterways and inlets, and wide jetties lined with little boats like fruits on a vine. Everywhere there was movement as vessels of all sizes went about their business: fishing trawlers, cruise ships, tankers and steamers. Huge derricks lined the docks, swinging crates round, ready for loading. The air was ripe with the tang of oil and fish. As they approached, James and Perry saw an eclectic front of mouldering red-brick warehouses and ornately designed houses and hotels, held back from the water by large plazas and promontories, bridges and walkways, busy with people and motorcars.

Perry bit his lip. 'How the hell are we going to get off?'

'Let's wait till the lorries drive away,' James said, 'and follow on foot.'

He and Perry waited up there, shivering in their damp clothes, hidden amid the smoke.

'You realize that if we're caught, the crew will think we're stowaways,' Perry pointed out. 'Stowaways on a cargo ship carrying top-secret weapons. If they don't shoot to kill, they'll haul us up before Whittaker, Herta—'

'And Blade.' James shivered as he patted the circuit board in his coat pocket. 'If he catches me with this . . .'

They looked at each other. Then Perry smiled. 'Been nice knowing you, James.'

James smiled back. 'Wish I could say the same.'

'Then do so, you ingrate.'

'It's occasionally been agreeable knowing you,' James conceded.

'That's better . . .'

They returned to the scene of their incarceration where, like a mighty drawbridge, the wall of the hold was being lowered down on mechanical chains to form a ramp. One by one, the vehicles began to roll off onto a private wharf emblazoned in blue and white Blade-Rise colours. A hundred yards away, a checkpoint with a barrier blocked the exit to the main thoroughfare. A guard stood beside it, ready to check permits and papers.

'Here goes . . .' The hold was brighter now, by daylight. Two crewmen stood at the exits, waving on the drivers, directing them towards the barrier.

'Now it's our turn,' James muttered. 'Rested, Perry?'

Perry took a deep breath. 'And in possession of a boundless energy, James.'

'Then here goes . . .'

The last lorry rumbled up the ramp onto the forecourt of the terminal – and James broke into a desperate, flat-out run after it, Perry at his heels. He almost slipped on a patch of oil, had nightmare visions of falling on his backside, but kept his balance and sprinted on, pushing himself harder.

One of the crewmen, a short, wiry man, had seen him. He shouted out, and James saw him come forward as if in slow motion, ready to tackle any intruder and bring him down.

James launched himself into the air as he ran, sailing straight over the outstretched arms . . . but the other crewman – black-skinned and hard-faced – was coming at him now. James couldn't alter his course; as he landed, he ducked down, skidded in a pool of water and kicked the man's feet out from under him. But as the man fell, he stuck out a leg to trip Perry, who went tumbling head over heels. The pair of them got to their feet amidst a chorus of angry cries.

The lorry up ahead was slowing; the driver must have seen the commotion. He steered hard left, trying to block James's path.

James swore and changed direction, ducking round the rear of the lorry while Perry dodged in front. Gulls wheeled and shrieked overhead as if laughing at their efforts to escape. Perhaps twenty feet up ahead James could see the white exit barrier. The guard turned, darted into the sentry box – for a fevered moment James thought he was hiding – and came out with a baton.

'Take the barrier!' James shouted to Perry – and made the sentry his target. James was now travelling so fast that he had shoulder-charged the man before the baton could do more than brush against his back. The momentum sent them both crashing into the sentry box – so hard that its back wall splintered under the impact. The guard let out a winded bellow, and lay there, stunned. James muttered an apology and ducked back out and under the barrier.

'*Bond!*'

James turned wildly at the sound of the voice, and saw Whittaker's gaunt figure on the upper deck of the ship; he was pointing his hook at him over the safety rail. Swearing

113

under his breath, James sprinted away, aware that the crewmen and the lorry driver were yelling at him too. He hared after Perry, who'd taken off along the forecourt, ducking through the traffic and into the cover of the crowds beyond.

James pelted after him into the streets, dodging this way and that. *Damn it, he saw me! Whittaker saw me!* When the controller unit was found to be missing from the crate, it wouldn't take a genius to figure out who had it—

Suddenly he heard a sharp squeal of brakes on the tarmac; then the thud of impact and a collective gasp from people gathered along the busy street.

James saw a fine 1930 Studebaker Commander in contrasting silver and burgundy coachwork at a standstill in the middle of the road . . . and Perry lying sprawled in front of it.

13
Strangers in a Strange Land

A babble of Dutch voices rose up. James couldn't understand a word, but the gesticulating driver was looking angry and upset, and someone was shouting '*Politie!*' James guessed that meant the police would soon be rolling up. Looking down, he saw blood on the road; it seemed to be leaking from Perry's right leg.

James broke through the gaggle of bystanders to crouch down beside his friend. 'Perry? Perry!' he whispered, reluctant to betray the fact that he was English in case Whittaker had already sent men in pursuit; people could already see that he and Perry were dressed the same. He felt a reassuring hand on his shoulder, then someone trying to pull him away. James shook off the well-meaning woman, slid an arm under Perry's back and eased him up into a sitting position.

Perry's eyes flicked open; they were wide with shock.

'Good God, m–my leg hurts!' He frowned. 'Sorry, James. Front fender to the shin. Is my kneecap still attached?'

Glancing around for signs of pursuit, James hushed him. 'We can't stay here,' he whispered. 'Can you move?'

Perry gasped as James helped him to stand, then put an arm around him and steered him away. People shouted out; James saw concern and doubt and anger on their faces. He attempted to wave a reassuring hand but quickly gave up and concentrated on supporting his friend's weight.

Perry's face was pale; he could hardly put any weight on his right leg, and moaned under his breath with every step.

'Keep moving,' urged James. 'Whittaker saw me at the wharf. He's bound to be sending someone after us.'

'I suppose they m–m–might have one or two questions.'

'I've got a few for them too.'

They stopped underneath an ornate wrought-iron bridge over a canal. It was dark down here, smelly and cold, but no one seemed to be paying them much heed. James took stock of the situation. The gash to Perry's leg was a couple of inches long, and deep; it was still pulsing with dark blood which had saturated his trouser leg and sock.

'Give it to m–me straight, Doctor,' Perry said, forcing a smile. 'Will it have to come off?'

'The sock? Almost certainly.' With a smile, James gently lifted Perry's leg: if it was raised higher than the heart, the bleeding ought to stop. 'We need to get this wound cleaned and dressed.'

'Wouldn't m–mind a change of clothes m–m–myself. We can manage both at Uncle's house . . .'

'You remember the address?'

'Eight, Brugsestraat.'

'Pardon me?'

'The Dutch never use one vowel when two will do.'

James half smiled. 'Surely if you turn up unannounced with a mangled leg, your aunt and uncle will hit the roof?'

'I told you: with luck, they'll be away, on one of their dull cruises.' Perry tried to move his leg and winced. 'Now, we m-m-must get to a railway station.'

'We have no money.'

'We can dodge the fare.'

'Like you dodged the Studebaker?' James gently lowered Perry's leg. 'Look, I'll find my way to the station.'

'Friend of mine here's batty about trains; I seem to recall there are two or three stations in Rotterdam.'

'Then I'm bound to find one in the end. Are you all right to stay here?'

'Lying still, doing nothing? First day of the holidays starting in fine style.' Perry forced a weak grin. 'I'll be brave. Watch out for dockers with a grudge.'

'I will.' James emerged from under the bridge into the bleak December sunlight and climbed the steps to the cobbled streets, trying to get his head straight. On the other side of the canal he saw a windmill, its four sails turning lazily in the wind. James shivered, kept his head down, turned his collar up against the cold.

Damn their luck! Their escape would've been a triumph, had it not been for the way in which it had ended! James was reminded once again of the thin line between success and failure. A single wrongly timed move, a single bad decision, and your fate could change completely.

Or a single overheard conversation . . . Herta had come to take components for the Steel Shadow from the back of the lorry; Whittaker was wise to her, wary of some sort of double-cross perhaps. But who exactly was this Grünner? Herta's loyalty was clearly to him; she'd told James she was only 'on loan' to Blade and Whittaker. Had the truth about Marcus's death been concealed to protect a business transaction? Was this the reason for the Fettes cover-up – to protect a large sum of money?

The thought sparked a cold anger in James . . . But right now he needed money himself, and there was only one way to procure that legally right now . . .

He found a telephone kiosk on the waterfront. It was almost twenty minutes before the international operator connected him through the many telephone exchanges to Pett Bottom – but, thank God, Aunt Charmian was at home and agreed to take the call with reversed charges.

'James, is that you?' She sounded relieved. 'When your train came in and you weren't aboard, and when Fettes told me you'd left—'

'I'm sorry, Aunt Charmian.'

'Where are you? I'm so glad to hear from you, but the operator said "the Netherlands". . .'

Taking a deep breath, and with fingers crossed, James explained that after the difficult term, he and Perry had felt the need to get away: on the spur of the moment they'd taken a ferry to Holland to visit Perry's relatives. He could tell that Charmian was sceptical – but she agreed to wire a few days' spending money through to the Rotterdamsche Bank.

'Only promise me,' she added, 'that this has nothing to do with Mr Blade and his company.'

Nothing got past Charmian, James thought wryly.

'Perry and I just thought it would be nice to visit the country Marcus might have gone on to. Sort of . . . say goodbye to him in a way we couldn't at Fettes.'

What he said wasn't exactly untrue, James reflected. He hated lying to his aunt, but he needed to get to the bottom of what was going on.

'Very well. You'll be back for Christmas.' It was more a statement than a question, and James could hear the steel behind it.

'Yes, of course,' he agreed, and gave her the address of Perry's relatives on Brugsestraat in The Hague. 'I'll bring you back the most wonderful Christmas gift.'

He was relieved to hear Charmian's smile through the tart reply: 'If it's paid for with my own money, I should hope so.'

After that, James tried asking passers-by for directions to the nearest railway station. There seemed to be conflicting responses to this, and when he asked which one would take him to Scheveningen, he soon learned that his pronunciation was wrong – it was more like *SHAY-va-ning-an*. He heard Rotterdam Maas station mentioned by several people, so he scouted it out.

It was located near the waterfront, a dull, functional building that resembled two enormous, dark wooden sheds with stepped roofs laid side by side. Natural light poured into the chilly terminus through vast glass semicircles arranged above the towering arched entrances. In a corner of the paved concourse James saw a small café, and his stomach growled at the smell of eggs and bacon and strong coffee.

119

Then, suddenly, he spotted the black man he'd brought down at the wharf peering at the crowds at the other end of the terminal.

James turned quickly, scanned the street for other questing figures he didn't want to see, and moved away at a jog-trot. At least Perry was still under the bridge where he'd left him. Pale and shivering, he'd torn off a length of his shirtsleeve and tied it around his leg.

'I'm starving hungry and dying of thirst,' Perry announced. 'Can we go?'

'In a minute.'

It was more like three. Perry gasped with pain as James helped him to stand up. 'Ha! Not at all conspicuous, are we!'

'Luckily the station's not far away. And now that it's been searched, we should be safe there – for a while at least.'

'Perhaps you can sit m-me down and I'll beg for small coins? I should soon scrounge us the necessary guilders to continue our trek.'

'It may come to that,' James admitted, helping Perry to limp through the streets as he retraced his steps to the station, keeping a sharp lookout for trouble. 'I'll check times and fares – after we've stoked our boilers a little.'

Once inside the terminal building, leaving Perry propped up against a wall, James checked that the precious circuit board was still in his coat pocket, then headed over to a table just as a middle-aged couple got up and left. One had left a mouthful of coffee, along with the remains of a sandwich; James swiped the leftover crusts and took the coffee cup over to Perry, who downed the dregs in a gulp, then swallowed the bread gratefully. James returned the cup to another table and palmed some sugar cubes. He surveyed the other tables, then, when the waiter gave him a dirty look, smiled blandly and backed away.

'Here, James!' Perry was waving to him in a state of some excitement.

He ran back, frowning, and handed over the sugar cubes. 'Seen something?'

'Deliverance, James! That girl up there!'

James followed Perry's gaze to the bridge that ran between the two platforms; a steam train in racing green was wheezing to a halt, cocooned in smoke, and James saw a boy of about their age looking down at it, clutching a notepad and pencil. 'Apart from that rail enthusiast, I don't see—'

'But that's *her*! I told you I had a friend who's batty about trains – that's *her*!' Perry shrugged. 'I m-m-mean, she's a bit of a spod – frightful company. I've had to put up with her since I was a young boy, but her heart's in the right place. She'll help us.'

'Who is she?' James asked.

'Her name's Kitty. Kitty Drift. Go over – quickly, James! You m-m-must!'

Baffled, James did as Perry bade, and ran up the steps to the bridge. As he got closer, he saw that Kitty's resemblance to a boy was superficial, emphasized by the baggy sweater, black trousers and shapeless raincoat she was wearing. She was not tall – barely five feet three, James estimated. Her red hair was worn in a scruffy bob, and the eyes behind large round glasses were wide-set and conker-brown. She had pale skin and a face that, even in repose, seemed amused by the world about her.

'Kitty Drift?' James said uncertainly.

'Yes?' The girl looked at him, and at once blushed a convincing shade of scarlet. 'Do I know you? I don't . . . I would remember someone like you. I don't know any men. Well, boys, but—' She broke off in a coughing fit, her eyes wide and startled; James got the impression that the coughing was to cover her embarrassment. 'Er, anyway, yes. I'm Kitty Drift.' She looked at him expectantly. 'Who-ever are you?'

'Bond. James Bond. I'm here with a friend who knows you – Perry Mandeville?'

'Oh, my life!' Kitty grimaced. 'What's Mandy doing here? Hasn't he persecuted me enough over the years?'

'Apparently not,' James said, shrugging helplessly. 'We really need your help.'

'You do?' She took a step closer to him, looked him up and down and smiled, revealing a slight gap between her front teeth. 'Oh, Mandy, Mandy. Very well – where is the dreadful rogue?'

James felt slightly protective. 'He's had an accident. A quarrel with a motorcar.'

'Not fatal? Ah, well.' Kitty grinned. 'I suppose I can spare a few minutes to say hello. Lead on, James Bond.'

James did. She bounced along at his elbow, striding out as if suddenly given fresh purpose.

Perry watched her approach. 'Ah, Drift, I was right – it *was* you. James, this is Kitty; Kitty—'

'Yes, yes,' Kitty broke in, 'your friend has handled the introductions, Mandy.'

'Good. Hand us some tin, could you?'

'Now, there's a welcome.' Kitty put her hands on her hips. 'Why should I hand you anything, beyond a cuff to the ear? You've been a comprehensive pain to me over the years.'

'I was m-merely m-m-masking my true feelings of adoration, Drift. Now, listen, James and I need to get to Scheveningen, but we're lacking in funds.' Perry gestured to his leg. 'This is liable to drop off if I don't get it seen to, so if you wouldn't m-m-mind . . .'

Kitty sighed. 'You're waiting in altogether the wrong station, you realize . . .'

'You'd know.' Perry looked at James. 'She collects the names and numbers of different engines. Out in all weathers in dumps like this.'

'I'm looking for something very rare. Very particular,' Kitty retorted. 'I certainly wasn't looking for *you!*'

'We'd be very grateful for your help, Kitty,' James said diplomatically.

'Well. That's good.' She smiled at him again. 'The line to Scheveningen runs from Hofplein – that's where you need to be. Or if you set off from the Delftsche Poort station, that will take you to Hollands Spoor at The Hague, and from there you can take the steam tramway to Scheveningen Beach. It's very regular.'

'Dear Lord,' Perry groaned. 'James, wake me when she's finished.'

'Shame the old broad-gauge tramway's been closed,' Kitty went on regardless, 'or we could have picked that up at Staatsspoor—'

'*We?*' James wondered.

'I can tell you'll get very lost without me.' She grew wistful.

'Ah, if only we could ride in style on one of the new diesels – have you seen them? The DE3s?'

James shook his head, feeling slightly overwhelmed.

'They're beautiful! A real leap in technology. To make them look more streamlined, the carriages are welded instead of riveted—'

'Not riveted? I can't imagine.' Perry pointed to his leg. 'Drift, you do realize I'm bleeding to death?'

'So why not get a cab—?' Kitty stopped herself. 'Oh, yes. No tin. Well, then, I suppose I'd best be your guide and take you to Hofplein.' She looked at James coyly. 'I was planning to go there later in any case. Watching out for my ultimate spot.'

'Ultimate spot?'

'One day. One happy day . . . !'

She led them back outside. A cold breeze was blowing in off the North Sea as they headed inland towards the centre of the city, James supporting Perry, who limped along painfully. Kitty's insistence on joining them was a good thing, he decided. Their pursuers would be looking for two boys, not the odd little party they now made.

The Hofplein terminus building consisted of a semicircular front building of white glazed brick that housed the privately owned Restaurant Loos, and a modest station hall accessible from an elevated gatehouse. Kitty kept up a near-constant running commentary as she bought them third-class tickets and led them into the carriage of an electric train – a *Blokkendozen*, apparently – with wooden slatted benches and large windows. Ornate ceiling lights glowed smokily in the gloom.

Perry settled himself uncomfortably on his seat. 'You really didn't need to come with us, Drift.'

'Once you reach your aunt and uncle's, Mandy, you can pay me back,' she informed him.

James breathed a sigh of relief as their train chuntered out over a reinforced-concrete viaduct, and Rotterdam was left behind. He sat beside Kitty and looked out of the window. The functional white bridge had been decorated with animal sculptures set in stucco.

'You know, this was the first concrete construction project in the entire Netherlands . . .' Kitty's cheeks reddened again. 'I'm sorry – that's boring, isn't it? I'm nervous, I think. Company makes me nervous, and I wasn't expecting it today. I always speak too much when I'm nervous.'

James smiled. 'Have you always been interested in trains? What do they call you types – gricers?'

'Sometimes. I don't like that word.' She wrinkled her nose. 'I think of myself as a *ferroequinologist*.'

'Do you,' he said, bemused.

'It means "a student of the iron horse".' Kitty inclined her head. 'The steam engine is a magical machine.'

I wouldn't want to wear one on my back, thought James, tapping the circuit board in his pocket.

'Its flying white breath . . . unvarying rhythmical pace . . .' Kitty sighed. 'It's tremendously exciting.'

Perry gave a pantomime yawn.

'It *is* exciting,' James agreed. *And it's also a relief*, he thought privately. To his left the sun was starting to set, warming him through the glass as the train rattled along. City scenes gave way to countryside; trees like thin brushes lined flat fields.

Long, straight channels crisscrossed them; James wasn't sure if they'd been cut deliberately for drainage, or if they'd formed naturally. There seemed to be so many rivers, great pools of water reflecting the grey-white of the winter sky. James put his hand on the circuit board in his pocket, and felt himself relax a little for the first time in an age.

'So what brings you here?' Kitty enquired. 'Just visiting family for Christmas, Mandy? How'd you dupe your friend into coming along?'

'I felt like a change of scene,' James said. 'How do you come to be in the Netherlands, Kitty? You sound as if you're from the north of England.'

'Oh dear, could you tell? Yes – Doncaster, to be precise. Daddy says the main purpose of my highly refined education was to stamp out any trace of regional accent to help me to "get on".' She laughed. 'Why should I change, anyway? But to answer your question, Daddy's a director of the Rhenish Railway Company – that's why we're here.' She turned to Perry. 'You know, whenever your uncle George takes the tramway from The Hague to Scheveningen, his carriage is almost certainly pulled by one of the Merryweather locomotives my father's firm supplied.'

'Just think of that, James!' Perry chirped with mock enthusiasm.

Kitty smiled tightly. 'I hope your leg falls off.'

James thought he might change the subject. 'So what's in your notebook, Kitty?'

'I record the number, name, type, classification, shed and date seen of all the engines I come across. It's all Daddy's fault. When I was young, he'd take me to the mainline station every weekend. Several lines converge in Doncaster, so there's lots to see.' Kitty slid her thick-rimmed glasses up her nose. 'It's not all about the notepad. Daddy used to take me shed-bunking – you know, sneaking into a locomotive shed – and cabbing too, where we'd ride with the drivers. I just got the bug, I suppose.' She looked at James, the embarrassed blush fading now; happy to be sharing her passion. 'I love the idea that all over a country there are tracks connected to every single locomotive that you have ever wanted to see . . . it's just a matter of finding them.'

James smiled. 'Are you looking for anything in particular?'

'I am! I call it the "Ghost Train".' She smiled self-consciously. 'Forgive me – I suppose I've always enjoyed melodrama. My Ghost Train is a train with no official livery.'

'Livery?'

'Yes – you know, the paint scheme, lettering, general design across a fleet of vehicles. This train . . .' She frowned at Perry's pantomime yawn. 'Well, I've seen it often over the last two years, travelling from Rotterdam to The Hague. No numbers, no name, no insignia. I've asked other spotters, but officially . . . my Ghost Train doesn't exist.' She shrugged. 'And yet I know that it *does* exist. So I'm trying to plot its course.'

'To *prove* its existence.' James inclined his head. 'You know, I thought that girls schooled abroad would be fixated on society dances and the like. It's refreshing to meet someone like you.'

'Is it?' The crimson glow in Kitty's cheeks returned. 'Well, not that I want to disappoint, but I am rather excited about attending a large party at the Hotel des Indes tomorrow.'

'Party?' Remembering Whittaker and Herta's strange

discussion, James sat up straighter on the hard wooden seat. 'Which party?'

'It's a tradition here among the *Hagenaars* – sorry, I mean, the posher types.' She shrugged. 'Each year the German Ambassador to the Netherlands hosts a grand Christmas party. It's one of the highlights of the calendar—'

'German Ambassador?' James pressed her. 'Who is he? What's his name?'

'Herr Konstantin Grünner,' Kitty said. 'Why? Is anything wrong?'

James and Perry were staring at each other.

There was so much that felt wrong, James didn't quite know where to begin.

14

Breaking, Entering, Crashing

Scheveningen was a quiet, picturesque suburb built around a slab of golden beach; as wintry twilight fell and the streetlamps glowed into life, its smart townhouses and well-trimmed lawns put James in mind of a painting on a chocolate box.

Perry's uncle and aunt lived on the spacious, spotless Brugsestraat, sited midway between Renbaan-Achterweg station and the long stretch of beach, which drew crowds even in winter. There was a restful atmosphere about the place.

James promptly broke it by cracking open the kitchen window with a large stone and fishing about for the latch.

Kitty looked scandalized but also enthralled as Perry kept lookout and James wriggled inside. 'What if you're caught?' she asked.

'I'm so cold and hungry, prison might come as a relief,' James quipped.

'It's a shame you can't come to Herr Grünner's party tomorrow,' Kitty said. 'The hotel serves truly marvellous food.'

James swung himself down onto the kitchen floor. 'I suppose you wouldn't give up your ticket for a starving man?'

'Not on your life. I've bought a frock and all sorts.' She tutted. 'Mandy, I always knew you had criminal tendencies, but to make your friend break into your aunt and uncle's just for a place to sleep . . .'

'You can't strictly call it breaking and entering,' said Perry. 'I'm family.'

'The blackest of black sheep,' Kitty said with a snort. 'You didn't even knock. You weren't expecting them to be in, were you?'

Leaving Perry to stammer the barest of explanations, James went through to the black-and-white tiled hall and found a mound of mail on the doormat; evidently no one had been here for some time. He opened the door to Kitty, who helped Perry hobble in.

'Knew it. George and Lettice are off on one of their pleasure jaunts.' Perry collapsed on a hard-backed chair beside the telephone table. 'Still, that should save some awkward questions.'

'Not from the neighbours,' James pointed out.

'You'll have to tell them you're here before they see lights on and call the police.' Kitty crouched down to sort through the post. 'Of course, I could always ask Daddy if you can stay with us . . .'

'You couldn't,' Perry retorted. 'Your father would keep an eye on us the whole time. It would be such a bore.'

'I'd get used to boredom, Mandy,' Kitty advised, still

arranging the post into piles. 'You won't be going far on that leg for a day or two.'

'Speaking of which, I'll boil some water and get the cut cleaned up,' James said, 'before gangrene sets in.'

'Gangrene?' Perry looked even paler as he pointed towards the kitchen. 'Go, nurse. Fetch!'

'Wait!' Kitty jumped up, brandishing an envelope. 'Here we are! I *knew* George Mandeville would have received one too.'

James stared. 'One what?' he asked.

'I recognize the envelope.' She tore open the creamy manila with a flourish, ignoring Perry's protests, and presented James with a stiff white card. 'Here you are, sir. One invitation to the German Ambassador's party tomorrow – the party that's clearly so significant to you both.'

James stared at the ornate seal at the top of the card, the neat Dutch script, and the swastikas printed in each bottom corner. 'George and Lettice Mandeville . . . ?'

'The party is for politicians, leaders of industry, the most successful businessmen,' Kitty explained. 'It's a very high-class affair.'

'Naturally Uncle George qualifies,' Perry said. 'Even so, you shouldn't have opened his post, Drift.'

'It's not like he's able to attend.' Kitty looked at James, the challenge in her eyes magnified by her glasses. 'But you could go in his place.'

Perry was incredulous. 'As George M–M–Mandeville?'

'I could hardly go as Lettice,' James said.

'Chances are the doorman will be none the wiser.' Kitty smiled. 'I don't know why you're so interested in old Grünner;

the old buffer's never grabbed my attention for more than twenty seconds. But it would be terribly funny if you came along and kept me company. Anyway, now I've aided and abetted you in your criminal undertakings, I'd best be away before the police descend on you.'

'Train numbers to write down?' Perry asked.

'Life to lead.' She shook hands with him and gave James a shy glance. 'See you tomorrow . . . George!'

The following evening saw James making for the Hotel des Indes; he shivered in the December drizzle as he looked around for signs of pursuit.

Aunt Charmian's telegraphed funds had bought him a smart new pair of black wingtip shoes and a raincoat to go with the dinner jacket and bow tie he'd hired from a tailor in the prestigious Noordeinde district.

'God knows, I wish I was going with you,' Perry had said as James prepared to leave. 'Laid up with only the wireless and a baked potato for company.'

'In the warm and dry,' James pointed out. 'Curled up in bed . . .'

'And with my m-mother and father ringing here every two seconds to check up on m-m-me.' Perry sighed. 'I should never have telephoned home. Too caring a son, I am, that's the trouble.'

'No, *you're* the trouble.'

'Seriously though, James. Blade and Whittaker will know you've got their special circuit board,' Perry reminded him. 'They've probably got m-m-men searching the streets for you.'

'Then they won't be looking for me at the party,' James said. 'I'll leave the controller unit hidden here. If they do happen to catch me and make me lead them to it, you'll just have to get me out of trouble, won't you?'

'And so I shall! I can rouse the neighbours once m-m-more . . .' The couple next door had called round to investigate, as Kitty had prophesied, and confirmed to Perry that his aunt and uncle were cruising the Mediterranean and would not return until after Christmas.

Sun and relaxation, James thought as he braved the biting wind along the darkened Frederikstraat in the centre of town. The pavement was laid with bricks in a herringbone design – an ornate carpet on either side of the long straight road. Grand residences in pastel colours stood alongside glass-fronted restaurants with candlelit booths and tables.

James's stomach grumbled when he saw the diners inside. Since reaching Scheveningen he'd slept for much of the time; then he and Perry had eaten their way through most of the tinned food in the larder. Only now, with danger stirring his blood, did he feel wide awake, ready for the challenge posed by his self-appointed mission.

That mission was simple: to spy on Whittaker and Herta, and see if they met the German Ambassador. If James could get proof that Blade-Rise was supplying arms to Germany through Grünner – names and places to go with the technology he'd managed to get hold of – then he could pass it on to someone who could help: his contact in the British Secret Intelligence Service, Agent Adam Elmhirst – an ally from his hair-raising adventure in Los Angeles a few months back – would surely be able to use the information . . .

James could still hear Marcus's terrible screams; still smarted at the way in which his honest testimony had been twisted to benefit Blade. *Yes*, he thought. *There will be payback.*

The Hotel des Indes dominated the corner of the central avenue known as Lange Voorhout, a stone's throw from the city's grand government buildings. Its burnt-ochre façade was lit by spotlights, and the flags of all European nations extended from its first-floor balconies, billowing in the stiff breeze. Luxury motorcars queued outside to disgorge their impeccably dressed passengers onto the red carpet. Doormen in tailored grey uniforms led each glamorous visitor to the revolving doors and surrendered them to the sumptuous marbled world inside.

James took a deep breath and walked as nonchalantly as he could to take his place in the queue. He knew he looked older than his years – he'd passed for eighteen on occasion – and he'd attended enough high-society functions to know how to behave just so. But if his identity was questioned . . .

He presented his invitation to the doorman, trying to convey the air of one for whom to be here at the Hotel des Indes was as natural as breathing! Woe betide any underling who kept him from his enjoyment of the party . . .

The doorman scanned the invitation politely. 'English?' he asked, and James nodded. 'Mrs Mandeville cannot attend?'

You have no idea, thought James, shaking his head.

The doorman returned the invitation with a deferential nod. James was through.

A marble staircase ran up to his left, the concierge and cloakrooms lay to his right. Trying to look nonchalant, he strode on into the palatial reception hall, and now his eye was drawn in many directions at once: he took in the solid marble pillars crowned with ornate stonework, the luxurious red velvet drapes, the thick red carpets, white marble floors and walls. The guests were checking in coats and bags at the cloakroom, or helping themselves to teetering glasses of champagne or fruit juice from silver trays. An enormous Christmas tree decked out in ribbons and lights stood in one corner, and festive wreaths of cedar, pine and holly lined the ochre walls.

James checked in his raincoat, which looked more functional than fashionable amidst all the furs. Then he climbed the magnificent staircase to the mezzanine level, where members of staff were directing guests to an enormous ballroom. James peeped inside: the orchestra was playing a romantic waltz, and guests whirled around the sprung wooden floor. Looking up, James saw that the high ceiling was swathed in aquamarine silk to create the impression of an ocean upon which chandeliers and Christmas decorations floated like festive boats.

Suddenly he caught sight of Whittaker, standing grim-faced at the door, his hook in his pocket, the stem of his empty champagne glass gripped in claw-like fingers. He looked as if he was waiting for someone. James backed away, not wanting to be seen by—

'Hey, where's the fire?' exclaimed a familiar voice. 'These heels are already destroying my feet, they don't need further assistance . . .'

James turned and his eyes widened. 'Kitty!'

'It would seem so.' The voice was the same, but her appearance was transformed. The baggy sweater had been replaced by an elegant black velvet dress with a cowl neck and draped slit sleeves. Her hair had been carefully teased into chic waves, and the glasses had gone, her large eyes expertly made up. With pearls around her neck and a champagne flute in her hand, she blended perfectly into her surroundings – much to James's surprise.

'How do you do, Mr Bond?' Kitty curtseyed grandly – then looked up at him, wide-eyed. 'Now, please can you tell me – are my eyes red? I'm wearing these new-fangled contact lenses and they feel dreadful. I can only wear them for a couple of hours at a time, and I worry they'll make me weep and smudge this make-up.'

'They're not at all red. You look very nice.'

'Very *nice*?' Kitty seemed unimpressed. 'Oh, my life, you make me sound like your maiden aunt!'

James smiled. 'Hardly that. It's quite a transformation.'

'Well, you can't just jot down an engine's number and believe you know all about her, James,' Kitty said, studying him. 'You have to observe her in action, do you see? Anticipate her arrival . . .'

'Her arrival. Yes.' Out of the corner of his eye, James saw a tall blonde in an evening gown of clinging mauve silk striding purposefully across the dance floor towards Whittaker. *Herta* . . . Her path would take her right past him. He needed cover, and quickly leaned in closer to Kitty. 'Mmm. What's that marvellous perfume?'

Kitty froze. 'I . . . I'm not wearing any perfume,' she said awkwardly.

'It's your natural scent, then.' James turned his face into her neck, angling it away from Herta until she'd passed. When he moved away again, he saw that Kitty's smile had grown somewhat fixed; his casual attention had been mistaken for something else.

'Well, you mustn't let me monopolize you,' he said quickly, his eye on Herta as she approached Whittaker. 'You must circulate.'

'I don't see why,' Kitty replied. 'These people are all ancient. I'm going to be patronized all night.' She linked arms with him and tried to tug him onward. 'Come on – let me introduce you to my father.'

James resisted. 'Kitty, I really don't think—'

'You can tell him you work for Mr Mandeville, and you're representing the firm. It'll be a hoot. Look, he's just over there, talking to poor Mr Blâde.'

With a start, James looked round and saw, across the room, the familiar hunched figure leaning on his cane: Hepworth Maximilian Blade, in a midnight-blue dinner jacket, which hung awkwardly over his mismatched shoulders. James saw that the hand clasping the cane was twisted, the fingers misshapen. His chauffeur, Carrel, and a large, dark-skinned bodyguard flanked him, ever alert to his every need.

James turned his back on the gathering, trying to stay composed. 'I've already met Mr Blade, back at school,' he said airily. 'I'm afraid he won't believe any story about working for George Mandeville.'

'That's a bore.' Kitty sighed. 'I'm surprised to hear that Mr Blade has travelled as far as Scotland. He daren't walk alone anywhere for fear of falling.'

'I suppose he felt the journey was worth it.'

'He owns a mansion in Wassenaar,' she went on. 'That's

the grandest part of town. They say that everything there is automated, to keep him safe . . .'

James was only half listening; he was looking for Whittaker and Herta. There was no sign of them now. 'I'm sure I'll meet your father later, Kitty, but right now, I think—'

A delicate tinging noise quietened the hubbub; a master of ceremonies, resplendent in red tailcoat, was ringing a delicate silver bell.

'I think it's the speeches,' James concluded, a little lamely.

The man made an announcement in Dutch, ending with the name 'Konstantin Grünner'.

James felt his heart pound as a man in his mid-fifties stepped forward; the guests responded with polite applause. *I'm truly in the lion's den tonight!* he thought. *And here comes the oldest of the pride . . .*

There was a cold, sober air about Grünner. He wore his grey hair very short, revealing a pink, puckered scar running down the right-hand side of his neck. His face was doughy, but the eyes behind the round, wire-rimmed glasses were piercing.

He spoke first in Dutch, and then continued in fluent English: 'Welcome to you all, my kind friends. I know why you are here – I don't mean here in this splendid hotel, thanks to the munificence of the Third Reich' – a pause for polite applause – 'but in Holland. Geographically, she sits at a strategic junction between Germany, Britain and France.'

Which will make the Netherlands a prime target for Nazi invasion when Hitler starts trying to grab his 'living space', James thought grimly.

'As can be witnessed by all those assembled here tonight,'

Grünner went on, 'this is an excellent place for gathering international business contracts . . .'

'And secret military intelligence,' James muttered as Grünner started again, this time in German. James wondered if Whittaker and Herta had already had their discussion with the Ambassador about the Steel Shadows and the controller unit, or if it was to follow later. The more he thought about it, the more he feared that Blade might be selling his incredible creation to the Nazis. A single platoon of Steel Shadows would form a military force greater than any in history . . .

A means of unleashing hell.

And the deal could be struck tonight.

15

For the Sake of Traitors

It was more vital than ever to learn exactly what Whittaker and Herta were planning here, James thought. Perhaps Grünner could lead him to their rendezvous. *Or perhaps I can be more proactive. They're not likely to talk in front of everybody at the party, so . . .*

'James?' Kitty grabbed his hand as he tried to slip away. 'Where are you going? I thought you wanted to hear the speech—'

'I've got no glass for the final toast,' James hissed. 'Do excuse me.'

'All right.' Kitty smiled hopefully. 'You'll hurry back?'

'You won't miss me,' James told her. *I only hope Blade and his cronies do.*

He took the elegant staircase down to the ground floor and approached the front desk with a face like thunder. 'Where is Herr Grünner's meeting to take place?' he demanded of the staff in fluent German. 'I am his junior assistant. The Ambassador has almost finished his speech and needs to know that all is in readiness!'

The man behind the desk looked baffled. 'Ready for what, sir? I don't know—'

'Find whoever does!' James snapped. 'This is urgent.'

Turning to a colleague, the man spoke quickly and softly before turning back to James, still puzzled. 'We have kept the cigar room for Herr Grünner's private meetings this evening – but surely he knows of this . . . ?'

'You misunderstood me,' James lied boldly. 'I said, I wish to see where this room is – I must inspect it for myself. Who will show me?'

'I assure you, our standards of cleaning are most high—'

'Who?'

The man gave a patient smile and signalled to his elderly colleague to lead the way. James tried to maintain an officious air as he followed the receptionist. Suddenly he realized that Whittaker and Herta might already be waiting for Grünner. Should he try to confront them with everything he'd learned?

James braced himself as they reached the cigar room – but sighed with relief to find it empty: he saw only elegant couches, mahogany tables and heavy glass ashtrays, a blue-black carpet and velvet drapes pulled across large French windows.

'I hope you are satisfied, sir?' The man's smile was forced.

'This all seems to be in order,' James concluded. 'You may go.'

'No, sir. I shall remain to ensure that no one enters the room ahead of Herr Grünner's arrival.'

'Well . . . excellent. I am glad to hear it.' James noted a door handle protruding through a gap in the curtains; the cigar room must give onto a patio, he thought. Which meant that the room could be accessed from outside . . . 'Thank you.' With a curt nod, James turned and left the room, walking quickly back down the passage. He could hear applause from the ballroom upstairs, swiftly followed by strains of music; Grünner must have finished his speech.

He looked at his watch and saw that it was nine forty-five. The meeting might take place any time now.

As James made his way back to the hotel reception, he took note of the layout, trying to work out how to reach the cigar room from the outside. There was a doorway behind the main staircase that ought to lead in the right direction . . .

Then, up on the mezzanine level, he caught sight of Kitty, leaning out over the banister rail as she peered around . . . and suddenly Herr Grünner appeared, walking stiffly down the stairs.

James hurried through the door he'd seen, along a passage and out into a courtyard. The cold night air made him shiver. The moonlight, broken up by passing clouds, was pale; no other guests were braving the elements out here – or so he assumed until he emerged through a stone arch and saw two figures huddled at a patio table outside the cigar room.

'Whittaker and Herta,' James breathed. So this was where they'd got to! Discreetly waiting out here until the meeting started.

Inside the room the curtains twitched; then the French windows opened a little, allowing light to spill onto the dark patio. Herta and Whittaker – who was holding a large briefcase — rose and went inside. The door closed behind them; the heavy curtains swallowed the light again.

James crouched down low, moving from table to table until at last he reached the doors. He put his ear close to the cold wet glass; he didn't dare touch it for fear of leaving a mark that would be spotted when the curtains were drawn again. The ornamental plants rustled in the wind, and James strained to hear the words spoken by those inside. Through the tiniest gap in the curtains he could glimpse part of the room.

'You see the photograph, yes?' Grünner's voice, his English careful and precise, was cold as he held out his wallet. 'Yes, I stood by Hitler from the beginning. It was my townhouse in Berlin that he used for the secret meetings that paved the way for him to become our leader.'

Most men would keep a picture of their family, James noted darkly.

'This document, signed by the Führer, gives me full author-ization to deal with you,' he continued.

Whittaker took the proffered piece of paper in his good hand. 'To make a deal, you mean?'

'To deal with you, yes. As I choose.'

The statement sounded ominous to James. He caught a glimpse of pale skin and golden hair as Herta approached the French windows.

Desperately he dived for cover behind the nearest table and chairs. Herta peered out of the window, caught between moonlight and shadow, her eyes oddly bright and other-worldly behind the glass. James stayed stock-still. She kept watch for over a minute before turning away and tugging the heavy curtains together.

James waited, shivering, for a minute or two, half expecting her to reappear, wraithlike, at the window. Then the noise of a door opening sent him edging round the table: a member of staff walked across the patio, vanishing down a well-kept pathway. James cursed: his vantage point was very exposed. *How long was the meeting due to last?* he wondered. *How much business was there still to be concluded?*

As he crept closer to the French windows, he heard Grünner say, 'I do not have long tonight. I will be missed . . . Now, I agree, the test film is most convincing. The problem of the motive units is overcome, yes?'

Whittaker reassured him immediately. 'My controller unit, taken in conjunction with the hydraulic interface, is capable of making all systems more efficient. The Steel Shadow can run for over thirty minutes before the steam-power backup kicks in.'

'Ah yes, this controller unit . . . I wanted to study it for myself . . .' Through the tiny gap in the curtains James saw Grünner pacing the room, hands clasped behind his back. 'Such a pity it is now lost.'

James thought of the gadget now in Perry's care. *Not entirely.*

Whittaker cleared his throat. 'The unit will be recovered. In the meantime Herta can confirm the improvements we've made. She's operated the Steel Shadow herself.'

'What of the high-voltage electrical test?' Grünner demanded.

'The Steel Shadow is still susceptible to such an attack,' Herta said quietly, 'despite our attempts to improve the insulation. My report has all the statistics for you.'

'The lightning-strike test brought about a fatality, I believe?'

Herta's voice was completely matter-of-fact: 'The original operator was electrocuted. As you suspected, the secondary systems could not handle the power surge.'

James felt his hands curl into fists. So here at last was the tawdry truth: Marcus had been killed deliberately in a callous experiment – an experiment intended to benefit Nazi Germany. He hadn't even died for his country.

'The test was a waste of time as well as a waste of a life,' Whittaker stated. 'Under ninety-nine per cent of battlefield conditions, this so-called *weakness* could not be exploited. In any case, the Steel Shadows are designed to spearhead an assault. They go in as shock troops, ready to perform pre-programmed assault movements—'

'But not in a thunderstorm, eh?' James heard an eerie, high-pitched noise, and suddenly realized that the Ambassador was laughing. 'Rain stops play? How British, yes?'

'They go in as shock troops, to be backed up by conventional forces,' Whittaker continued, ignoring him.

'Rain stops play, yes . . .' Grünner's amusement faded; he scratched the scar on his neck. 'You know, my dear Whittaker, I did so desire to see this new controller unit. Stolen by a boy from your school – isn't that your story?'

'It's the truth,' Whittaker insisted. 'The same boy Herta involved in the cover-up for the fatality.'

'I thought he would make a good scapegoat,' Herta said. 'It would make the official report more convincing.'

'Instead, you've turned him into some kind of crusader.' Whittaker's tone was withering. 'I don't know how Bond got aboard the ship or found that part, but we *will* get the controller unit back.'

Want to bet? James thought darkly. It felt surreal, listening in to a conversation about himself. He looked around, worried that at any moment the patio would fill with noisy partygoers and he would have to leave.

'There's no real cause for alarm,' Whittaker was saying. 'Now that the problems in its construction have been solved, a new controller unit can be assembled from the notes and blueprints. Mr Blade has already given the order . . . he'll be here presently – he will tell you himself. The final delivery of all outstanding materials will reach you tomorrow.'

Damn it, James thought. *Taking that controller has barely slowed them down at all.*

'You have seen Dr Whittaker's notes, Herta?' Grünner enquired. 'Not the official ones intended for my eyes, but the full originals?'

'*Ja,*' she said, her voice sounding so close that James almost recoiled, afraid she was about to open the curtains again. 'I studied the papers in depth while at Fettes.'

'You can't have,' Whittaker protested indignantly.

'I cracked the code you worked into the notes to keep them secret. They are most comprehensive: your pioneering study of the overall principles, your scientific breakthroughs in the miniaturization of componentry—'

'Do not look so shocked, Dr Whittaker, please!' Grünner's voice dripped sarcasm. 'It could be worse, yes? The resourceful young Master Bond could have stolen these notes also! Do we know their whereabouts?'

'Currently they are safely locked in a trunk at Blade's residence in Wassenaar,' Herta said.

'How . . . ?' Whittaker sounded shaken. 'How do you know that?'

'I know what you and Blade have been discussing in secret,' she informed him. 'I made it my business to locate those notes. After all, I did not see Bond take the controller unit that you had refused to give me. I wished to be certain that you and Blade had not given away the only means to recreate it.'

'This is a breach of trust,' Whittaker protested, 'and furthermore—'

'For years now Blade has been drip-feeding me details of this project, piece by piece.' Grünner was gradually losing his temper. 'My country has paid over the odds for Blade-Rise arms and munitions in order to secure the Steel Shadows – and the means by which Nazi superiority will be asserted over the world . . .'

So Blade really is *a traitor.* James felt rocked by the unfolding proof. *He's dealing with the enemy for massive profits, giving Grünner and his Nazi bosses the means to mount an attack . . .*

'Now, on the eve of completion and delivery, the all-important controller unit conveniently goes missing.' Grünner's voice grew more threatening. 'Perhaps Blade thinks to double-cross me, yes? To show this marvellous unit to another buyer. The Russians, or the Japanese . . . or others who would seek to prevent the growth of Nazi influence?'

'I refuse to listen to this paranoid drivel.' James could imagine the veins standing out on Whittaker's temples, his eyes bulging. 'Let Blade convince you when he—'

'Your arrogance is so very British, Dr Whittaker. It will be the death of you.'

'Go to hell—' Whittaker broke off.

As he watched through the curtains, James saw why: Grünner had stepped forward, a gun in his hand; its silencer jabbed at Whittaker's chest.

'I don't believe you take me seriously.' The Ambassador was smiling, his face shiny with sweat. 'And, you know, the power I represent – the irresistible power of the Reich – must be respected.'

'You . . . you can't kill me!'

'I cannot allow knowledge of the Steel Shadows to go any further.' Grünner shrugged. 'It is Blade's project, first and foremost; I feel he should aid the Nazi war effort more . . . whole-heartedly. But you, Whittaker? Herta tells me you are a most annoying man to work with, yes? And since we know we can get hold of your private notes . . .'

James backed away from the French windows. *I've got to get help*, he thought. *Create a diversion . . . set off a fire alarm or—*

The curtains were suddenly ripped aside and Whittaker filled the space, eyes bulging as he felt for the door handle. James dived back behind the nearest table, but he knew he was too late: Whittaker had seen him, frowned, opened his mouth to shout.

But Grünner's gun had already fired. The bullet threw Whittaker forward and he bounced off the glass. As his arms flailed, his metal hook struck his temple and stayed there – its cruel point caught in his own flesh. Still staring at James, hook raised in a limp and bloody salute, Whittaker sank slowly to his knees.

It was all James could do not to be sick. He tried to control his breathing, to keep absolutely still. Already Herta was at the French windows, yanking the curtains closed, hiding

149

Whittaker's body from sight. On trembling legs, James crept closer again.

'Shall I clear this away?' Herta was asking.

'Leave him there for now. Let Blade see what has happened to his underling. It will be instructive, I think.' Someone clapped their hands; Grünner, James supposed. 'I will not be kept waiting any longer. Fetch Blade. I have a proposition to put to him – which he will accept, of course – and then you will go with him to his house to collect the notes.'

'Very good, sir,' Herta said.

Which way will she leave the room? James wondered. Fearing the worst, he scurried behind the nearest table just as the handle to the French windows jerked and twisted down. Herta emerged, looking as if nothing untoward had happened. She turned right, to rejoin the party. As the heavy curtains stirred in the breeze, James saw the tall figure of Grünner watching her go. His face showed the faintest of satisfied smiles.

Then the door clicked shut.

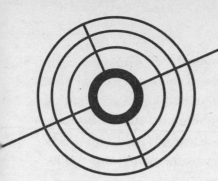

16
Tooth and Claw

James didn't hesitate. He headed left along a paved path, making his way round to the rear of the hotel.

If I hadn't taken that circuit board, he thought, *Whittaker might not be lying dead right now*. Perhaps he should feel guilty about it, but in truth he felt nothing; not even a sense of justice for Marcus now that one of his killers was dead too.

Until I can act on all I've learned, I've achieved nothing, he realized.

The clear priority was getting hold of Whittaker's notes before Grünner and Herta – and Blade himself. Two people had died already, both victims of that egotistical traitor. If James could get his hands on the files as well as the controller unit, it might sabotage Blade's deal with Grünner – and he'd have enough evidence to get Agent Elmhirst on board: Blade could be prosecuted and British national security protected.

That would be some revenge, James decided. That would be perfect.

But how the hell to make it happen?

Barriers had been erected across a small service lane that led to the laundry and kitchen areas. James ran quickly along it in the other direction, wishing he'd still got his raincoat. He had to find a taxicab. Kitty had told him where Blade's mansion was . . . What was the name of the place again . . . ?

The service road emerged onto a quiet back street that led to the Lange Voorhout. James pelted across the wide avenue, his new shoes chafing at his heels; to his left, a dark channel of water separated the street from the looming palaces on the other side. As he quickened his pace, he saw revellers piling into the back of an Austin 12 taxi. He ran after it, then stood and stared helplessly as it pulled away.

At the T-junction ahead James emerged onto a busier street: bars and cafés were still open. There had to be other taxicabs, he thought . . .

Gasping for breath now, he pounded along the street. Damn it – no sign of a taxi anywhere! James saw his slender head start dwindling with every passing minute.

Without checking for traffic, he flew across a side street, and a car had to slam on its brakes, its elongated bonnet almost knocking him down. Startled, James turned as the horn rasped and the driver shouted in Dutch through the window. Then he realized what this car – a Fiat 510S – was . . .

'A taxicab!' He grinned, went over to the driver, and tried to shake the gesticulating hand. 'You're free? You can take me?' He pulled the last of the money Aunt Charmian had wired from his inside pocket and pushed a bill into the driver's hand. 'Please!' He had no idea how much it was worth, but when he scrambled into the back of the cab, the driver pulled away without complaint.

'Thank you,' James panted as the Fiat turned left, back the way he had come. 'Speak English?'

The driver grunted, noncommittal.

'I need to go to Wassenaar!' James tried again. 'Do you know Hepworth Blade's residence in Wassenaar?'

'Blade-Rise man?' The driver looked at him strangely, then grunted again. 'Yes.'

'There, please. Quickly.' James tensed as the driver accelerated away. He'd wasted twenty minutes already. How long would he have before Herta and Blade arrived?

The taxi took the wide avenue leading back into the centre of town. To James's right, the shimmering surface of a canal shone palely in the moonlight, its banks packed with boats moored one behind the other, bumping gently in the wind. The cab crossed over it onto another wide road that led sharply downhill. A huge hexagonal church tower loomed out of the darkness, taking James by surprise.

The driver noticed his reaction. 'Grote of Sint-Jacobskerk.'

'Jacob?' James echoed the pronunciation, feeling the 'y' sound of the letter J in his mouth, as in German.

'In English is *James*,' said the driver.

James smiled despite himself. The Great Church of Saint James! Were the gods watching over him tonight? Or was it an omen: after all, one could only reach sainthood after death . . . He shivered, and sat back in his seat, noting landmarks only automatically from then on – should the need arise to retrace his journey.

Within fifteen minutes they had left the city and were

motoring through a more rural landscape. To the right was dense woodland; to the left, magnificent mansions stood in manicured grounds.

Then the taxi slowed and turned off the main road onto a series of quieter streets, where houses peeped from behind great hedges. Finally they turned left into a cul-de-sac and stopped; the driver slapped the wheel with both hands. 'Blade is here,' he said, and held out his hand for more money.

Peering out into the darkness, James surrendered all the change he had left in his pocket. The driver did not object, and James quickly got out. The taxi turned round and went back the way it had come, leaving him standing in the glow of a solitary streetlamp. On either side, tall hedges of thorny pyracantha disguised metal fences topped with rolls of barbed wire. At the end of the cul-de-sac stood a huge set of wrought-iron gates. Through them, James could see lawns bordered by cushioned safety rails. Yes, this must be Blade's place; even the gardens were designed with his protection in mind. Beyond them the pale moon illuminated a huge mansion.

James knew that the only way to survey the area would be from on high – which meant shinning up the streetlamp. Well, at least there were no neighbours around who might notice him. He took off his dinner jacket and slung it over his shoulder before holding onto the dark fluted metal and climbing all the way up to the ornate electric lantern sprouting from the top. Its light was so bright it masked much of the area around him, and the glass so hot he couldn't bear to hold on for long. James shifted precariously, clinging on with his legs while wrapping his jacket over his bare hands so he could take hold more effectively and block the light. He was trying to assess whether he could climb up into the pyracantha without damaging himself when he heard the throaty thrum of a motorcar engine.

Herta, so soon?

He'd hoped to have longer . . . Dropping quickly back to ground level, James crouched down against the hedge as headlights swept over the tarmac only a few feet from his face. Sleek and powerful, the silver Tatra 77 rolled up to the imposing gates – and with a low hydraulic throb and a rattle, they slowly swung open. James watched, fascinated. The mechanism was ingenious: the gates responded to a radio signal from inside the motorcar, he guessed.

James couldn't see inside the Tatra: Herta must be in there with Blade, he guessed.

As the big car headed round a bend in the drive, the gates began to swing shut. James rolled out from his hiding place and sprinted forward, hurling himself through the closing gap. He hit the ground hard, scrambled up and, keeping low, headed onto the lawn. He glimpsed red taillights disappearing fifty feet ahead, and went cautiously in pursuit, skirting the edges of the driveway, dodging from tree to tree. Ahead of him, Blade's mansion looked like the archetypal haunted house.

As the Tatra reached the entrance, James heard a series of barks go up, followed by deep snarls. He felt fear travel along his spine. Guard dogs. *Attack* dogs. The sound was growing closer, louder.

He turned to run, but knew he'd never reach the gates in time. Big, powerful shapes were already hurtling past the car, bounding towards him, ivory fangs bared, ready to tear him apart.

He was sprinting towards the nearest tree when the first dog caught up, its bulk slamming into him. Brought down, winded, James rolled onto his back – to find the Alsatian's frothing jaws snapping in his face. Its heavy paws pinned him down, claws ripping his shirt. He gripped the animal by the throat, trying to push the huge head away. Then another beast pounced on his legs. James felt teeth clamping around his shin, scissoring into the flesh. He tried to protect his body with his arms, but a third Alsatian grabbed his elbow in its jaws. James opened his mouth, ready to scream—

Then, all at once, the attack stopped. As if at some invisible command, the dogs turned and trotted back towards the house. For a few moments James lay there, frozen with shock before getting onto all fours; he peered after the vanishing Alsatians.

Staying stock-still in the shadows, James saw that Herta and Blade had emerged from the car. 'Don't know what's got into them,' Blade said, apparently quite relaxed . . . even though, James saw, Herta had a gun pointed straight at him. Carrel, the chauffeur, was holding something up in the air – a metal sphere about the size of a cricket ball. The Alsatians ignored the little group, making straight for their kennels, James assumed. *How is he doing that?* he wondered. Then he remembered the electronic gates that had opened at some sort of radio-controlled signal. Perhaps the dogs were responding to a similar signal in the sphere, analogous to a dog whistle, and Blade used it to stop them running wild.

Now Herta was training her gun on Carrel, who opened

the front door of the mansion. While Blade slowly shuffled inside after him, followed by Herta, James checked himself for damage. Aside from a gash in his hip and a loose flap of skin on his calf, it seemed he'd got away with scrapes and bruises.

In front of him, the front door had been left open. *Something's going my way at least*, James thought. He waited a couple of minutes, gritting his teeth against the pain in his leg. Then, afraid that whatever had stopped the dogs might wear off, he approached the door and stealthily entered the house.

He found himself in an enormous hallway. To his surprise, the black floor shifted slightly underfoot – it was soft, like rubber. In the bright light of the electric chandelier he saw that the walls were thickly carpeted. *In case Blade falls*, James supposed. *He's customized his house for his condition.*

Off to the right was a door that led into a study. All the furniture had padded corners, James saw, and the floor and walls were cushioned, like a padded cell. To his left was a staircase, the balustrade covered in spongy foam rubber; the steps in rubber slabs. A large walk-on platform lift ran vertically up next to the staircase, designed to carry someone up to the first floor. Since the platform was at the foot of the stairs, James realized Blade and the others must still be on this level.

Ahead of him was a set of double doors leading into a large drawing room. He went in and looked around. There was no clutter, no mess, no antiques; just a couch in the middle of the room beside a film projector that pointed at the wall. Tall beakers stood fixed to the side of the couch, a rubber straw extending up from each to avoid the need for glassware. An open doorway on the far side led to an equally minimalist dining room.

James wondered how large the mansion was. If he listened out, he would surely hear where Blade—

'*Now, sir!*' Carrel bellowed from beyond the dining room, his voice immediately obscured by a crash and clatter of something heavy falling.

'What the hell . . . ?' James hurried into the dining room and made for the double doors at the end of it, throwing them open. A well-lit corridor clad with padded leather stretched left and right; sounds of violence carried from the left, and James quickened his pace. Blade couldn't fight; it had to be Carrel versus Herta. The chauffeur must've jumped her so that Blade could hobble clear.

The course of action was obvious to James. If he let Carrel and Herta carry on with the fight, there would be no one to stop him finding and taking Whittaker's files . . .

He skidded to a stop as Carrel came flying out of a doorway to his left, his cheek bleeding from a deep cut. The chauffeur hit the soft wall and sank to his knees, unconscious. Herta strode out after him, a small, flat semi-automatic pistol aimed at his chest.

'No!' James launched himself at her. Herta brought the gun up – but too late; his hands closed on the barrel and twisted it round in her fingers. As they fell back through the doorway into a large white room, she dropped the gun, while James caught a glimpse of filing cabinets lining the far wall. *Whittaker's notes*, he thought. *They must've come here to fetch them.*

They hit the soft floor together, James on top. But the next moment Herta had bucked and rolled over; James was now pinned against the floor. She brought her elbow down towards his neck, but he pulled in his chin . . . The blow sent white sparks across his vision but made her grunt in pain too. James quickly grabbed hold of her hair and yanked hard. She gasped, arched her back and brought the gun butt down into his sternum. The pain made him gasp for breath, and before he knew it Herta had torn herself free. James rolled over and tried to pin her down by her wrists, but he was too slow. She slithered away, rolled over backwards, snatched up the gun and got to her feet.

James stared up into the barrel of a Colt 1908 Vest Pocket pistol. Herta's finger twitched on the trigger.

17

House of Traps

J ames lashed out with his heel and struck Herta on the shin, kicking her feet from under her. As she fell, he punched her in the jaw, all his weight behind the blow. With a grunt, she let go of the gun and collapsed on the floor, out cold.

'Stay that way,' James hissed.

He quickly checked on Carrel; the gash in his cheek looked nasty but he'd be all right. Rummaging through the chauffeur's pockets, James found the keys to the Tatra on a key ring that was attached to the spherical gadget that called off the dogs – and, please God, would open the gates too. He stuffed it in his pocket, and checked the room with the filing cabinets.

Lying on the floor was a large, tan leather trunk.

The Steel Shadow files?

James knelt beside the trunk, wincing as he put weight on his injured leg, and opened it. It was stuffed full of papers covered in diagrams, notes and equations that made no sense at all to him — but that didn't detract from his feeling of elation. *Done it!* He'd got hold of Whittaker's files which, taken together with the controller unit, would surely sabotage Blade's scheme to—

Where *was* Blade, anyway? Gone to call for help?

In which case, thought James, *it's time to leave.* He closed the trunk and picked it up; it was heavy and cumbersome. Not to worry. All he had to do was get it into the car before the dogs came back for seconds . . .

As James stepped out into the corridor, he heard something approaching. For a moment he couldn't move, haunted by that sound of grinding machinery, regular and repetitive. He'd first heard something like it in the grounds at Fettes, and again deep in the quarry at Thornhill Abbey. But this . . .

A bizarre, giant figure appeared round the corner, moving stiffly. The framework was in the shape of a man, with extending mechanical hands that clenched and unclenched. In place of the metal armour he'd seen on the Steel Shadow, there was only thick foam rubber, enveloping the man inside to keep him from harm, holding him in place as it nudged forward like some grotesque, life-size clockwork toy.

Blade's eyes glared out through the thick plastic visor. '*I wasn't expecting you, Bond.*' His voice boomed out over loudspeakers embedded in the suit. '*I'm tired of your meddling. Put down the files.*'

James turned with the trunk and headed back towards the dining room. But as he made to turn the door handle, metal shutters slid down from the ceiling; the doors were sealed off.

'*This house was built and automated to my specifications,*' Blade said, his voice rasping out over the speakers. '*Like this suit, it exists to protect me . . . and to defend against intruders.*'

Searching round for another exit, James followed the corridor past the dining room and found another doorway. As he turned the handle, an identical shutter slid down, almost taking his hand off.

James felt sick. *Now that the system's active, opening any door brings the shutters down.* Trying to keep calm, he carried on along the corridor, ears filled with the ominous whir of Blade's protective suit: It could move only slowly, but it was inexorable.

It'll never tire, James realized, *and here I am, exhausted already.*

'*Put down the files!*' Blade's rasping voice rang out again.

James found another door and, in desperation, hurled the heavy trunk against it to smash it open. This one led to a large stairway stretching down into shadow; another platform lift stood there, ready to carry its passenger to the lower level.

Crippled or not, James thought, *in that suit, Blade can follow me anywhere.* He started to run down the soft rubber steps, then gasped as a burning, toxic stink filled his nostrils.

The foam rubber of the stairs was melting. His new shoes were sticking to the stuff, sinking into it, trapping him there . . .

'*An ingenious idea, don't you think?*' Blade's voice reached him from the corridor. '*When the house is on "lockdown", heating panels under each step kick in to slow down intruders . . .*'

Desperately, James hurled the trunk down the stairs – it fell too fast to be caught in the same way – and started tearing at his laces, undoing both shoes. Then he threw himself down the soft, rubbery steps in much the same way, rolling down as fast as he could, stinking black goo coating his dinner jacket, until he hit the floor at the bottom. *At least it's a soft landing.*

Choking, he got up and reached out for a light switch – and an electric shock pulsed up his arm, making him cry out and fall back. *What have I triggered now?* The lights came on to reveal a spacious workshop, fully kitted out with benches and tools and separate work areas. James swore: the windows were set high in the walls, impossible to reach.

Blade shuffled up to the top of the stairs in his outlandish protective suit. As he stepped onto the platform, it hummed smoothly into life, carrying him down.

Feeling sick with fear, clutching the trunk, James forced himself to look around, to plan a course of action. *Don't blunder into anything else.* What could he do? As soon as he tried to climb the stairs, he'd be stuck . . .

The workshop was clearly designed to be used by staff under Blade's supervision – how else to explain the jagged sheets of metal, the mechanized tools and welding torches that Blade could not risk using, and areas of solid concrete flooring to support the equipment. James spotted what looked like a large gun, connected by rubber tubing to several pressurized canisters. He ran over and tried to make sense of the connections: a bulky melting pot with a handle on one side and a nozzle on the other was mounted above a kind of oversized Bunsen burner. Compressed air, fed to the burner, would intensify the flame so that whatever was inside heated quickly, to be sprayed out through the nozzle . . .

It fires metal! James realized, observing the solidified silver spatters all over the wall behind. At Fettes, Blade had talked of spraying metal onto a circuit board for greater efficiency . . .

James switched on the accelerated heating chamber. Behind him, he could hear the platform still whining its way down. *'There's nowhere to run, Bond,'* Blade shouted. *'Don't make this harder than it already is.'*

'What will you do this time?' James replied. 'Frame me for Whittaker's death like you framed me for Marcus's?'

'Tell me where the controller unit is.'

'Go to hell.' The heavy, cumbersome device was heating up fast; James grabbed hold of the insulated handle and heaved the spray gun round to face Blade. As he pulled the trigger, molten metal spat from the nozzle in a stream of red-hot sparks, mostly coating the floor. Blade retreated out of range.

All he has to do is wait for the fuel to run out and then come and get me. James looked with dismay at the smoking silver pool spreading over the floor before him. How could he cross that with no shoes?

'I did assure you that was no use as a weapon, Bond,' Blade jeered. *'Any minute now . . .'*

He's trying to intimidate you. James kept his finger on the trigger. *Ignore him—*

With a clank, a large grille in the wall behind him and two in the ceiling above swung open, and thick white foam exploded outward. It hit James – a foul, reeking, chemical mess – and threw him to the floor. The flame-spray machine hissed and sizzled as the melting pot was engulfed and the jet of molten metal extinguished.

'A fire would do the most terrible damage here,' Blade said as the

foam went on surging from unseen reservoirs in the walls and ceiling. '*So, before the tools here are used, the safety systems must be disengaged . . .*'

James could hardly breathe, and he struggled to keep his balance on the slippery floor. He heard Blade's suit rumble forward, unbothered by the foam; clutching metal hands extended towards him.

At last the deluge ended, the last of the foam falling in thick spatters. Feverishly, James crawled through the mess; his fingers grappled with the catches on Whittaker's trunk until he'd got the lid open.

Blade stopped dead. '*What are you doing?*'

'How many years . . . did it take to build up . . . these precious notes and papers?' James was panting for breath. 'How would you like me to stamp them into this sludge?'

No answer came from the speakers.

'I can't hear you . . .' With renewed strength, on hands and knees, James pushed the open trunk ahead of him, circling carefully round Blade. The suit stood there like a statue, no movement, no—

Just as James thought he was out of reach, the suit swivelled round and both arms lunged for him. James pushed the trunk forward with all his might, so that Blade's mechanical hands closed on nothing but foam.

'*Leave those!*' Now, finally, Blade seemed scared, and the realization was sweet. '*You don't understand – I need them. I need the controller unit . . .*'

'*I* need to stay alive,' James muttered. He closed the lid of the trunk and ran up the smoking, ruined stairs as lightly as he could: foam-saturated socks prevented his feet from sticking. He reached the top with a euphoric sense of victory; he knew that Blade could never catch him now.

Without looking back, the trunk clutched close to his chest, James skidded along the leather-padded corridor. *One of these doors must lead to the way out . . .*

A harsh scraping noise made him freeze. It was coming from the dining room, on the other side of the shutters.

No. It *was* the shutters, sliding back up into the ceiling.

Someone had taken the house out of lockdown. Carrel was the obvious candidate; as Blade's chauffeur and body-guard, he would surely know how to, but why would he do so now . . . ?

Because he's been forced to.

As James staggered on, he glanced round. Herta was standing in the corridor, the gun in her hand again.

'Stop!' she shouted.

Go to hell. Sweating, exhausted, James skidded out into the hallway. *Why didn't I take the gun?!*

He reached the front door just as Herta emerged into the hall. She gave him no second warning; she opened fire.

18
Threat on All Sides

The noise of the gunshot hammered at James's ears, but the sturdy oak door was already shutting behind him, stopping the bullet dead.

He saw the Tatra parked on the drive, wrenched open the driver's door and got in, pushing the trunk onto the seat beside him. His senses felt shattered but he forced himself to focus on the set-up: the steering wheel, a futuristic-looking circle in brushed aluminium, was set in the middle of the dashboard, white-rimmed dials and meters surrounding it like satellites. Rather than individual seats, there was a single leather banquette stretching from one side to the other.

Hoping for the best, James fumbled with the petrol–air mix control, set it to strong, and hit the button on the dash. The engine came straight to life. He brought up the hand throttle to engage the main carburettor, set the petrol mix halfway, put the car into gear and pulled away, twisting the steering wheel round hard – just as Herta threw open the front door. A bullet shattered the passenger window as James accelerated, his wet, stockinged foot nearly sliding off the pedal, praying the car wouldn't stall. He veered off the drive onto the soft lawn, desperate to reach the cover of the trees, then, safely behind a row of larches, headed for the gates. They swung slowly open as he approached; Carrel must have left the device switched on. Now, like Blade, James thought, Herta was stuck there with no means of controlling the patrol dogs – and no way to follow him.

He let out a shaky breath and drove out into the cul-de-sac, heading for the main road. The Tatra was powerful, but he slowed down and tried to get his breathing back under control, to push what had happened out of his mind and focus on the road.

It was no good. He was soaked through, and stinking, the chemicals making his cuts sting. He kept reliving the horrors he'd seen: Blade inside his machine, lurching ever closer; Whittaker, the hook lodged in his temple; and his killer, Grünner – the man whose orders had led directly to Marcus's death – Grünner with his whining laugh and staring grey eyes . . .

Please God, James thought, looking at the trunk beside him, *let there be something in these files that incriminates him and Blade.* He knew that only hard evidence would cut it for Agent Elmhirst; proof that no one could argue with. Only then could something concrete be done. Only then would Marcus's death not have been in vain.

James turned onto the main road back to The Hague, hoping that the way back to Scheveningen would be well signposted. He drove as fast as he dared, making for the coast. However, he soon got lost in the maze of streets that made up the smart suburb – until he passed Renbaan-Achterweg station, the nearest to the Mandevilles' townhouse on Brugsestraat. With a sigh of relief, he turned left and followed the route he'd taken the day before with Perry and Kitty, leaving the car a little distance away: he didn't want to lead anyone looking for the Tatra straight to his hideout.

James limped the rest of the way in wet socks, the trunk with the files held tightly under his arm. But just as he entered Brugsestraat, he saw another Tatra 77 parked outside the dark house.

He felt a sick pulse in his stomach. This Tatra was coloured deep burgundy. It must just be a coincidence that it was parked there . . .

And that the front door was standing ajar?

James swore. What if Blade, or one of his lackeys, had recognized him at the party? He'd posed as George Mandeville . . . it was hardly a great stretch for a pursuer to start the trail at the man's address. But instead of finding James, they'd have found . . .

'Perry,' he breathed. He set the trunk down under the hedge in the front garden and cautiously approached the door. He opened it enough to slip inside. All he could hear was the ticking of the grandfather clock, the distant roar of a motorcycle somewhere in the streets beyond.

Then the hall light snapped on. James blinked fiercely, bracing himself.

Blade's bodyguard from the party, tall and broad, with features that might have been Indonesian, stood at the entrance to the kitchen – with one muscular arm clamped tightly about . . .

'Kitty?' James frowned, and clenched his fists. 'What is this?'

'I'm so sorry, James!' Kitty, still dressed in her evening finery, looked scared and dishevelled. 'Mr Blade saw me with you during Mr Grünner's speech; he asked where you were staying. I said you were here, alone.'

Alone? James looked up the stairs, then back at Kitty, who shook her head a fraction. So Perry hadn't been found. Not yet.

'Daddy wanted to stay at the party, and I was tired, and Blade said Mr Van Diemen here would drive me home . . .' Kitty looked up at her captor. 'Instead he forced me to bring him here and wait for you.'

'Since we couldn't find you at the party . . .' Van Diemen stared at James from under heavy lids. 'Mr Blade wants the item you took. Where is it?'

'You know, I'm glad you're here, James,' Kitty broke in, 'because now I can do *this*.' Suddenly she stamped her pointed heel down on Van Diemen's foot, elbowed him in the stomach and then pulled hard on the arm clamped around her. The bodyguard was sent somersaulting over her head; he hit the tiled wooden floor on his coccyx, crying out with pain. He rolled into a crouching position, and James started forward to follow up the attack – before recoiling in alarm as a heavy vase fell from above. It crashed down on the back of Van Diemen's head. Kitty shrieked, while the bodyguard said nothing, out for the count.

'M-m-marksmanship of the highest order!' Perry hooted

from upstairs. 'I was waiting for him to come into the line of fire. Do hope Auntie wasn't too fond of that horrible thing.'

'I don't suppose she even knew him,' James joked as he frisked Van Diemen for weapons – after Herta, he was taking no chances. 'That was quite a move you pulled, Kitty.'

She shrugged. 'These shoes have been agony all night. I was glad to share the pain with somebody else.'

James discovered that the man was carrying a Beretta Model 418, a handsome gun, hidden in a shoulder holster. 'I was actually referring to the judo.'

'Oh, that. That's for self-defence. Daddy wouldn't let me out train-copping by myself until I was at least a first dan.'

'And what about me?' cried Perry, limping downstairs.

James pocketed Van Diemen's car keys and smiled. 'Good shot, Perry.'

'When I heard the door being forced, I wasn't sure what to do,' Perry admitted. 'With this leg, I'm neither use nor ornament – which rather gave m-me the idea.'

'I'm very nearly impressed, Mandy. Very nearly.' Kitty stared at James as he pocketed the gun, taking in his dishevelled appearance. 'God, James, the state of you!'

'Yes, what's been happening?' Perry asked as he reached the lower steps. 'And what the hell are we going to do with this Van Diemen character?'

'We can't stay here,' said James. 'It's not safe. Is the controller unit where I left it in the boiler cupboard?'

'No.' Perry tossed the cloth-wrapped bundle to him. 'I took it into personal custody until you returned.'

'Then, once I've changed into whatever fresh clothes your uncle has, let's get going.' Holding the controller unit tightly,

James started up the stairs. 'I've got some stories to share – and some secret files to go with them. That is, if you're interested . . . ?'

Kitty glanced at Perry, and they both nodded. 'Get on with it, James, for God's sake!'

Twenty minutes later James was driving Kitty and Perry away in Van Diemen's burgundy Tatra 77; he'd switched because Carrel's silver version had taken several bullets, and there was more fuel in this tank. As James drove out of The Hague and back towards Rotterdam, he appreciated the smooth ride: the motorcar handled beautifully.

Three stolen cars in as many days, he reflected. *This is becoming a habit.*

He had planned to drop Kitty at her house, but she wouldn't hear of it. 'I was kidnapped and I damn well want to know why.' She had telephoned her half-asleep mother to say that Mr Blade had dropped her off at a friend's house ('It's sort of true,' she argued), and demanded James account for his evening.

Having brought her and Perry up to speed on everything that had happened, James parked under a streetlight on the quiet outskirts of Rotterdam and got into the back with the other two. At least he smelled better now – though the navy shirt and black jumper were very snug beneath his coat, and the hems of his borrowed tweed trousers waved well above his scuffed school shoes. *Perhaps I'll set a trend*, he thought wryly.

The 77 was designed with comfort in mind: as there was no driveshaft beneath the car, the floor was flat, which meant that six adults could be seated comfortably in the rear across

174

the two cream leather bench seats, one facing forward and the other back. The generous windows meant that the interior was brightly illuminated by the streetlamp.

Kitty had spread the files over the cream leather banquette to the rear. She'd swapped her high heels for a more practical pair of flats with a scalloped trim, and now wore black French-finish linen slacks and a white blouse: all belonged to Perry's aunt. Her glasses were back in place, the thick contact lenses discarded, and the frames lent her a studious air.

'There's a whole lot of stuff here,' she remarked, scanning the pages. 'Cargo shipments from British ports to Rotterdam, going back to the twenties . . . Orders for things with serial numbers; no names, it seems . . .'

'And there are reams of equations that would fox the m-m-masters back at Fettes, I'm sure,' Perry added. 'Diagrams too.' He tapped a piece of paper, bringing it to James's attention. 'Looks like the thing we saw at Ruskie . . .'

'This must be research that led to the Steel Shadow,' James surmised.

'And *this*.' Kitty had snatched up a typed sheet of times and stations. 'Oh, this. This, *this!*'

James looked over, confused. 'What is it? Train times?'

'Yes. No. Oh!' Kitty looked ready to swoon. 'If only I had my notebook! No, I don't need it. I know those timings off by heart. Oh, my life . . .'

'Stop flapping, Drift,' Perry complained. 'What's wrong with you?'

'My Ghost Train. The one I told you about' – Kitty put her hand on James's knee – 'when *he* bothered to ask. No official livery, no regular route.' She whipped off her glasses and studied James. 'I think this might be its timetable. It last ran from Rotterdam two days ago, at two p.m.'

James found himself swept up in her sudden excitement. 'Ran where?'

'Its final destination says *Winter Immer*.'

'*Immer?*' said Perry.

'German for *always*,' James told him. '*Winter* is spelled the same in both languages – though of course, the W in German is pronounced like a V: *Vinter*.'

Kitty's dark eyes gleamed. 'I've seen the Ghost Train myself between Rotterdam and The Hague, and other train-coppers have reported it out as far as Nijmegen, heading east . . .'

'Making for the German border,' James breathed. 'All right. What else is on the timetable?'

'A stop at four forty-six a.m. today, marked *Schaduw Nieuw Oost*.' Kitty paused impressively. 'Meaning, *New East Shadow*.'

'There's a station called that?'

'Not officially. It might be a code . . .' she suggested.

'M-m-might be anything,' Perry said sourly.

'Well, we'd better work out what the hell it is, and fast.' James checked the numbers, heart pounding. 'Because our Ghost Train is due to stop at this shadow station in just a few hours from now.'

19

Riding the Rods

'Are you hungry?' It was four a.m., and Kitty was standing by the railway track beside James, her spirits unflagging. 'I'm absolutely famished. Luckily I've got a sandwich in my coat pocket. The canapés at these parties are never enough, so I take extra fuel for the journey home. Never got a chance last night, so . . .' She pulled out a white package. 'Edam and apple all right for you? Slightly squashed, I'm afraid . . .'

'Please, you have it.' James was trying not to limp; his calf was very sore. Following Kitty's directions, he'd driven them as close to this spot in the wilderness as possible, but Perry was having to sit out the endeavour. With his gammy leg, he knew he couldn't keep up, so he'd stayed in the Tatra; he reckoned he could just about drive it himself, at least to somewhere with a telephone kiosk. Perry's mission was to get hold of Adam Elmhirst back in Britain and tell him what was happening – with best regards from James Bond.

That was the idea, in any case.

James was holding onto the controller unit, keeping it separate from the files, so their eggs weren't all in one basket. Hopefully it would also encourage Adam Elmhirst to act when James got hold of him; then things would surely start to move. In the meantime Perry could stay at the Drifts' house until James and Kitty returned.

James gazed around at the empty moonlit countryside; only the occasional tree to break up the low-lying landscape. He couldn't shake the feeling that they were being followed; that Blade or Grünner or both had put agents on their tail. For the twentieth time he checked that the controller unit was still in his pocket.

'Kitty,' James said, 'are you sure this is the place we need to be?'

'I'm staking my reputation on it. Ooh, *steak!* Wouldn't that be heavenly right now?' She offered James the sandwich again, but he shook his head. 'All right, then, my reasoning for coming here in search of the New East Shadow . . . Well, back in 1843, the station, Nieuw Oosteinde, was located on the crossing with the Laan van Nieuw Oosteinde, the Avenue of the New East End. It was named after the New East End Inn.'

James yawned, his breath misting out in the cold. Kitty sounded like a schoolmistress, and with her thick glasses was starting to look the part. 'Perhaps I *will* have a bit of your sandwich. Sounds as if I'll need to keep my strength up.'

'So rude.' She pulled a face but let him take a bite. 'Well, the station closed in 1864, and a new one didn't open until 1907 – same location, only they'd electrified the track by then. We rode the Old Line yesterday, remember? The first electrified railway in the Netherlands.'

'Is this going somewhere?' James wondered.

'Yes,' she said. 'To Leiden one way, and Utrecht in the other.'

'Kitty . . .'

'Oh, all right. Sorry, James. Well, in the forty-odd years between the old station closing and the new one opening, there was an attempt to build a separate branch line a mile or so north of the Old Line, making stops in Voorburg and Zoetermeer before picking up the main Utrecht line at Gouda—'

'Not that this lecture isn't fascinating,' James murmured, 'but . . .'

'The point is, this branch line was never finished. Money didn't materialize; investors pulled out. The existing track was left lying there, unfinished and unusable. *Unless* . . . years later . . . someone added to it in some way.'

James grasped where this was going. 'You think Blade could've used some of this unfinished track for his cargo shipments?'

'Well, he isn't short of influence in these parts, is he? He could have built an extension from the main line for his own private use – with a secret stop at an equally secret New East Shadow station along the way, before journeying on towards Germany – probably joining the State Railway line, if it travels through Nijmegen – and on to *Winter Immer*.' Kitty tapped the side of her nose, leaving a smear of butter there. 'Who says that a sound knowledge of railway networks is a dull thing to fill your head with, eh?'

'Not me.' James held up his fingers in a salute. 'Scout's honour.'

'I should hope not.' Kitty hugged herself for warmth as they walked on. 'So watch out for the freight train.'

James nodded. 'I'll do more than watch out for it. I told you, if it comes along, I'm jumping aboard.'

'It's called "catching on the fly",' Kitty informed him. 'And I think you mean *we* are jumping aboard.'

James looked doubtful.

'I'm not settling for just another glimpse of my Ghost Train, James,' Kitty retorted. 'Not after all this time. For your information, I've hopped freights on the fly plenty of times. I've ridden the rods.'

'Rods?'

'The Ghost Train runs old stock – probably the same freight cars it's been pulling since the twenties. These old wooden carriages are often reinforced with steel joists running lengthways, so they can carry heavier loads. Gives you something to hold onto, or even lie back on.'

'Kitty,' James tried again, 'getting aboard is only the start of it. We don't know where the train's going or what to expect when it arrives.'

'I don't need looking after, if that's what you're implying.'

'I just mean that—'

'Oh, hush now. We can always jump off when the train slows for the freight yard. Anyway' – Kitty winked, a slow, careful gesture – 'I might be wrong about all this.'

'If you are, and if the Ghost Train fails to haunt us this morning . . .' James stared down the dark, unending track. 'I suppose it's down to the police to halt Blade's operation with the evidence we have.'

'And that would kill you, wouldn't it?' Kitty looked at him thoughtfully. 'Most boys your age would be happy enough to duck out after so many near scrapes. And yet here you are, looking for more.'

James thrust his hands into his pockets. 'If we discover exactly where Blade's been sending his weapons, investigators will know where to start looking for proof.' He looked down at his feet. 'I need to know that I did everything I could for . . . for Marcus.'

'Ah, I see.' Kitty brushed sandwich crumbs off her coat. 'I thought perhaps you thought you needed revenge.'

James stared at her, but said nothing.

'I know you lost your poor friend,' Kitty went on, 'and you want people to know what really happened, and why. But the likes of Blade and Grünner – they're powerful people. If they killed one young man in his prime—'

'The bigger they are, the heavier they fall,' James said, shrugging. 'I suppose that once I start something, I need to see it through. Besides . . . I couldn't let you catch your Ghost Train all alone, could I?'

Kitty half smiled. 'It's been a mystery I thought I'd never solve.' Her gaze hardened. 'Wait . . . You don't think a girl like me should be allowed her own adventures?'

'I've seen that you can handle yourself,' James said quickly. 'I just don't want to feel that I involved you in—'

'Well, you bloody well *have* involved me. I was practically abducted tonight, thanks to you. But if you think that makes me your responsibility, forget it. Tonight it's about the Ghost Train, and that means you're in *my* adventure.' She paused, then leaned forward and kissed him clumsily on the cheek. 'Welcome aboard.'

James's surprise turned to a smile. 'Well, thank you. But there'll be no adventure at all unless your precious train comes.'

'The timetable says— Shh.' Kitty held up her sandwich for silence. James took another bite from the end, and she shushed him again. 'Listen.'

James did. 'Listen to what?'

'Such a romantic, hopeful sound . . .' Kitty's smile was broad and warm. 'Here she comes, right on time.'

Now James heard it, stealing into the night – and spotted the first smoke signals in the distance. The Ghost Train was approaching. He felt his nerves tingle, his tiredness fade and the blood surge through his veins as he readied himself for action. He looked around: open ground; nowhere to shelter apart from a few low tussocks of grass. 'There's our cover,' he said. 'Keep down out of sight.'

'I hope they don't spot our breath.' Kitty huffed out mist in James's face as she joined him in the wet grass. 'I wonder how long the train will be. It's best to make for the middle section.'

'Why's that?'

'Furthest from the driver at the front and brake van at the rear. With heavy freight, the brakeman may have to apply the brake to help the driver regulate the speed and keep the buffers tight.'

'Yes, of course.' James nodded. 'And with any luck, we'll be far enough away from the crew in the locomotive . . . They

182

shouldn't notice us in the dark.' He sized up the train as it came into view. It was moving at perhaps twenty-five miles an hour, ploughing relentlessly through the landscape.

'It'll slow for the bend in the tracks here,' Kitty told him. 'You know, there's a saying amongst freight-hoppers. If you can't count the bolts on each wheel, don't do it. It's going too fast.'

'Sensible advice,' James commented.

'You'll jump anyway, won't you? Fool . . .'

He smiled at her, and she smiled back.

The dark engine was moving closer, etching a path between the flat countryside and the blue-black sky. The brakes made a grating sound, and steam gusted and bellowed from the chimney, trailing wraithlike behind it. James could see no numbers on the engine, no insignia, just as Kitty had described it. He glimpsed two men up front in the cab, huddled together. As he watched them, he felt again for the circuit board in his pocket . . .

'On your marks,' Kitty breathed, 'get ready . . .'

'Go!' James ran full pelt towards the moving train. Through the billowing smoke and smuts he searched out the containers rumbling by, each built around a steel frame, with wooden walls, floor, roof and doors. In the filthy air he could barely see the wheels, let alone count the bolts . . .

But he could see the metal ladder running from the foot-plate to the roof, used by the loading crew to guide cargo lowered from above.

'Go on!' Kitty shouted over the din from behind him.

James sprinted alongside the train as fast as he could, trying not to choke, hands reaching for the rungs of the ladder. As it began to pick up speed, he leaped, grabbed hold and swung his feet onto the lowest rung. The train's whistle shrieked, as if in alarm, but James clung on, shivering in the cold, his fingers already growing numb. The train swayed along the track, making him rock to and fro. He looked round for Kitty. Had she made it? Was she aboard?

'Here!' Kitty's voice carried to him over the clank of the wheels on the track. As the smoke cleared a little, James saw a hand waving at him from under the freight car. With a start, he leaned out to peer down, and saw Kitty lying flat out on her back, braced over two of the metal joists that stretched under the carriage, just as she'd described.

'Nothing like local knowledge, eh?' James called to her. 'Shall I come down to you or are you coming up to me?'

'My bones are being shaken to jelly!' Kitty clung on, her lips set with determination. 'Will the door open?'

James edged his foot onto the running board, leaned across and grabbed the handle of the freight car's sliding door. It wouldn't budge.

'Must be locked,' came Kitty's verdict. 'Damn.'

'Did we expect anything else?' James shrugged. 'I suppose the ghosts on the Ghost Train walk straight through. Well, we're too conspicuous out here.'

'I don't fancy climbing along to the next car to see if it's the same story,' Kitty called up to him. 'But you stick out like a sore thumb up there.'

'A frozen thumb,' James corrected her. Gingerly he lay down on the running board and prepared to manoeuvre himself down to join her.

'Wait till we slow down!' Kitty yelled.

James's nerve faltered for a moment; the train was going fast, and he knew that she was right: a slip would leave him sliced in two or pulverized by the wheels. But he was so cold out here: the driving wind was dehydrating him; soon cramp would set in, his extremities would lose sensation . . . If he was going to change position, it needed to be now.

Holding onto the lowest rung of the ladder with both hands, James swung his feet under the carriage, just inches from the deadly wheels, his feet feeling for the steel joists. The train rocked, almost throwing him off, but he clung on grimly. Kitty swung herself onto the next joist, which ran along the middle of the freight car's underside, clearing a space for him. It was terrifying, holding on with only one hand as he reached down for the joist. Then, suddenly, he was underneath the carriage, twisting round and grabbing hold of the steel strut beneath him. In the enclosed space, the noise was deafening; the ground rushed along beneath him, barely more than a foot from his nose.

'My God.' James looked at Kitty – a dark shadow beside him. 'You say you've done this before?'

'Never while the train was actually moving,' she admitted. 'I can't say I'm of a mind to repeat the experience.'

James silently agreed as he clung on. His head throbbed from the cacophony, and he felt nauseous from the endless rocking motion. He wondered where the hell the train was headed, and what awaited them there . . .

20

Shadow Factory

The train thundered on for mile after mile. The sky was lightening, and James could now see Kitty clearly.

'What kind of a crew would a freight train have?' he wondered.

'I suppose a minimum of a driver and a fireman, to check the steam pressure, the water, the fire . . .'

James smiled in spite of his discomfort, impressed by her knowledge. 'Those two up front, then, and the brakeman to the rear. Only three to steer clear of. Could be worse, I suppose.' He tried to ignore the bitter cold and the pins and needles in his limbs. 'Although I'm not sure this journey could be.'

'It has to end soon,' Kitty told him, clearly trying to reassure herself too. 'We came aboard around twenty-five miles from Utrecht and haven't switched to the new line yet.'

We'd better switch before long, thought James, his eyes closing wearily, head pounding.

A sudden piercing screech from the rear of the train made him jolt. The guard in the brake van was slowing them down.

Kitty looked hopeful. 'Sounds like we're nearly there.'

'We should jump off now while we can,' James said. 'Find out where we are—'

'How do you suggest we do that?' She nodded to the ground, still racing by a foot below them. 'We'll just have to stay out of sight and hope we can get off while it's in the yard – or find a better position for jumping clear once it's set off again, before it picks up too much speed.'

James stared at her. 'You're taking all this very coolly.'

'That'll be the cold numbing my brain,' Kitty said, inclining her head. James knew she was trying to act as if she was fine, but sensed the fear behind the façade.

He felt something similar himself. If he'd guessed that his private crusade for justice for Marcus would lead him here, caught up in a web of high-level treachery at the cutting edge of weapons development . . . might he have given up and walked away? No, he decided. It was pointless even to think that way. The moment, the 'right now' – whatever the risk and opportunity it held – had to be his only focus. *Wherever I go*, James thought, *there I am.*

With a worm's-eye view of the world, he couldn't see much. But as the train slowed to a crawl, James heard heavy gates being rolled open; two men, one on each side of the rails, exchanging greetings in Dutch with the train crew. The locomotive advanced slowly into darkness, as if into a tunnel, and then the daylight was replaced by harsh yellow overhead electric lights. It grew warmer, thank God, and there was a smell of diesel and cordite. The two men closed the gates behind them.

'Where are we?' James whispered as the train finally creaked and hissed to a halt.

'It's like no rail shed I've ever been in.' Kitty listened for a moment, then lowered herself onto the track and rolled sideways to the edge of the carriage, her dark eyes looking around.

Slowly, painfully, James let go of his joist and dropped down too. He felt for the circuit board in his pocket, then, still on his back, wriggled over to the other side of the train and peeped out.

It was a huge industrial depot, as big as an aircraft hangar, with huge sheets of frosted glass in the roof. Wooden crates and pallets were stacked in neat piles, and James could hear the grind and hiss of hydraulics nearby; a forklift truck rolled past.

'Looks like a warehouse or something,' Kitty whispered.

But there were also conveyor belts, lathes, welding stations, all standing quiet now. The rails ran clear across the hangar – on the far side was a colossal sliding door to allow the train straight out the other side.

'It's not a warehouse, it's a factory.' James rolled back under the train, closer to Kitty. 'A factory built around its own railway yard, so the product can be loaded aboard out of sight.'

'Helps the train remain a secret: it never stops at regular stations, and never runs at the same time twice.' Kitty gave a low whistle. 'And this is all run by Blade-Rise . . . You think my Ghost Train's been jam-packed with illegal arms going to Germany all these years?'

'That's my best guess, yes,' James said. 'In direct contra-vention of the terms of the peace treaty signed after the war.'

'But during the last couple of years Hitler's been quite open about his intentions to re-arm Germany – restoring national pride and all that – it's no big secret. The Nazis can make their own weapons, so why still buy from Blade-Rise?'

'Because Grünner has been waiting for the Steel Shadow to be finalized; then he can present it to Hitler and take all the glory,' James said sourly. 'They must have paid a lot for the prototype. I've seen it in action. It would be worth huge amounts to get hold of that.'

'But if you saw it being tested in Scotland,' said Kitty, 'it must have been sent over on the same ship as you and Mandeville.'

'Right. So the question is, what's being loaded onto this train now?' James looked around for other staff or security men, but everything was silent. 'Production seems to have stopped here.'

'Perhaps they've already made the last batch of weapons, and now they're clearing out—'

James put a warning finger to his lips as, over the hiss of the locomotive, he heard approaching footsteps and voices. The brakeman, in dark blue overalls and a donkey jacket, had got down from the car at the rear and joined the two men who'd closed the doors. He called to the driver up front.

'You speak Dutch?' James whispered.

'Not as much as I ought,' Kitty confessed. 'The brakeman said something about thirty minutes to get some rest. The

190

fireman said there's a good fire and plenty of pressure and they'll get straight out afterwards.'

'Sounds as if they're on a tight schedule.' James looked at her. 'Which means, so are we. You stay here – I want to have a look around.'

Kitty put a hand to his chest to stop him as a clang reverberated through the shed and, with a rusty squeal, a neighbouring container was unlocked and its door dragged open. A minute later a workman's booted feet came into view – a third staff member – and the container above them was unlocked and opened too. The man turned and moved away, heading for the forklift.

James crawled out from under the train. From his vantage point he could see only the one workman, but he knew others might arrive at any time. He glanced inside their container, which was empty, then moved swiftly along to check the next one. Four crates were stacked along the side.

What was inside them?

James hung back behind a workbench as the man, wearing plain dark overalls, set about loading the last crates and pallets into the freight car. James saw that some tools had been left discarded on the floor; he picked up a hammer and a chisel and a screwdriver, wincing when he realized that his palms were covered in blisters. He watched as the last pallets went on, then the man closed the doors and locked them. Presumably master keys were held at every stop, so the trains could be accessed at all times. James looked down at his stolen tools and hoped that he could open the door the hard way.

The workman left the cavernous shed, and James crept quietly back to where he'd left Kitty under the train . . .

To find that she had gone.

James felt fear clench a fist in his guts. He looked around wildly – *she's been captured, she's hurt, they've killed her* – only to see her peep out from behind the freight car a few feet away, a cheeky smile on her face.

'What took you so long?' she whispered. 'Look, we can ride the couplings. Not very safe, but if we're to jump off before the train builds up too much speed . . .' She trailed off; she must have seen the look on his face. 'What is it?'

'I'm not jumping off,' said James. 'I've decided. I have to stop this train.'

'It *is* stopped.'

'I mean, I can't let whatever's on board reach Germany.' James continued on to the front of the train, looking up at the huge, glossy black locomotive. He climbed into the cab – he'd always wanted to drive one of these, he thought – then opened the door to the firebox, basking for a moment in the blaze from the glowing coals. Like any boy alive, he understood the basic principles: the heat from the firebox slowly warmed the water in the boiler around it. When the water was hot enough, it turned to steam, and when the steam pressure was high enough, the driver opened the regulator valve, feeding it into the locomotive's dense nest of cylinders. The pressure of the steam forced pistons back and forth, which in turn moved the driving rods connected to the wheels. The hotter the fire, the greater the steam, the faster you could go.

James marvelled at the elegance of the system; for all the dirt and sweat and brute strength that went into it, here was a beautifully designed process, a miracle of engineering.

He turned to Kitty. 'How do we break it?'

'Sabotage, you mean?' Kitty looked worried. 'Er . . . we could put sand in the oil boxes . . .'

'Do you see any sand?'

'Oh, to be on Scheveningen Beach again.' Kitty chewed her lip. 'The firebox, then – if the water level dropped far enough to leave the top plate of the firebox uncovered, the steam pressure ought to pull it apart.'

'So we've got to stop the fireman doing his job,' James realized. 'Whatever we do to the train here, they've got staff and resources to fix it. I'll have to wait till we're underway.'

'Hijack a moving train and take on two men? It's suicide.' Kitty looked deeply unhappy. 'Who do you think you are – Richard Hannay from those silly novels?'

James half smiled. 'Let's hope we can destroy a firebox in fewer than thirty-nine steps. Come on – let's get back under-cover. They've been gone twenty minutes; in another ten . . .'

He led Kitty back to the freight carriage. Long minutes passed with only the hissing of the train and the hum of the electric lights to mark them. Finally they heard movement from somewhere outside the depot: a door opened, and men's voices approached.

The brakeman trooped back to the rear of the train. '*Volgende halte, Düsseldorf. We zullen op tijd terug zijn voor Kerstmis.*'

Dutch wasn't so dissimilar to German, James realized. 'Düsseldorf is the next stop?'

'And he said they'd be back in time for Christmas!' Kitty translated, her eyes alight now. 'That's it, then: the last part of the Ghost Train mystery. From here, it could take four or five hours to get to Düsseldorf, I suppose. And then . . .' Her excitement faltered. 'Christmas . . . I'd almost forgotten.

Doesn't that sound wonderfully normal? It's nearly Christmas, James.'

He tried to offer a reassuring smile. 'Stay here, Kitty,' he suggested suddenly. 'Sneak out and make for the Old Line; get back to your father; spread the news that *Winter Immer* is in Düsseldorf. The authorities can change the signals and halt the train.'

She gave a dismissive snort. 'You don't believe that. By the time I've got back, made anyone believe me—'

'That's why I've got to try my way too.'

'You'll get yourself killed. Is that what Marcus would have wanted?'

James made no reply.

'Very well. I *will* stay here and find a way out.' Kitty wiped at her eyes crossly. 'Not because you're gallantly telling me to, but because if we both commit suicide, then no one will ever know where the Ghost Train was going, will they?'

James heard the slam of the door to the brake van. 'There are empty crates behind that workbench over there,' he said urgently. 'If you hide out till everyone's left—'

'I'll find a way.' Kitty looked at him. 'When we first met, I thought, this can't truly be a friend of Mandeville's, can he? So self-possessed, so mature . . .' She shook her head, turned and, keeping low, stole quietly away.

James watched her go, wishing he could call her back, realizing that he had nothing to say in any case. He tucked the tools he'd taken inside his waistband and considered what he had to do. Back to riding the rods? No, not this time. Scrambling back up onto the carriage in broad daylight while the train was moving really *was* suicidal.

There was only one other option. James ducked out from under the car and swiftly climbed up onto the couplings as Kitty had suggested, one foot on the metal buffers connecting it to the car in front, one on the parallel chain that held them in place. He leaned back against the container wall, knowing that if he fell between the carriages while the train was in motion, he'd be crushed.

The same men who'd opened the doors that led into the depot now opened the exit doors. Then they moved across to the far side of the building, out of sight. *Obliging*, thought James. The hissing of the boiler as coal clattered into the firebox was growing steadier, stronger. A sudden loud rattle made him jump, and he realized that the two men were pulling on chains to open the glass windows in the roof, letting out the steam and smoke.

At last, edging forward slowly, the train began to move out. James gave silent thanks to any celestial being that might be listening.

Then he saw that the man who'd driven the forklift was now standing by the exit. James shrank back, trying to make himself as small as possible.

As if in slow motion, the man's head turned towards him.

21
Wrong Side of the Tracks

The man's blue eyes widened at the sight of James clinging on between the carriages. The steaming locomotive was already out of the depot, so he couldn't alert the driver and fireman. Instead he lunged forward to try and haul off the intruder. James pulled the chisel out of his waistband and brought it down so that the flat of the blade struck the bridge of the man's nose; it brought forth a yell and a stream of blood. Hands covering his nose, the man never saw James's foot – which connected with his chest and propelled him backwards against the wall. He slid to the ground in a daze.

'One less for you to deal with, I hope, Kitty,' James muttered. He looked about for any sign that the two men opening the windows had heard anything, and was reassured.

But a slow, painful squeal told him that the brakes had been applied.

The brakeman, he realized. He must be aware that some-thing untoward had happened.

Impulsively, James jumped off the slowing train, keeping the carriages between him and the other two men, and pelted back up the track towards the brake van. Once they were properly underway the brakeman would be looking out of the cupola in the roof, but at the moment there was still too much smoke to see if he was there or if—

As James reached the brake van, the door flew open into his face. It was like running into a wall, and he rebounded, his head ringing, and he dropped the hammer and screwdriver as he hit the ground. Through the pain behind his eyes, James saw the brakeman jump down to attack him.

No, he thought, grabbing the hammer and smashing it into the man's knee. He fell down, yelling in agony, as James threw himself inside the brake van. He turned the braking wheel round and round to release the brake – but he feared he was too late. The train wasn't picking up speed; the driver must have put on the brakes in the locomotive.

James heard more shouting. Still woozy, he pushed his head up into the cupola to peer out – and saw Kitty strug-gling in the grip of the forklift man, who was back on his feet. The other two were now waiting for the train to come to a stop so that they could cross the tracks to join him.

If he was going to help her, James knew he had to move fast. He hunted around for anything he could use – and saw a long wooden pole with a twisted metal end (for uncoupling wagons, he supposed); a milk bottle full of paraffin for the side and tail lamps; and something that looked like a square-ended baseball bat . . . a brake stick, that was it – he'd seen them used to lever down the handbrakes of wagons—

The door to the carriage was thrown open and the brakeman reappeared. James grabbed the milk bottle and threw the paraffin into his face. The man staggered back, clawing at his eyes, framed in the doorway, until a hefty jab with the end of the long pole ejected him back onto the concrete.

'James!' Kitty shouted.

He grabbed the square-ended bat, jumped out of the brake van and ran towards her. Before he could reach her, she had bent over double and flipped the forklift man against the side of the train. James raised the bat, but this time the man stayed down.

Kitty gave James a brief hug. 'I'm sorry – that thug saw me before I could hide.'

James turned and saw a man scrambling between the carriages, a revolver in his hand. James brought the bat down onto his knuckles, and he dropped the gun. There was no time to retrieve it – the other man had a revolver too; he fired a warning shot into the air.

'Come on!' James seized Kitty's hand, and together they raced for the open doors, hearing another gunshot as they burst through. The cold morning air woke James's senses, made him feel sharper. But he soon realized that the game was up: the train had come to a halt, and the driver and fireman had jumped out; both were armed.

James stopped and squeezed Kitty's hand. 'They've got us,' he panted. 'Put up your hands.'

She said nothing, but James remembered her words: *If we both commit suicide, then no one will ever know where the Ghost Train was going, will they?*

Suddenly he heard footsteps coming up behind him. James's legs gave way even before he felt the blow to his neck, and blackness closed about him.

When he was young, James had loved falling asleep in the back of his parents' car; lying safe and warm under his blanket on the rear seat. If he opened his eyes, he could see flashes of light amidst the dark, and his mother's face in profile, her hand on his father's shoulder.

When he woke up, for a few perfect seconds, rocked by the motion and calmed by the sight of the white sky above him, James thought he was safe. Then reality intervened, and he saw where he was: back in the brake van, lying against Kitty, hands and ankles bound. His head was splitting; even small movements made him wince with nausea. Kitty was asleep, or unconscious, breathing softly. The brakeman was looking out through the cupola, watching the track ahead. He glanced down, and James closed his eyes again. *Feign sleep*, he told himself, but almost immediately succumbed to the blackness for real.

The next time his senses returned he was aware of the rhythm of the train slowing as the brakeman spun the wheel and increased the friction. James turned his head; it hurt a little less now. Through the windows he saw thick woodland pressing in close, as if trying to smother all trace of the train. The cold scent of wet fir trees filled the air, along with paraffin from the lamps and coal from the little fire burning in the stove. Smoke blew back from the stack past the windows.

Suddenly they were swamped in darkness. *A tunnel*, James realized. The train was heading gently downwards, the gradient slowly increasing. Electric lanterns had been screwed into the tunnel wall, black cables connecting them like arteries. The train was doing maybe five miles per hour now, snaking slowly deeper.

It's like we're being swallowed up, James thought. Though his hands were tied he reached for Kitty's fingers behind him. She did not react, still dead to the world; he felt a sullen moment of envy.

Finally the track levelled out and the train came to a huffing stop in a large space lit by spotlights. When the brakeman opened the door, James glimpsed two men standing outside. They were all in grey, from their greatcoats, breeches and caps to the pallor of their skin. The only exception was the glossy black of their belts and jackboots. James saw the distinctive patch on their left sleeves – an eagle with wings spread above a swastika.

They're not regular German Army, he realized with a shiver. *They're SS* – the elite armed wing of the Nazi Party's 'Protection Squadron'. He'd read about the SS – the men who'd murdered so many in Hitler's great 'blood purge' in the summer. James knew that all members had sworn a fanatical oath of loyalty to their Führer.

A tall, slim girl came past them and entered the van. Her grey tunic and skirt aped the uniform of the soldiers, but her face as she looked at James was far more expressive.

'Well, well. James Bond.' Herta all but licked her lips. 'What a pleasure it is to see you again.'

James said nothing. His head was still throbbing, but he forced himself to meet her gaze.

'You've proved most resourceful, unravelling our little secrets. You've come so far . . . and now, here you are at the heart of things. A military research bunker constructed beneath a most delightful forested area south of Düsseldorf. A bunker designed to endure for always . . . until hell freezes over.'

'*That's* why this place was marked as *Winter Immer*,' James breathed. 'Winter Always.'

'Correct! So you made good use of the files you took from me . . .' The brakeman passed her a familiar cloth-wrapped bundle; taken, James realized dismally, from his pocket while he slept. 'You made less good use of the controller unit, hmm? Well, thank you for returning it to us. Oh, and incidentally, those files you took? They have been recovered from the back of Blade's car. Clumsy.'

'Sorry to disappoint.' James looked away. *No mention of Perry? Please tell me he got away, at least.*

'But the past is old news, eh, James? I bet you've been wondering what this train was bringing here on its last trip, hmm?' Herta sucked in her cheeks and nodded thoughtfully. 'Dying to know, I should imagine.'

James tried to rouse his brain into thinking instead of merely reacting. What did she want with him? He could try playing the innocent, but after clobbering her at Blade's place, that would hardly wash . . . Or he could exaggerate everything he knew, impress her so that she kept him alive for questioning. 'I'd guess you were shipping over the parts of the Steel Shadow suit that needed further tests after the demonstration at Ruskie.'

'So well informed. But . . . Steel Shadow *singular*?' Herta

202

shook her head. 'Our agreement with Mr Blade was that he should supply four Steel Shadows with fully functional controller units.'

'Four of those things . . . ?'

'You took the original controller, the only one in the country at that time. Herr Grünner wanted it at once because time is tight and he must conduct the most exhaustive tests.' Herta's eyes widened. 'But now we have Blade to help. The other Steel Shadows are being unloaded as we speak.'

'Why are you telling me all this?' James wondered.

'Because you have earned your answers.' Herta paused and crouched down beside him. 'Even better' – she leaned in and placed her hand around his throat – 'you get to *participate* in the answers.' She squeezed, and James couldn't help but give a gasp. 'I imagine you're breathless with excitement?'

James held her gaze; but as his vision started to swim, he saw her raise a black canister.

'Before we start, a little mental preparation is needed,' Herta told him. 'When I'm sure you're going to take a deep enough breath . . .'

James was suffocating; his lungs burning, his vision darkening.

Finally Herta let go of his neck. He gasped for air, and immediately she sprayed the cold mist into his open mouth. The taste was rank, burning his throat. 'What is that stuff?'

'An experimental nerve agent,' she said. 'It relaxes some muscles, temporarily paralyses others. When given in excess, it extends sleep and clouds the memory.'

James felt dizzy. 'That's what you used on me after Marcus . . .'

'Yes. But this time you're getting the correct dosage for its intended use.' Before he blacked out, James heard Herta add, 'And your little girlfriend gets the same.'

22

Man and the Machine

A sinister hissing and bubbling woke James from his sleep. The stale tang of rubber filled his nostrils and he couldn't see clearly. A gas mask had been pressed over his face. When he tried to remove it, he found his arm wouldn't respond.

What the hell . . . ? He wasn't tied up, but standing, arms out to his sides, as if crucified. He tried to turn his head, but something hard – a helmet or a crash hat – had been strapped over the gas mask. Through round lenses he saw that his arms and upper body were encased in silver bindings, that he was held inside a metal frame. He felt many inches taller. The susurrant hubble-bubble of steam hissed in his ear like a devil on his back.

Oh my God, James realized, sweating now, though his throat was bone-dry. *I'm inside a Steel Shadow.*

'*Lift your legs as if marching.*' The command – spoken in a harsh German accent – boomed out of loudspeakers around him. '*Once you make a movement, the Shadow will imitate it mechanically. March. Exaggerate the movements, like a child. Strong, definite movements are needed to power the drive systems.'*

Confused, disorientated, James did as the voice ordered just to make it stop. He raised one leg into the air; it felt heavy, weighed down – until, with a buzz of motors, the weight lifted and his leg was carried forward, landing with a metal thump that he barely felt. He lifted the other leg in the same way; a strain at first, and then—

James found that his legs were now lurching forward of their own accord. He remembered the complex set of braces and callipers that had engulfed Herta's lower body at Ruskie. 'Get me out!' he shouted through the mask, his voice sounding muffled over the hiss and whir of moving parts about him. Leaning to the left as he tried to pull his right leg free, he found the automaton bearing left too. By turning his body right, he started to head in that direction.

'Control is intuitive, you see?' The voice sounded smug. *'Now press the large round button near your left palm to reset the engine.'*

What? James fumbled with numb fingers. Looking down, he saw a row of small square buttons built into a steel bar-grip in his hand and, sure enough, one large round button. He slapped his palm against the disc and the Shadow stopped. James still had one foot in the air, and automatically tried to lower it. With a whine of hydraulics, the steel suit responded.

Keep calm. James tried to slow his breathing. *Keep control.* He knew that he'd been put into this thing for a reason, and that in time that reason would become clear.

The realization brought no comfort at all.

James tried to focus on his surroundings. He seemed to be

inside a kind of cave, the lighting a sodium glare, the walls dank folds of solid rock. He reasoned he was still inside the hidden bunker. Ahead of him was a wall of white concrete.

'*Advance,*' came the command. '*March forward as before. You must do this.*'

Must . . . ? James was feeling just like he had when he'd first woken after finding Marcus, dazed and uncertain. He lifted his leg in an exaggerated movement, and the Shadow responded again, breaking into its automatic stride. The wall loomed up and James pressed the disc again. Again, the suit stopped, his left foot coming down hard on the floor.

'*Now raise your left arm and strike the barrier in front of you,*' the disembodied voice commanded.

James tried to raise his arms; they felt as if they were made of lead. Pressure built over his shoulders and triceps, and the metal casing about him juddered; prickles ran down the back of his neck like electricity.

'*Move with strength, don't twitch.*' The voice sounded impatient. '*The Shadow will respond to smooth, confident movements . . .*'

Will it? James tried to throw a punch as if he were unencumbered. This time the suit was easier to shift. He heard the clang of metal on rock but felt no impact. The air was thick with white dust, and he saw that there was a crack in the concrete.

'*Strike again,*' said the voice. '*Dr Weissmann, assist the operator. Prime assault manoeuvre three.*'

James caught a movement at the periphery of his vision. Someone had reached inside his mobile cage; they pressed down on the fingers of his left hand three times, then retreated.

'*Now, Bond, try again.*'

This time there was an eager growl of mechanics from within the steel frame. He gasped when he saw that he was punching the concrete like a mechanized battering ram. His arm, suspended by flexible cables within the steel cradle, rocked but barely felt involved. James watched, astounded, as the concrete crumbled and fell apart before his eyes, reduced to rubble. To be wielding such power . . . To be able to wreak such destruction with merely a gesture. The feeling was beguiling.

'*Lift your right arm. Press the button beside your right index finger.*'

Intrigued to know what else he could do, James raised his right arm towards his chest and did as he was ordered. Machine guns mounted on the Shadow's wrist spat bullets through the clouds of concrete dust. James felt his upper body twist from left to right and back again in a sweep of gunfire. A spotlight snapped onto another wall a few yards further back; it showed a group of British soldiers cringing away. James stared as the bullets went on pumping out of his Steel Shadow arm, reducing the image to rubble.

The firing stopped. Numb, James lowered his extended right arm.

'Sehr gut. *The Steel Shadow has successfully breached the simulated machine-gun emplacement and eliminated all enemy forces,*' came the voice.

With a bubble and a hiss, the hum stopped and the steel framework was still. James stood trapped within it, marvelling at the raw power of Blade and Whittaker's invention.

A slow hand–clap started up. '*Very good.*' Even through the mask and helmet James recognized the new voice. *'Yes, the film footage cannot do justice to such a solid performance.'*

James gasped as the helmet was lifted off his head and the protective mask pulled away.

A thin man in a white coat clutching a microphone – the man who'd directed James's movements in the Steel Shadow – stepped aside as a bulkier man strode forward: Grünner. The man who'd ordered the experiment that had killed Marcus up in the trunk room at Fettes – so long ago, it seemed to James. The pale, round, expressionless face was glistening with sweat, the uniformed chest swelling with each hoarse breath. This was no longer the polite, stuffy Ambassador wishing further success to all in 1935. He wore a grey peaked cap with silver piping; in the centre was the metal *Totenkopf* – the SS death's head – and above that, in nickel, the Nazi eagle with its wreath and swastika. James could only guess at the insignias and decorations on Grünner's shoulders and chest, but clearly this man had risen far in the Nazi Party. Beyond him, two soldiers stood to attention beside a metal door built into the cavern, along with two men in white lab coats, presumably technicians.

'How do you feel, James, hmm?' Grünner sounded polite, almost fatherly, but the thin smile told its own story. 'Not too many ill-effects, I hope. Blade, what do you think of your new operator?'

'Blade?' James tried to marshal his senses. Judging by the echo, the cave must be enormous, although only one end of it was currently lit; the rest was in darkness. Now that the helmet had been removed, at least he could turn his head. First he looked around – in vain – for Kitty. Instead he saw,

a few yards to his left, accompanied by a battered-looking Carrel and Van Diemen, the twisted figure of Hepworth Blade.

James felt a bitter pleasure at the sight of the traitor sitting there in his wheelchair, helpless. 'You didn't get away, then. Couldn't escape from your dirty deal with your paymaster there.'

Blade's face was emotionless. 'Herta extricated me from the machine,' he said briefly.

'And I provided her with guards to assist her in the task,' Grünner added. 'Accidents must be prevented. Blade's mind is a most valuable asset to the Reich. And you, Bond – you also shall be an asset, I think.'

I wouldn't bet on it. James struggled against the metal straps that held him in place. His body felt strangely hollow, but sensation was returning to his hands and feet. 'Let me out of this thing.'

'Ah, my boy, I cannot do that.' Grünner gave his strange, high-pitched laugh. 'Look at you both, each as trapped as the other in your own way.'

Blade's face was twitching with anger. 'Damn it, Grünner—'

'*Stabsscharführer* Grünner, thank you, Blade.' The pasty face had darkened in reproach, the voice was hard. 'To the world I must present the face of Konstantin Grünner, the dull civil servant stuck behind a desk in The Hague. As German Ambassador to such a strategically positioned country, I am perfectly placed to gain any information that might be of interest to the Reich – but here in my own domain, you will kindly show me the same respect I receive from my Führer.'

Blade stared at him with those indomitable eyes. 'Perhaps I will show respect, *Stabsscharführer*, when you make an attempt to earn it.'

'You think I have not, eh?' Grünner was smiling again as he turned to James. 'Ah, Bond, let me explain fully. Herr Blade is not happy to be here, you see. To the outside world, it will be as if he has disappeared. The twisted arms baron – gone, overnight! His business empire will come crashing down . . .' He nodded sympathetically to Blade. 'How long before it comes to light that you've been selling weapons illegally, do you suppose?'

Blade made no reply.

'And you, my boy, the crusading orphan born from the Scottish peasantry . . . will you be missed? You, who came to avenge your friend's quite senseless death . . . Along with your little girlfriend.'

'What have you done with Kitty?' James demanded.

Grünner did not reply; merely looked from him to Blade for a few seconds. 'I understand the need for revenge. I understand the need to correct injustice . . . such as the injustice of the treaties that ended the last war. Treaties that robbed our people of wealth and honour, our rights as a nation—'

'Treaties that you both contravened in any case.' James glared at Blade. 'You sold weapons, and he bought them.'

'Hitler was a long way from power when I began my dealings with the German Army.' Blade's twisted face sneered. 'You were only given your non-commissioned rank, *Stabsscharführer* Grünner, to reward your loyalty to the Nazis in those wilderness years. Why did you bring me here? I can't imagine it was to demonstrate to me my own exo-suits?'

'Hepworth Blade, the great visionary, finds something beyond his imagination?' Grünner laughed again. 'Well, it was your imagination that fired the Steel Shadow project. And at long last, it is complete. I feel sure that Herr Hitler will be captivated by the possibilities that exo-suits afford our soldiers in time of war.'

'Yet this is how you repay me!' Blade shouted. 'You steal my files, you coerce me into coming here in person—'

'Is that all you have to complain about?' James exploded. 'You sold out your country for personal gain—'

'Be quiet.' Hardly looking at James, Grünner reached up and gave him a sharp cuff, his attention fixed upon Blade. 'Over the years Germany has paid a very great deal for your services. As I have told you, from now on, you will apply your inventive genius to the Nazi special weapons pro- gramme. You will oversee development of the next generation of exo-suits, helping and inspiring our own scientists.'

'Ridiculous!' Blade stared up at Carrel and Van Diemen, who in turn looked around at the armed soldiers. 'I will not be held here against my will.'

'*You will do as I command!*' Nostrils flaring, Grünner marched up to Blade and slapped him with the back of his hand.

Blade cried out in pain as his head was jerked sideways by the blow. Both Carrel and Van Diemen made to defend their employer, but Grünner's soldiers raised their long-barrelled semi-automatic Mauser C96 pistols. The bodyguards stopped in their tracks.

James stared at the German Ambassador, feeling helpless, and hating it.

'You disgust me, Blade. You know that?' Grünner gripped

Blade's misshapen hand in his, and began to squeeze. 'But it's your brain I require; not that repulsive prison you call a body. To think that such ugliness could also be so fragile!' He leaned closer, laughing shrilly. 'If I choose, I can have your every limb broken in a dozen places. Imagine the pain of it, Blade – the fearful anticipation . . . To know that your body will unleash bone to fill the gaps: bowing your legs, distorting your arms, freezing your form into such nightmare aspects—'

'Leave him alone,' James called out hoarsely. God knew he hated Blade, but to treat him like this . . .

Grünner ignored him. He started to stroke Blade's hair as if petting a dog. 'All that pain and suffering – perhaps it will concentrate your genius, eh, as you work to distract yourself.' He looked over at James and smiled. 'You will be no better than the boy here, locked into one of your suits!'

Blade met his eyes with a look of hatred. 'You have . . . the Steel Shadows now. You have recovered the notes. You can study the circuitry, the components, make more, equip an army . . .'

'Ah, indeed we can.' Grünner pinched Blade's cheek playfully. 'But, no, we will not do this, thank you.'

Blade's brows drew together in a frown. 'No?'

'There would be no point, you see. We acquired exclusive rights to your Steel Shadows not because we want to make more – but simply because we do not want other nations to possess such technology. We are – how do you say? – "cornering the market".'

All at once James heard the steaming whisper of a hydraulic press; a door was opening somewhere in the darkness beyond the broken concrete. There was a metallic scrape, and then the clank of heavy footsteps. A static charge was building in the air. The damp hairs on the back of James's neck were prickling.

'Have you not guessed, Blade?' Grünner's voice was full of self-congratulation. 'We do not require your inferior exo-suits. We have created better ones.'

Suddenly lights snapped on, illuminating more of the cavern, and revealing a solid steel chamber in the middle of the space, its door gaping open. James stared at the thing that had emerged – another mechanical exo-skeleton, the frame blood-red, less bulky than the Steel Shadow, the sinews simpler but still formidable. Within it stood Herta, in a crimson protective suit, wires and leads protruding from every joint into the tough metal framework. One arm ended in a fearsome pair of shears, the other in the blackened metal spout of a flame-thrower. There was no steam-fired engine bubbling on her back; in place of that, assorted cables fed back from the frame into a rack of bell jars and batteries, perhaps nine feet square, the power-lines paying out behind her as she strode forward.

'There, Blade, you see? A high-powered exo-suit – initially modelled on your Steel Shadow, but with improvements that make it far superior.' Grünner grinned as he gestured towards it, pure childish delight on his flabby face. 'Tomorrow, in front of representatives of the German military, I shall prove it.'

James strained to move, but it was as if he was made of metal himself. He watched helplessly as Herta, smiling in the centre of her high-tensile web of red steel, stepped forward and brought the snapping shears down towards his face.

23
Blood Banners

Grünner stepped away from Blade and held up a cautioning hand. 'Now, now,' he said to Herta.

She slowly closed the blades.

'A very much smoother response, Blade, no? And pound for pound, twenty per cent stronger and more resilient than your Steel Shadows.' Grünner looked smug. 'How arrogant you have been, Blade, to think that you alone could create such a weapon. Oh, yes, it was your genius – and Dr Whittaker's – that set us on this course, but we have learned quickly. We have an exo-suit programme of our own.'

'And that's why they killed Whittaker and kidnapped you once the Steel Shadows were complete,' James murmured, looking at Blade. 'To stop you making more for anyone else.'

'Ah, such a bright boy. But he talks too much, I think.' With an eerie laugh, Grünner came across to James and put a finger to his neck. 'Herta, prepare to tear out his throat.'

'No . . .' James strained against the heavy bonds still tying him to the Steel Shadow, as the shears sprang open again, and Herta's arm lowered them into position on either side of his Adam's apple – as if ready to remove it.

'For God's sake, man!' Blade snapped. 'There's no need for this.'

Grünner shook his head as if bemused by the comment.

James held stock-still; he didn't even dare to close his eyes. He imagined the twin blades carving through his throat, severing arteries, his breath bubbling with blood . . .

'Very well. Enough.' Grünner signalled Herta to step back, and she obeyed, the shears retracting. 'Of course I cannot kill him! Not if tomorrow's demonstration of the exo-suits is to go ahead, eh?'

'Demonstration?' James tried to keep his voice steady. 'That's why I'm in this thing?'

'And you have made a promising start. But do not fear, you will be given training in your Steel Shadow. It would be most unsporting were you not fully acquainted with your only means of defence against the *Blutbanner*, eh?' Grünner gazed at Herta in her exo-suit as a farmer might at his prize bull. 'This is what we call our suit, you see: the *Blutbanner* – or Blood Flag. Historically it was the red flag presented to feudal lords as a symbol of their absolute right to rule; as far back as the thirteenth century the *Blutbanner* was carried into war.'

I don't need a history lesson, thought James.

'And now?' Grünner sounded as if he was giving a speech to his beloved Führer. 'Now we take power from the future to fully realize the ambitions of history. We shall plant our red

216

flags – our *Blutbanners* – in the soil of our enemies, and so assure our triumph.'

'You're using radio control to enhance the suit's operation, aren't you?' Blade actually seemed impressed. 'I know the Russians have been experimenting with unmanned tanks operated remotely, and I have even made small inroads myself . . .'

James shuddered. 'I remember.'

'This technology – and the ambition – is somewhat more advanced.' Grünner had clearly been looking forward to this moment. 'Portable and mobile high-frequency radio equipment allows the suit operator to communicate requirements to his superior officer in real time. Should he lack the skills for the job, an expert from the support crew can guide him remotely . . .'

James peered into the metal chamber from which Herta had emerged, and saw a figure crouched over what might have been the controls of a radio set.

Grünner was enjoying himself. 'A rather more elegant solution, wouldn't you say, Blade, than relying solely on pre-programmed general moves that can be anticipated and countered—?'

'Elegant?' Blade gestured at the bank of cables. 'How do you expect to carry such a cumbersome power supply into combat? Not to mention a second dedicated operator to man the radio.'

'Perhaps your Steel Grunts will guard these things, eh?' Grünner said, pacing slowly around Herta. 'Your creation is inferior to the *Blutbanner*, but it might be useful in a support role.'

'The cables, then . . .' Blade went on. 'They can be severed, and then what will feed energy to your—?'

'Enough. This is but an early incarnation of what will one day fight in our name.' Grünner pointed at him. 'Now that you are here you will take the project to the next level. Yes, the transmission of energy could be improved, but there are so many possibilities for the *Blutbanner* programme, Blade. I invite you to embrace them. I *insist* upon it.'

'Think of the body itself,' said Herta, 'alive with electricity, an *internal* power source we carry with us at all times – imagine if that could be harnessed to run the exo-suit. Or if we could store the power of a lightning bolt in the batteries of the *Blutbanner*.'

'Is that why you killed Marcus in the lightning storm?' James asked grimly. 'You were there in the lab that night – I heard you—'

'Grünner sent me to Fettes, ostensibly to assist Dr Whittaker . . . but really to confirm the Steel Shadow's weaknesses.' Herta shrugged. 'I convinced the fool that his new controller unit could convert high-voltage energy into reserve power. In truth, I was merely measuring the electrical current required to bypass the Shadow's insulation, kill the operator inside and overload the controller units.'

'A blueprint for murder,' Blade said softly.

'We wanted to discover your invention's Achilles' heel, Blade – in case you have cheated us, and sold the design to other powers.' Grünner smiled smugly. 'However, we will not dwell on the weaknesses of your exo-suit at tomorrow's demonstration but on its strengths – so that the victory of the *Blutbanner* will seem all the more impressive.'

'And so you look more impressive to Hitler?' James was starting to feel ill – just like he had when he woke up in the sanatorium at Fettes; a reaction to the nerve agent. He licked his cracked lips and let his head fall forward. 'I think I might be sick. Can I get out of this thing now?'

'You may take a short rest,' Grünner agreed. 'The demonstration will take place at noon tomorrow: three Steel Shadows against two *Blutbanner*s in a special testing site here in the bunker. One of the Shadows will be piloted by young Bond here, the others by your two bodyguards, Blade.'

'Civilians?' Blade roared. 'Are you insane?'

'Not at all. But forgive me – to maintain standards, this division of the SS recruits only German nationals between the ages of seventeen and twenty-three who can prove their Aryan ancestry back to 1800, who are unmarried and have no criminal record.' Grünner gave a thin smile. 'Such men do not grow on trees, eh? It would be such a waste to use them in this manner. I am grateful to have alternatives.'

James looked him in the eye. 'I'm still at school.'

'Big enough to fight.'

'And who will be fighting in your own exo-suits?'

'As it is close to Christmas, I intend to indulge in a small amusement.' Grünner's eyes were shining with anticipation. 'The *Blutbanner* suits are so simple and powerful to operate . . . why – even a schoolgirl could use one! Look . . .'

A second *Blutbanner* stomped uncertainly out of the metal chamber. Bound helplessly within the crimson shell was a terrified red-haired girl, her brown eyes unfocused.

'Kitty . . .' James whispered.

'It is not wise to think of her as Kitty now, James,' said Herta. 'Consider her instead as the girl who is going to kill you.'

★ ★ ★

The words reverberated through James's thoughts as he lay in his Spartan guest room.

He'd shouted to Kitty that they'd be all right, but the words rang hollow as James was removed from the Shadow and escorted to his room. It held nothing more than a bed, a cupboard and a toilet in one corner – but then, it was simply a place to rest before his next training session.

The girl who is going to kill you . . .

James closed his eyes, but he couldn't block out the image of Kitty, her face pale with terror, eyes still vacant after the dose of nerve agent. To fight in an arena for the gratification of a crowd! It was horrific, barbaric, like the gladiatorial combat of imperial Rome.

A cold knot of tension formed in James's stomach. *If they want to see a fight, I'll damn well give them one*, he vowed. But the thought of going up against Kitty . . . flicking through sets of pre-programmed moves in the hope of finding one that might prolong his life by a few seconds.

I can't fight you, Kitty, he thought. *There must be some way out . . .*

There has *to be.*

24
Blade Sharp

Later that afternoon, when the door opened with a creak, James struggled to open his eyes. A guard stood in the doorway holding out the black insulated overalls of a Shadow operator for him to put on.

Once changed, he was marched along endless passages – they were wide enough to accommodate vehicles, he realized, for behind him a horn sounded, and a light armoured car – an open-topped variant of the Soviet D-8 by the looks of it drove past, a technician sat back to back with the driver, a large machine gun beside him. James was gradually becoming aware of the scale of this research centre.

He fantasized about overpowering his guard, setting Kitty free, hijacking the armoured car . . . imagined stealing a Mauser and shooting Grünner . . . He'd already witnessed so much death – more than anyone should ever see – and while sometimes he tried to pretend it hadn't changed him, he knew deep down that he had been deeply affected.

To kill someone at point-blank range, in cold blood. Could he ever do such a thing?

Tomorrow he was being thrown into an arena where, if he failed to do so, he would be killed for sure.

James tried to concentrate on his surroundings, memorizing certain features in case they helped him at a later date. But building in his mind was the cold certainty that there would be no way out.

You can't give up now, he told himself sternly. *You fought so hard to find this place. It can't all be for nothing.*

As he and his escort turned down yet another passage, he heard the growl of an engine approaching, and another D-8 trundled towards them, carrying machine parts to areas unknown. He felt a throb underfoot; the rush of ventilators masked a deeper, more powerful hum. Where was he being taken?

At last the guard opened a door and they stepped into a large, noisy industrial space carved out from a cavern, dominated by an enormous furnace; a metal mountain with a foundry built around it, the top protruding through the ceiling to vent somewhere above ground. Workers in protective overalls were skimming slag from the molten metal, then pouring it into moulds, casting machine parts. Others worked with blowtorches, welding or correcting the scarlet skeleton of a *Blutbanner*.

In one corner, well away from the foundry, was a gigantic workshop. Blade sat there in his wheelchair, a guard watching him from a few feet away. Of the bodyguards there was no sign. Beside him stood a Steel Shadow; it put James in mind of an iron maiden from a torture chamber of old.

His memory of being removed from the suit was hazy – he'd still been suffering the effects of the nerve-agent spray – but still he hated and feared the thing. It opened vertically down the middle to allow the operator to clamber inside; it must have already been adjusted to fit his form. Once the operator was inside, he would be secured to the internal connectors. Finally the front of the frame would be closed around him, the steam power stoked and primed, and armour plating attached to seal and protect the soft flesh parcel inside.

James shuddered and looked away as his escort left him with Blade, who studied James for a moment.

'Ah, Bond,' he said. 'I'm supposed to run you through the attack and defence manoeuvres possible in the Shadow.'

James stared at him. 'You're actually going along with this? Your own bodyguards—'

'Are in their rooms, being treated with the nerve agent as we speak.' Blade's face was as unreadable as ever. 'I developed it while trying to find relief from pain. Without it, the physical stresses of using the exo-skeleton would severely damage the body.' He wheeled himself over to the Shadow. 'Don't worry, there's still enough in your body from the dose Herta gave you.'

'*Beeilen sie*,' the guard shouted, urging them to hurry.

'Step inside the Steel Shadow, Bond. I need to optimize all connections so you're served by it as well as possible.'

'You mean you want your stupid suits to be served as well as possible. Last night you were trying to kill me yourself.'

'I was trying to contain you, for your own sake, until this affair was over.'

'*Affair?*' James felt frustration kick into anger. 'You're helping the Nazis just to save your own skin—'

'Quieten down,' Blade hissed, 'for God's sake, boy!' He paused for a moment. 'Life is a gift; you don't just give it away – you keep a damn tight hold of it for as long as you're able, however hard things get.'

'Is that why you're doing whatever Grünner asks?'

The guard frowned at James and gestured to the Steel Shadow. Reluctantly he stepped inside, and Blade carefully adjusted the links and catches that would secure him to the exo-suit.

'I underestimated Grünner, I confess. It seems that he has followed his dream as . . . devoutly as I have followed mine.' No emotion played on Blade's tight, immobile face. 'I have always dreamed of a protective suit that would let me walk without help; that would make me strong . . . allow me to live without fear.' Blade hesitated, looking down at his warped fingers. 'Me . . . and others who suffer as I do, disabled. Excluded.'

'I saw that thing you wore at your house. Saw what it could do.' James glanced around. 'But you didn't stop at building that, did you? You designed the Steel Shadow for soldiers. Designed it to kill.'

'A weapon can *save* lives as well as take them. Would you rather we dug ourselves into trenches for years all over again?' Blade connected a cable to the leg frame, and a low hum started up. 'As I told you at your school, the search for the ultimate weapons of war extends technology. These are

224

literally the first steps for the exo-suit. We are already decades ahead of our time.'

James scoffed. 'Well, wearing this . . . I can't see much future for myself.'

'I must seem insensitive, I suppose.' Blade sank back into his wheelchair, rolling his eyes towards the bored guard behind him. 'Bond, we're all Grünner's prisoners. If we are to live through this, we must work together.'

James snorted. 'Against Britain? Forget it. I'm not joining you after all you've done.'

'All I've done . . . ?' Blade lowered his voice. 'Have you any conception of how much the Steel Shadow has cost to develop? Without the sale of those illegal arms to boost Blade-Rise's capital, we could never have funded it . . .' His lips pulled taut in a sly smile. 'That is why the British government authorized me to sell those illegal weapons to Germany in the first place.'

James stared as the whispered words sank in. '*Authorized* you?'

'The British government has known all along that I've been secretly helping to arm the Germans.' Blade gave a wheezing laugh that bubbled somewhere in his lungs. 'I'd struggle to ride the white charger, true enough, but the fact is, Bond . . . I'm a bloody hero.'

25
Brushes with Destiny

James stared at Blade. 'You expect me to believe you're one of the good guys now?'

'Show me a "good guy", Bond.' Blade seemed amused. 'However handsome and fair, or twisted and ugly, inside all men lies an explosive mix of the noble and the inexcusable. How brightly they explode depends on how the fuse is placed and who lights it.'

'*Kein geschwätz.*' The guard stepped forward again, his gun aimed menacingly. '*Wieder mit der arbeit.*'

His mind racing, James held still as Blade continued to connect him to the suit. Suddenly he heard shouts from the smelting area near the furnace; molten metal had spilled out of a mould and one of the workers was clutching his arm, crying out in agony. The guard was summoned to help by his colleague.

'It's been a long game, Bond, with the highest stakes,'

Blade went on. 'When I first conceived the exo-suit with Dr Whittaker, his thinking was so advanced that every part of the design had to be built from scratch. Rather than pool resources with a competitor in the arms trade, I turned to the government.'

'Why would they help you?' James asked.

'Because I have a reputation for genius.' There was no conceit in Blade's voice; for him it was simply a fact. 'The British Secret Intelligence Service knew that Germany had already begun small-scale re-armament in secret. If I supplied some weapons, I could make valuable contacts that would help SIS monitor the scale of German ambition; that was their thinking.'

'Like a double agent?'

'If you wish to be melodramatic about it, yes,' Blade said. 'And, of course, it meant that the Germans would be contributing handsomely towards the cost of developing a secret weapon for Britain. Whittaker appreciated that little irony.'

'He was in on the trick too?' James said wonderingly.

'From the start.' Blade kept his voice low. 'Your precious Head at Fettes wasn't the only man with space and resources commandeered for the project, you know. Whittaker also worked in temporary labs set up at Glenalmond School, Loretto, Merchiston . . .'

'Off the radar of industrial spies?'

'Secrecy was paramount. That's why Stephenson's death – and your attempted interference – had to be stage-managed into schoolboy high-jinx.'

Don't remind me, thought James darkly. 'But you handed the Shadows over to Grünner.' He winced as Blade's fingers caught the skin on the back of his arm. 'Four finished models.'

'With good reason. You don't think this is the Nazi's only top-secret weapons research centre, do you?' Blade looked up at him. 'Imagine if you could find and destroy those places. It would set Germany's war effort back years.'

'How *could* you find them?' James wondered.

'Come now, Bond. What's the one thing that will inevitably be taken to a top-secret weapons research centre?'

With a soft groan, James realized: 'A top-secret weapon.'

'Such as a Steel Shadow.' Blade gave a twisted smile. 'To that end, we have concealed a radio transmitter within each segment of the Steel Shadow's outer skeleton.'

James stared. 'They can be tracked?'

'In a best-case scenario, the suits would be dismantled and sent for testing at many different facilities – so those facilities could be marked down for destruction.'

'That was before you knew that Grünner already had his *Blutbanner*; the suits are staying here to be destroyed.'

'So Grünner says,' Blade said. 'He would never admit my suit's superiority in any case. But while they're kept here for the demonstration, they're all transmitting their signal as one.' He lowered his voice still further. 'And between you evading me at the house and Herta herding me here at gunpoint, I was able to get a message through to SIS back in London.'

James felt hope like a glimmer of warmth. 'Then . . . help could be coming.'

'There's always a chance. If we can capture the *Blutbanner* technology for Britain's use . . . or sabotage it somehow.' A new determination had crept into Blade's voice. 'That's why

I'm telling you this, Bond. However hopeless things seem, you must *use* your time. That includes when you're fighting in the Shadow tomorrow.'

'Grünner must be confident about his Nazi suits if he's pitting just two of them against three of yours.'

'Yes. He must.' Blade completed the final connection and sank back into his wheelchair, pale and exhausted. 'Well, now that we've established that I'm a selfless hero, I'll have to see what can be done about those blessed *Blutbanner*, won't I?'

Blade's bravado brought James little comfort; the evening passed like a cold, slow nightmare. He was taken back to the first cavern, where Herta was waiting with Carrel and Van Diemen. Both men were still dazed by the nerve agent; they'd been crammed into the Steel Shadows and forced to march around, fumbling with their controls. The deep shushing of the steam dynamos on their backs made the mechanical suits sound alarmingly alive.

Were the suits really signalling their location? James wondered. Could the transmission truly penetrate all that solid rock above them?

At least the practice run gave James an opportunity to check out his surroundings. The metal chamber, protected by thick armour plating, stood in the middle of the space like the *spina* of the Roman Circus Maximus; it was tall enough to provide useful cover. James thought of the radio controllers safely hidden inside their bunker, ready to orchestrate the impending carnage. How he longed to feel secure and shielded himself!

Then he remembered watching the demonstration back in

Ruskie – the way the mortars had been fired at Herta; the way she'd emerged from the firestorm, unscathed. The suits must offer an incredible level of protection; enough to keep operators alive for a time . . .

Or to prolong their suffering.

No, James said to himself. He mustn't look at it like that. Suffering was a part of life, but how you chose to deal with it was down to you.

And if I'm made to suffer, I'm going to damn well dish it out too, somehow . . .

Herta worked with the technicians to teach James, Carrel and Van Diemen the physical movements that would prime the suit for pre-programmed manoeuvres, and the sequence of controls needed to activate them. There was far too much to take in, particularly as they were already exhausted. But then, James thought, they were hardly expected to prosper in this contest. Right now, the built-in machine guns were empty of ammo; he wondered if they would be armed tomorrow.

Finally they were helped out of the Shadows.

'What weapons will your suits use?' Van Diemen asked Herta. 'Shears won't stop machine guns.'

'The *Blutbanner* limbs can accommodate many combat options.' Herta's smile was knowing. 'The better you know how to operate your suit, the longer you will last.'

'Right. It'll be a walk in the park,' Carrel said. 'Well, I'm not fighting girls for the pleasure of old men. It's sick.'

Van Diemen looked across at James. 'If none of us fight, they'll have no demonstration.'

Herta was about to reply when Grünner's voice crackled over loudspeakers set high up in the darkness above them. '*The*

231

demonstration will go ahead, gentlemen.' Lights came on in the rocky ceiling – to reveal glass panels in the wall and a viewing area with carved wooden seats beyond. Grunner was standing at the window and speaking into a microphone. '*If you refuse to operate the Shadows, I shall be forced to demonstrate to my guests how the* Blutbanners *tear apart the opposition . . . slowly. So very slowly.*'

James felt his stomach clench with fear, saw Carrel and Van Diemen look grimly at each other.

'*You may opt to use the Shadow defensively, or you may choose to fight,*' Grünner went on. '*If you fight well, then your lives will be spared.*'

'He really *does* think he's a Roman emperor,' James muttered, then called out: 'Spare them for what?'

'So that you may continue to work for me here. I shall need experienced volunteers to pilot our suits, to refine them further . . .' Grünner paused. 'If you show obedience, loyalty, honour – these things shall be rewarded.'

The lights went out, leaving the space above them in thick darkness. Van Diemen and Carrel were clearly thinking the proposition over.

'You surely can't believe that guff?' James said incredulously. 'Grünner's lying. He's got to be.'

Back in his room, after a brief supper, James could only doze fitfully in spite of his exhaustion. The clock on his table said it was one a.m., then three. Time was rushing past, a countdown to the trial by combat.

Thoughts of Blade and his spectacular bluff raced through his head. The game with the Steel Shadows had been audacious, but ultimately futile; the exo-suits had long since been overtaken by superior technologies. The true cause of Marcus's death had been hushed up to protect an irrelevant fiction.

James found it hard to revise his opinion of Blade. He was vainglorious and self-serving, a brilliant opportunist – James supposed this was a plus when you were making underhand alliances in the interests of national defence. Things were never as simple and straightforward as they appeared, but even so . . . could Blade be counted on to defy Grünner now?

James longed for sleep, but he kept hearing noises outside: footsteps, knocks, a D–8 droning past. Even when it was quiet, apprehension woke him with a jerk each time his eyes closed. His fingers were blistered from working the controls in the metal gauntlets, and the skin around his eyes was swollen and tender; a side-effect of the nerve agent, he guessed.

At seven-thirty a guard told James to get dressed, ready for breakfast with the other hostages in a private room off the main canteen. Buttered rye toast and scrambled eggs had been laid out for them. James's heart thumped when he saw Kitty already sitting there. Herta stood behind her – looking pale and exhausted, James noted with satisfaction – armed not with a gun but with a hypodermic syringe.

We're too valuable to be shot, thought James.

'The condemned men will enjoy a hearty meal.' Herta smiled wanly. '*Frohe Weihnachten.*'

'Christmas and last supper both at once,' Carrel said.

'Peace and goodwill to all,' Kitty murmured.

Of course, James realized, it was Christmas Eve tomorrow. Right now he ought to be sat with Charmian by the fireside at Pett Bottom, gifts beneath the tree, carols rising from the wireless. The thought made his present misery almost too much to bear; quickly he swept the sentiments away.

James tried to sit next to Kitty, but the guard directed him to the next table. She looked over at him, and he saw that some of the old fire still showed in her dark eyes. *Good*, he thought. *She hasn't given up*.

'James, are you all right?' she called over, then stopped and shook her head. 'Sorry, stupid question. I told myself I wouldn't ask anything so ridiculous, but in a situation like this – not that I—'

'I'm fine,' he told her.

'I believe you.' Kitty glanced at Herta. 'She's had me in that wretched man-sized tank feeding honey to guards from a silver spoon.'

James frowned.

Herta smiled at his puzzlement. 'Kitty is going to feed honey to our VIPs. It will be an amusing way to show the precision with which the *Blutbanner* can be controlled. Think of the applications.'

Van Diemen swallowed down his mouthful of toast. 'I've had a bellyful of it.'

'Under an ordnance expert's hand, an operator can defuse a bomb – or construct and position one just where it is needed,' Herta told him.

James raised an eyebrow at her. 'You know, I didn't think the Nazis allowed women in the SS . . .'

'They don't, officially. Not yet.' Herta took a swig of

coffee and licked her lips. 'But as my reputation and standing grows, who knows where I may end up.'

'Dead?' he suggested.

'Hark at who's talking.' She looked coolly across at him. 'The contest begins at noon. You have a little under three-and-a-half hours before it begins.'

The door opened and Grünner appeared, looking as serious and sober as ever; the guards saluted him respectfully. He snapped his fingers at Herta, who hurried over. James tried to listen in on the conversation, but it was only about the positioning of the fourth Steel Shadow; it was going to be put on display in an anteroom so that the generals could see it up close before watching the others in action. Grünner and Herta left the room, deep in discussion, and the guards closed the door behind them.

'Here we are, then,' Kitty said stoutly. She was trying so hard to be brave, James thought. 'I . . . I keep remembering the train . . . If I hadn't got myself caught, then perhaps—'

'*I* was spotted first,' said James. 'Anyway, deciding who's *to* blame won't help us.'

Kitty snorted. 'Nothing can now.'

'It's not hopeless,' Van Diemen insisted. 'The boss says people take one look at him and think he's incapable of doing anything. All his life he's been proving them wrong.'

'He's not facing this,' Carrel pointed out, 'is he?'

James wanted to tell them what Blade had revealed, but even if it was true, words of comfort would surely be futile. 'Kitty,' he said, 'whatever happens today—'

The guard behind him cuffed him about the ear. 'Eat. Not talk.'

235

James finished his meal, not tasting a mouthful, and the guard marched him back out of the room. *Here I go again*, he thought.

He looked back to Kitty and summoned up a smile. She raised her hand in a forlorn gesture, like a goodbye.

26

Countdown to Carnage

The base soon began to buzz with activity. James was escorted back to his room to change into the insulated overalls. The smell of them made him feel sick.

James, Van Diemen and Carrel were taken in an armoured car to the foundry workshop, where Blade was waiting in his wheelchair. The four Steel Shadows stood behind him like statues, polished to a gleam. *If rescue really is coming*, thought James, *it had better hurry*.

Two-and-a-half hours left.

'This is your final chance to familiarize yourself with the exo-suits and their commands,' Blade announced. 'To confirm that the controls are correctly adjusted for your height, weight and grip – and to test your fast-release mechanisms. Bond, if you would care to step inside yours.'

A guard pushed James forward. He climbed reluctantly into the frame, and as he did so, he realized that something was different. A thick metal cylinder shaped like a C, with the smallest of gaps between the two ends, had been secured inside the left fist of the exo-suit. Insulated copper wire had been wound tightly about it, and the whole assembly connected to the innards of the suit.

He was about to ask, 'What's this?' but Blade shook his head, discreetly indicating the watching guard. James saw that Van Diemen – though not Carrel – had found something similar in his own Shadow.

Can we trust you, Blade? James longed to ask.

Blade's face remained impassive. 'I've done all I can. There's just one more thing.' He looked from James to Van Diemen. 'A way to work an Achilles' heel to your advantage. At the end you'll find the electro—'

'Seal him in the Shadow,' the guard interrupted, before he could say any more. 'They must be ready.'

'Yes, they must.' Grünner had entered the workshop, immaculate in his SS uniform, and was hurrying towards them. 'The finishing touches have been made to the cavern. Our test volunteers must be ready before the first VIP guests arrive—'

'Here is the inspection model.' Blade wheeled himself quickly forwards, stopping beside the fourth of the Steel Shadows. 'I trust it meets with your approval, *Stabsscharführer?*'

Grünner stared at Blade. 'I will have it transported to the antechamber. And your soldiers to the demonstration cavern.'

'They are *your* soldiers,' Blade corrected him, 'fighting *your* battle.'

Grünner smiled. 'But now *my* war is *your* war.'

'Yes . . .' Blade smiled back. 'I feel this is so, *Stabsscharführer* Grünner.'

James tensed as two guards closed the Steel Shadow frame around him like a snare. He moved his hand to cover the mysterious addition to his suit; Blade had clearly been trying to distract Grünner. But what did this device do, and how could it help?

Van Diemen, Carrel and James were each put through their paces, lifting arms and legs while circuits were checked and final adjustments made.

'No more tests,' Grünner decreed at last. 'You stand and fight, come what may.'

'Still three of us against two of your suits?' Carrel asked, glaring at him. 'What are you planning?'

Grünner ignored him. 'Your steam power is good for fifteen minutes of combat.' The high-pitched laugh rose at the back of his throat. 'Use them well.'

'Am I permitted to attend the demonstration?' Blade wanted to know.

'I'm afraid I have another task for you,' Grünner informed him. 'Your two customized Tatras are being brought from the rail terminus to be melted down. They are too conspicuous.' He lowered his voice. 'In any case, you will shortly be losing your chauffeur. I would like you to oversee their dismantling and disposal in the furnace.'

James watched for Blade's reaction to this humiliation, but he merely gave a thin, twisted smile. 'As you wish, *Stabsscharführer.*'

Grünner was watching too. 'You are most compliant today,' he said, almost as if disappointed.

'I agree with Charles Darwin,' Blade replied. 'It is not the strongest of the species that survives, nor the most intelligent . . . but rather, that which is able to adapt.'

With a clank of chain-gears, the foundry's loading-bay door slid open to allow the handsome burgundy Tatra in. Behind it came the silver model that James had first seen on the drive at Fettes, a hundred years ago and a million miles away. A place he'd most likely never see again.

Adapt or die, he thought.

A soldier signalled from the doorway.

'It is time,' Grünner announced.

Transport was waiting for them outside the foundry: a large flatbed trailer towed by a customized open-topped D-8. James, Carrel and Van Diemen climbed stiffly aboard. James wondered about using the suit's capabilities to try to escape, but with the armour shield, gas mask and protective helmet not yet in place, he knew he wouldn't last a minute. A single bullet would penetrate the steel lattice and kill him.

Heart beating faster as he got down off the transporter, James saw the clock mounted on the wall. It was close to eleven. One hour until the ordeal began.

James was herded with Van Diemen and Carrel through the thick metal doors and inside the cavern, where soldiers and staff were taking orders from Herta and a team of technicians. He saw that two huge, hardened-concrete walls, over ten feet high, had been erected crossways between the rocky walls and the *spina*.

As Herta came over, James saw Van Diemen mask the addition to his suit and did the same. *What is this thing?* he wondered. *And how can it possibly help me . . . ?*

Luckily Herta seemed more interested in self-congratulation than in examining the Shadows. 'These walls are five feet thick and constructed over a steel framework,' she said.

'You will be on this side of this wall; Kitty and I will be on the far side of the other one. At the starting signal, we will attempt to break through our wall to reach you, and you will attempt to break through your wall to get to us. And do please remember – you're fighting for your lives.'

'What about the girl's life?' Van Diemen said. 'What about yours?'

'This is war,' said Herta simply, and beckoned to a guard. 'Watch them,' she ordered. 'Armour is not to be fitted until T minus thirty minutes. If they try anything, shoot to wound. They can still fight.'

Carrel watched as she went to inspect one of the remote control units. 'Yes,' he breathed, 'and we will.'

'What the hell is this thing Blade's added to the suit?' James asked.

'Huh?' Carrel looked blank.

'It's got to be a weapon,' Van Diemen said quietly. 'Something heavy-duty. But what the hell do we do to arm it?'

'I don't have one,' Carrel said, frowning. 'Why do you two have one and I don't?'

The guard shouted at them to be quiet.

'Perhaps Blade ran out of time,' James hissed.

'If we can't work it,' Van Diemen said, 'we're no better off in any—'

The guard fired a warning shot that chipped the rock by James's feet, and they all fell silent. James stood there, sweating into his suit. With no more to go on, how could they ever hope to use the weapon and learn what it did?

Time crawled while workers scurried about their tasks: scaling ladders to correct the lighting, or adjusting the power rig that fed the *Blutbanners*. James had identified the cables as a target – put them out of action, and the Nazi exo-suits would cease to function. But it seemed that some of the power units had been buried in the top of the thick concrete wall, while the trailing cables had been encased in metal alloy.

Forty-five minutes to go, James realized suddenly.

The Nazi VIPs would have arrived by now. He imagined them crowding round the Steel Shadow in the ante-chamber . . . pictured Kitty in the *Blutbanner*, feeding honey to an amused general – to appreciative applause from the other onlookers . . .

His blood boiled.

Forty minutes . . .

James gazed around the cavern, looking for anything that might give him cover or some possible advantage. There was a deep crevice in the far wall; it was too narrow to shelter in, but would possibly be a weak point. At first he'd considered attacking the metal chamber in the middle – taking out the remote controllers rather than the *Blutbanners* themselves so that Kitty could at least act for herself – but upon closer scrutiny he saw that he hadn't a hope. The metal walls were over two feet thick: nothing was bringing that place down in a hurry.

Thirty-five minutes . . .

A siren blared and staff filed away, out of sight. James eyed the metal doors to the arena and decided that these must be his target. If he could hammer them down and escape into the base beyond, he might just make it out of here. Succeed or fail, it would be better than playing Grünner's sick game.

'What about the spray?' Carrel shouted. 'Without that, these things will shake us apart.'

'No nerve spray,' came the technician's response in halting English. 'Not needed.'

'To even up the odds,' Van Diemen guessed. 'They think we'll be in too much pain to take them down.'

'We can't fight Kitty, in any case,' James insisted.

The others looked at him, but said nothing.

With just thirty minutes to go, another siren sounded. Technicians crowded in to fit the armour plating to the Steel Shadows. James stood there as the rubber gas mask was stretched over his face, as the helmet was pressed down over his head. His breathing sounded hoarse in his ears; his vision was obscured by the thick plastic lenses. A trickle of sweat ran down the back of his neck. He looked up into the space where he knew the viewing window was. The audience would be gathering there even now.

Mr Bond, we're ready for your close-up . . .

James felt pressure at his back. The steam generator was being fed coal. With a whoosh, flames took hold. The first hisses followed, and he felt heat along his backbone. His heart was banging in his chest.

Fifteen minutes . . .

The same as the lifespan of the Steel Shadow, James thought. *Once they've stoked us up and set us off, we'll have whatever's left in the can and no more.*

A technician directed them to their wall. Once this had been demolished . . . the battle would begin. James spotted lights in the viewing area high above, and imagined keen eyes upon them. Out of the darkness on the other side of the cavern he could hear grinding gears, and adrenalin surged through his veins. He recognized the sound of the *Blutbanners*.

Herta would be coming for him soon — and, he realized with a heavy heart, Kitty too. James chewed his lip as the splutter and rush from the engine on his back grew louder. The portable furnace was pushing up the pistons; the batteries in the suit were sending power along the connectors. Tension balled in James's stomach, making every limb tremble. He forced himself to breathe slowly and deeply. The concrete barricade before him filled his vision. *What do we do?* he wondered, his flesh crawling. *What the hell do we do when the siren—*

The blare was deafening.

It's begun.

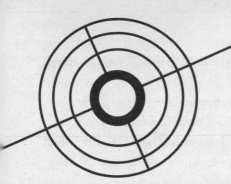

27
Battle Royale

Carrel raised his left arm and thrust it towards the wall, activating the hammer-punch action. James watched, detached, as the metal fist began beating against the concrete. But then, above the hammering, he heard Carrel's agonized wail. Without the nerve agent, the impact of each hydraulically accelerated blow jarred his bones. Carrel stopped just as Van Diemen started to kick the base of the wall.

James looked across and heard a booming from behind the *Blutbanners'* wall. Cracks were already forming. Was the concrete weaker there? he wondered. How much had this contest been rigged?

'Come on, James!' Carrel bellowed. 'If we all work at it together . . .'

'We should go over there,' James shouted back. 'Surprise Herta when she comes through.'

'Those things will be better armed than us,' Van Diemen pointed out.

'That's why we have to use surprise!'

'You're just a kid,' Carrel said. 'You do what we say.'

But James had already started marching round to the other side of the wall, priming the controls, the steam like a dragon's breath at his back.

He cancelled the forward stride – just as a *Blutbanner* broke through its wall in a storm of dust and debris. It was fast – much faster than the Shadow. The dark metal blur smashed into James, and he glimpsed Herta's face through the facemask, her teeth bared. He turned away, praying he could keep his balance, as a fierce torrent of flame was directed at his face. The asbestos shield deflected the blaze, but the gas mask lenses turned red, and heat prickled through his body. James raised his right arm and hit the command code to launch the machine guns. Bullets spat into the firestorm as he backed away awkwardly, as if wading through treacle.

Suddenly he stopped firing as a terrible thought struck him: *What if I hit Kitty?*

His breathing inside the mask was fast and loud, his heart was hammering and he could barely see through a thick white mist. Gas, or a smoke grenade to add to the confusion? Where was Herta now?

More gunfire sliced through the smoke. Seeing the top of the concrete barricade, James raised his gun arm higher and fired again, hoping somehow to hit the power supply.

Out of nowhere, another impact slammed into him, head on. Now, through the crimson framework, James could see Kitty's frightened face, though the rest of the suit was obscured in the smoke and gloom. He grimaced as the *Blutbanner* forced him backwards; his retreating steps were jerky: he couldn't halt her advance, couldn't prime the suit to shift forwards as he needed to. *Backing up at this speed*, he thought, *we must be nearing—*

James yelled as he felt himself smash against the wall. His hand had closed around Blade's new addition – but of course he had no clue as to how to activate it. Kitty was shouting something at him; he saw that tears were running down her face. Suddenly a dark fist came smashing into his armour; the impact struck sparks from his side. Another blow sent pain jarring through his bones. James found himself trapped against the wall, and swung his forearm across his body for protection. Two more jolts shocked through him; he imagined the steel armour bending, caving in . . .

He thrust forward with all his strength, driving Kitty back a couple of steps. Then he primed his own striking arm and unleashed a flurry of punches, targeting her left arm. James cried out with the pain, but it was enough to shift her sideways. He pressed the button to stop the attack, then marched past her.

But to where? James wondered frantically. *Attacking the doors means turning my back on the* Blutbanners. At least Kitty was at the edge of the cave, out of harm's way for now. Though her remote operator was no doubt already steering her back into the thick of the action . . .

The contest had barely lasted a minute, and already James's suit was badly damaged and his left arm was throbbing. A horrendous stench was filling his nostrils, turning his stomach—

Oh, God.

Striding through the smoke, James saw that one of the Shadows was down on its knees, burning. Was it Carrel or Van Diemen? He couldn't tell – but Herta was in front of it, shears extended and working their way right inside the suit; she must have sliced through the cables and command wires, breaking the Shadow's electronic backbone. Then she'd simply reached in with her other arm and poured on the flames. The man inside was soon ablaze.

James stared at the scene in horror. He suddenly recognized what was left of the features beneath the mask: they belonged to Van Diemen.

All at once something slammed into James from behind. Kitty again, pushing him forward. He turned, but she had already grabbed hold of his machine-gun arm.

He saw the strain in her face as she closed her eyes, unable to watch what she was being forced to do. James tried in vain to pull clear. *You can't give up!* he told himself. Servomotors whirred and caught as he fought to stop her twisting his arm behind his back, but it was no use; strain as he might, James knew he was losing the contest. The *Blutbanner* was simply stronger than the Shadow.

James imagined the VIPs in the gallery looking down as he fought for his life, some dispassionate, others excited. *See, the boy's friend is being forced to kill him by radio control! Now we can make our worst enemies serve us in any way we choose!* Were they placing bets on how long he would take to die? Were they shaking Grünner by the hand, congratulating him on his canny strategies—?

A great crash followed by a clanging, like two steam

locomotives running into each other head on, suddenly set James free. He spun round through 180 degrees, almost toppling over – to find that Carrel had come running out of the smoke and knocked Kitty aside. She grabbed hold of him, and they whirled in a nightmare dance across the floor.

James saw too that Herta had extricated herself from Van Diemen's exo-suit; it was left on the floor, steam pouring from the unit that bubbled uselessly on the back.

Now she was heading towards him.

This is it, James thought. *Do or die*. The Shadows came armed with five hundred rounds, and he started to let her have them. Bullets ricocheted wildly off her exo-suit, but they didn't slow her for a second. She brought up her shears and grabbed hold of the barrel of his machine gun, distorting the metal. The stream of bullets stopped, the weapon out of commission. James tore his arm away, backed off.

For a few seconds Herta paused while she manipulated controls inside the *Blutbanner*. With a heavy judder of compressed air, the shears attachment was ejected, and a metal spike, two feet long, slid out of the framework in its place. She pulled back her forearm, and then the spike was lashing out towards James's face.

He parried the blow with his gun arm. The spike caught in the framework, very nearly slicing clear through his forearm. They were jammed together now; he waited for her to pull away and stab him again, but instead he felt a strange thrum, as if a charge was building.

Electricity.

'Your friend Marcus didn't die for nothing!' Herta shouted.

'Thanks to him, we know exactly how much electric charge it will take to fry your suit, and you with it!'

She's going to send the force of a lightning bolt through me, James thought desperately. He brought up his free arm, ready to prime the hammer-punch. If he had to die, he'd die raining down blows on the steel bars that protected Herta's face.

But before he could launch his attack, James realized that the C-shaped length of wire-clad metal by his hand was growing hotter. The next moment Herta's suit was lurching towards him, drawn inexorably towards his hand.

Electro . . . All at once James made sense of the riddle. *It's an electro*magnet. *And it's started working* . . .

It's drawing on Herta's electric charge to power itself!

James almost laughed as he remembered Blade's words. *Turn an Achilles' heel to your advantage!*

Then Herta was falling forward: just as he triggered the hammer-punch, the *Blutbanner*'s neck was drawn to the end of his suit's metal fist. The electromagnet kept her pinned there, shaken around like a rag doll. Herta screamed as her body was jolted to and fro inside the suit. Cables pulled free and components sparked.

Then the wire about the iron core burned through, the electromagnet blew, and Herta was thrown backwards; as she did so, the spike came free. Desperately she launched her flame-thrower, and James felt the blistering heat – until she stumbled over Van Diemen's corpse and went flying with an almighty crash. The flames continued to gush out, the mechanism jammed.

James stood there, barely able to believe he was still alive – when he was brought back to reality by Kitty's scream. He turned to see Carrel's Shadow suit face-down on the ground – and looked away as the foot of her *Blutbanner* smashed down on the back of its head. Then she turned, marching over to help Herta.

James started forward grimly, ready to intercept her, but soon realized the danger. Herta's flame-thrower was still licking fiercely at the pressurized steam generator on Van Diemen's back.

'Kitty, look out!' James shouted – as the machine blew apart. Herta shrieked as the scalding water engulfed her. The sound died as quickly as she did.

Meanwhile Kitty had been thrown backwards by the blast. James hit the release button on his Shadow, and his battered frame sprang apart. He climbed out, but then felt a shaking hand close on his bruised arm.

It was Carrel.

'Great minds, huh?' he said. 'Lucky I jumped ship *before* she stamped my head to mush.'

'We've got to get Kitty out too,' James shouted. 'Come on—'

But it seemed that the powers up above had declared the demonstration over. The metal doors to the cavern burst open and four SS men entered, taking aim with their Mauser machine pistols.

28
Hell Down Here

James raised his hands in surrender, but Carrel turned and sprinted back towards his fallen Shadow. 'The machine gun—' he began.

His words were cut off as the SS guards opened fire, and his body jerked and spun in the hail of bullets. James threw himself to the floor beside Kitty, using her suit as cover. Panting for breath, his body aching, he knew with a terrible sense of finality that there was nothing more he could do now. The soldiers were already advancing, ready to empty their bullets into him.

'James?' Kitty shouted. 'I . . . I don't think the radio control is working any more.'

He realized that, face down in her exo-suit, she couldn't see what was coming. 'That's good,' he whispered. 'It's all right, now, Kitty. Quite all right. We have all—'

He was interrupted by a wild rev of engines as an armoured

car ploughed through the double doors. It braked sharply, skidding in a wide arc. The soldiers turned and opened fire on it. As they did so, Kitty fired her flame-thrower at their legs. 'I'm sorry!' she yelled as their uniforms caught fire and they cried out in pain, dropping their guns as they tried to put out the flames.

'*Quite all right*, he says,' Kitty grumbled.

A familiar face, though now trembling and terrified, popped up into sight from inside the D-8. 'Get in, then, for m-m-mercy's sake.'

'Perry?' James stood there, mouth open in amazement, until the sharp prang of the *Blutbanner*'s fast-release catch brought him back to reality. He helped Kitty out of the frame and over to the armoured car, lifting her up and dumping her unceremoniously inside before scrambling in after her. Perry quickly put the car in gear and headed back out.

James and Kitty clung to each other like half-drowned mariners washed up on the shore. 'Where the hell did you spring from, Perry?' James asked.

'The same bloody m-m-motorcar you left m-me to rot in! Blade's burgundy Tatra 77.' Perry screeched round a corner, his knuckles white on the steering wheel. 'When you went off to find your Ghost Train, I felt so tired, I had to have a kip. I was too scared to stay in the back, so I crawled into the trunk space, out of sight. When I woke up, the car was moving! It was heading for . . . well, for this dreadful hole, to be precise.'

'Grünner was rounding up all traces of Blade,' James explained.

'And brought you along for the ride.' Kitty's laugh bordered on the hysterical. 'Isn't that perfect, James? The hell we went through to end up here – and Mandy here gets chauffeur-driven!'

'I've been slowly starving to death,' Perry protested. 'I only came out of hiding when they started breaking the bloody car up for scrap.'

James looked at him in amazement. 'And, what, you over-powered the guards?'

'There was only one,' Perry admitted. 'He got such a shock when I jumped out, he banged the back of his head against that m–m–monumental furnace. I picked up his gun, and old Blade covered the other workers while I tied them up.'

'Blade?' Kitty began. 'But I thought . . .'

James quickly told her all about Blade's long game, trailing off as he recognized the route Perry was taking. 'Wait – we're going back to the foundry now? Why didn't Blade come with you?'

'He said there was something he needed to do first.'

'I suppose it's not such a bad idea to head for the foundry,' Kitty said uneasily. 'After all, Grünner's men will be expecting us to make for the exit. They're probably waiting there to pick us off as we approach.'

'And to escort their VIPs out,' James agreed. 'I can't imagine this will help Grünner's standing.'

'Or ours,' said Kitty. 'He's probably organizing a search-and-destroy mission right now.'

James put his head in his hands and rubbed his aching temples. Euphoria was already fading, to be replaced by the grim realization that safety was still a very long way away.

Perry brought the little armoured car to a halt at a cross-roads in the passages. 'Which way was it, now?'

'Right, I think,' James said.

'Shhh.' Kitty was sitting up straight, listening. 'Do you hear that?'

James held his breath. Then, over the quiet rush of fans pushing air down into the bunker, he did hear it: a *boom, boom, boom*, regular and precise. Getting louder and closer.

'Oh, no . . .' Kitty whispered.

Perry turned to look at her. 'What is it?'

It came round the corner to their left: the fourth Steel Shadow; the one that had been left on display and was, apparently, good to go.

Konstantin Grünner had climbed inside – no insulation suit, no helmet or mask – and now he was coming after them. A great metal machine-gun arm swung up and shook loose a hail of bullets. The armoured rear of the D-8 shook under the onslaught.

'Drive!' James pushed Kitty down flat and slapped Perry's shoulder. 'Go! *Go!*'

Perry hit the accelerator pedal and the car pulled away, just as the rear tyres burst under bullet-fire. The armoured car skidded drunkenly to the right and smashed against the wall, nearly throwing James loose. He ducked again as Grünner's guns went on blazing.

'Come on!' Perry yelled, slamming his fists against the steering wheel. With the back tyres blown, it felt as if the car were towing a parachute.

'Grünner's gaining on us!' Kitty shouted.

'Park this thing across the corridor, Perry,' James told him. 'Block the way. It might slow him down while we run for it.'

Perry heaved hard left on the wheel, and the vehicle's

battered front bumper chewed into the rock of the corridor wall. Kitty jumped down and James scrambled after her, then opened the driver's door for Perry and hauled him out. Grünner fired again, and James led his friends in a crouching charge for the cover of the next corner, the D-8 taking the bullets behind them like a barricade.

'We've got to reach the foundry!' James shouted. 'The Shadow is Blade's brainchild. He'll know best how to stop it. He'll have a plan.'

'He'd better,' Kitty panted, keeping pace with Perry just behind James. The sledgehammer slam of metal on metal echoed behind them; Grünner was already fighting his way through.

James's lungs felt like they might burst as he finally saw the foundry's loading-bay doors ahead. As he led the others inside, he saw that he was right. Blade *did* have a plan. Sweating and dishevelled, he was sitting in his wheelchair beside some kind of mortar – aimed straight at them.

'Good God. I didn't think anyone would survive that demonstration.' Blade searched their faces. 'Carrel, Van Diemen – are they . . . ?'

'Dead,' James hissed, gasping for breath. 'I'd have joined them if not for that electromagnet you installed. But they helped take down Herta, at least.'

Blade nodded and looked away.

James motioned for Kitty and Perry to close and bolt the loading-bay doors, then turned back to Blade. 'Sir, Grünner's coming after us. He's in the last of the Steel Shadows.'

'The last . . . ?' Blade turned to the mortar beside him. 'Well, this is a Blade-Rise 12 mortar. Found it in the storeroom over there.' He gestured painfully behind the workshop. 'One of the weapons I sold to the Nazis. I suppose it's fitting that I use it now.'

'Sir, you said it yourself – we need more than a mortar to stop a Steel Shadow.' James started towards the storeroom. 'Let's see what other weapons we can find—'

He broke off as the foundry doors buckled inward under some colossal impact.

Kitty flinched. 'Grünner.'

'No time to get more firepower,' Blade said, as another ringing blow made the huge steel hinges jumped in the wall.

'Wait. The Tatra . . .' James breathed. The burgundy one was partially dismantled, but the silver 77 was still intact; he raced over to open the driver's door. 'It's not quite a tank, but it should slow Grünner down. You two take cover in the other.'

'But James—' Kitty protested.

'Come on. While we can.' Perry started to drag her away. 'Knock him flat, James.'

James swung himself into the driver's seat and started the engine first time. He looked over at Blade. 'If I get this wrong . . .'

'No.' Blade had got out of the wheelchair; he was trembling as he held himself upright, looking down at his misshapen hands. 'I told you, Bond – use your time well, every last second. Whatever cards you're dealt, play them as best you can.'

There was another splintering crash, and the door was finally smashed in. Grünner stood there, kicking away the remains.

James revved the Tatra's engine and then released the

handbrake. With a screech of rubber, the sleek silver motorcar accelerated towards the Steel Shadow.

'Ha! You really think so, little boy?' Grünner raised his metal arms high above his head, and brought them down on the vehicle's bonnet just a fraction before it hit.

James cried out as the impact threw him forwards. He cracked his head on the steering wheel as the windscreen shattered and the suspension collapsed. He stared, dazed, as a large metal claw pushed inside and groped for his neck through a curtain of steam.

Grünner's still standing, James realized. *I failed. I—*

'Get the hell away, boy!' Blade bellowed. He was still standing, leaning on the mortar as his thick fingers grappled with a shell. 'My whole life I've maintained that weapons save lives – don't you damn well prove me wrong now . . .'

James grasped the handle, threw open the door and rolled out before Grünner's steel pincers could get hold of him. With the breath still beaten from his body, he crawled across the filthy foundry floor towards the burgundy Tatra. Kitty pushed open the door and she and Perry helped him clamber inside.

'Not a hope, Blade.' Grünner forced the caved-in hulk of the silver car away from him and raised his machine-gun arm. 'You'll be dead before you can fire at me . . .'

'I'm not about to fire at you, Grünner.' Blade turned stiffly away to face the furnace, and stuffed the shell down hard inside the mortar.

'Oh my God . . .' James slammed the Tatra's door as the shell whooshed out, closed his eyes as Blade's twisted body jumped and jerked with a never-known freedom as it was thrown forward by Grünner's bullets, and then—

The explosion was incandescent, its thunder like hell cracking open. James was thrown against his friends as the Tatra was sent skidding across the ground.

James peered out of the car window as the echoes of the blast petered out. Grünner still stood, immovable, his high-pitched squeal of a giggle building into hysteria. 'You lose, Blade! You lose.'

Kitty bit her knuckle. 'After all that, we're still going to die.'

Perry pulled at the Tatra's door handle. 'Come on, we can still run—'

'Wait.' James pointed at the furnace. 'I think Blade knew just what he was doing . . .'

Hairline cracks had formed in the base of the furnace where the mortar had struck. One of the cracks widened, and a stream of white-hot copper, heated to more than 12,000 degrees centigrade, burst from inside.

Grünner's laughter cut dead as his hateful face filled with horrified disbelief. 'No. *No!*'

'Oh, my life.' Kitty crossed herself. 'There must be industrial coolers on the level below us, to drain the heat from that furnace. Vats of cold water. If the molten copper touches it . . .'

James was no boffin, but he knew that the difference in temperature between superheated molten metal and cold water would cause massive explosions of vapour, huge pressure waves that—

This time, the explosion was truly colossal. A tsunami of

260

white-hot copper and debris was thrown up from the base of the furnace. Blade's body simply disappeared as coke, cast iron and slag blasted through the air. Moulds and machinery were torn loose and tossed about. The burgundy Tatra was shunted out of the open loading-bay doors to smash against the wall; James clung onto the seat as Kitty and Perry were thrown against him.

Through the broken passenger window he saw Grünner standing in the eye of the storm. The molten copper had pooled around him, setting fire to the tyres of the silver car beside him. *The heat must be unbearable*, James thought. Grünner tried to retreat, but the molten copper had welded the feet of his exo-suit to the floor. He couldn't move, couldn't stop the slow toasting of his flesh.

By the time his heart finally gave out, Konstantin Grünner had been roasted black, arms still reaching for the heavens from inside his metal coffin.

29

Peace and Goodwill

Shaking, James helped Kitty and Perry out of the battered Tatra. The foundry and the workshop were all but consumed by flames. He looked at the remains of the Steel Shadow, and wondered if it was still transmitting its signal; if the searchers were still hoping to be led into the darkest corners of Nazi science.

Kitty broke into a trembling run, and James and Perry fell into step beside her. 'Mr Blade . . . He never stood a chance.'

James nodded. 'He played his hand the best he could.'

'But the storeroom back there is chock full of amm-m-mo,' Perry said. 'If that goes up. . .'

Kitty swore as the ceiling started to fall in. 'The whole place is already falling apart.'

'We have to keep going,' James said.

Within minutes, they reached the wreck of the armoured car they'd abandoned; it had been torn almost in two by

Grünner in the last Steel Shadow. Then they heard the sound of an engine approaching. James, Perry and Kitty hid behind the wreck as another armoured car rolled past the crossroads from left to right ahead of them, crowded with injured soldiers. One was crying over and over, '*Müssen wir zur Abfahrt . . .*'

'They're making for the exit,' James realized. 'There must be a roadway in and out, as well as the train line.'

'Of course. The Tatras were driven inside.' Perry climbed over the wreck and hurried along the corridor. 'Follow that m–m–motorcar!'

James hurried after him with Kitty, and was about to take the lead when further explosions shook through the floor and he fell beside Perry. The boys clung together as dust and rubble showered about them, but Kitty was thrown down a side-tunnel, rolling over and over.

'Kitty, no!' James reached helplessly after her, covering his head as more debris collapsed from the ceiling. 'No—!'

'Yes!' Kitty hollered back in reply. 'Yes, yes, YES!' James and Perry looked at each other as the trembling in the floor subsided – then heard the diesel growl of an engine. Warily, James got to his feet and waded through the thick dust haze into the side-tunnel.

Kitty was perched on the passenger seat of an abandoned D8. 'Come on then, boys, for heaven's sake!'

James checked that Perry was safe and following, then climbed into the driver's seat. He drove carefully over the debris in the corridor then accelerated away through the wide passages.

'You'd think they'd pin up an exit sign,' Perry fretted.

As James rounded a corner, he braked sharply at the sight

of another armoured car travelling ahead of them. 'With luck, this lot will know the way.'

He followed the car out at a safe distance, onto a service road that led up to the surface. Lights hung down from the cracked roof, flickering, and fresh smoke was following them out from the doomed Nazi base. James thought of Blade and Whittaker, of Carrel and Van Diemen, and the sacrifices they'd made. Most of all, he thought of Marcus. The lightning strike that had killed his friend back at Fettes had set James on the path to avenging him – and let him play his part in bringing down the whole sickening project.

He heard Blade's voice in his head: *Weapons save lives . . .*

And all at once James thought: *Is that what I'm becoming?*

He pressed down on the pedal. *Let this whole place burn to dust. Let every trace of the exo-suits be gone.*

If we fight wars as if we're machines, how much worse will our conflicts become?

Kitty yawned loudly.

'How can you think of sleep at a time like this, Drift,' Perry muttered. 'What kind of a desperate spy and brigand are you?'

'A tired one,' said Kitty, 'who wants to go home.'

'Me too.' James smiled as he spotted daylight up ahead. The exit barriers stood open, the sentry boxes abandoned.

They emerged into the German pine forest. Behind them, black smoke poured out of the entrance, and they felt tremors from deep underground. But James took a deep breath of fresh air; it hurt his lungs, telling him that he was still alive; that he still had a chance to do better. His first priority was to find a public telephone so he could call Aunt Charmian and tell her he loved her; that he would be home with her again *so schnell wie möglich*. With luck and swift transport, he could keep his promise and travel back to England tomorrow on Christmas Eve to join her in time for the big day. Time was precious, and there were many things left unsaid.

'Kitty . . .' James turned to her. 'There's something I need to know; something only you can tell me.'

Her eyes met his through her glasses, dark and solemn. 'Yes?'

'Yes.' He smiled. 'What time's the next train from Düsseldorf to The Hague, and can Perry and I stay over at your place tonight?'

'Splendid idea,' Perry said brightly. 'Company and a little looking after.'

Kitty raised a mock-haughty eyebrow. 'Not too boring for you?'

'Right now, "boring" sounds like heaven.'

'Well, I do believe there's a diesel that leaves Düsseldorf at 18.03. And yes, Daddy will be so glad to find that I'm safe and sound, he'll agree to anything. He usually does.' Kitty leaned in and kissed James on the lips. 'A happy Christmas to you, Mr Bond.'

James looked at her and smiled. 'And I didn't even notice the mistletoe.'

'Never m-m-mind the m-mush,' said Perry. 'There'd just better be a restaurant car on this train, that's all. I'm starved.'

James smiled. 'I only hope we can find our way to the station.'

'What? But we m-must!' Perry stood up in the armoured car and peered around. 'Hello? Directions, anyone?'

'Maybe we'll pass Blade's Shadow-hunters on their way here,' James said, 'and they can give us pointers . . .'

'You know, I still can't believe Blade was on the side of the angels after all.'

Kitty snorted. 'You think there's an angelic side to *any* of this, Mandy . . . ?'

James drove on through the forest, joining in with the banter, aware that none of them could bear to talk about what they'd seen down in the bunker; not yet. There would be a time for that, he supposed. In the meantime, as the first cold stars speckled the twilight, they could celebrate their survival.

Feel the joy of clinging on.

Acknowledgements

I am extremely grateful for the enthusiasm and generosity of Gemma Gray and Craig Marshall at Fettes College, Edinburgh, who have helped me so much in researching the school as James would have found it.

I would also like to thank several Old Fettesians for sharing their personal recollections of the school in the 1930s: Mr Iain MacLaren, Dr Hugh MacPhail, Sir Robert Sanders, Professor Ian Stewart, Mr Ian Hall and Mr Neil Irvine.

Gratitude too to Rachel Griffiths-Johnson for supplying judo expertise and Evelien Pieterse at Het Spoorwegmuseum in Utrecht for assistance with period Dutch rail detail.

For their work on helping to shape this novel, special thanks to Sophie Wilson, Ruth Knowles, Corinne Turner, Jo Lane, Mainga Bhima and Philippa Milnes-Smith.

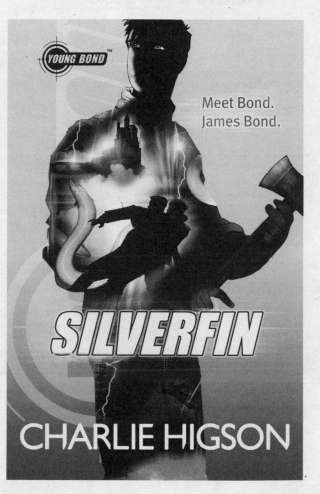

Blood in the Water

The boy crept up to the fence and looked around. There was the familiar sign . . .

KEEP OUT!
PRIVATE PROPERTY.
TRESPASSERS WILL BE SHOT.

And hanging next to it, just to make sure that the message was clearly understood, were the bodies of several dead animals. Strung up like criminals, wire twisted round their broken necks.

He knew them so well; they were almost like old friends. There were rabbits with their eyes pecked out, tattered black crows with broken wings, a couple of foxes, a few rats, even a wildcat and a pine marten. In all the days he'd been coming here the boy had watched them slowly rotting away, until some of them were little more than flaps of dirty leather and yellow bones. But there were a couple of fresh ones since yesterday, a squirrel and another fox.

Which meant that someone had been back.

In his thick brown poacher's jacket and heavy green cotton trousers the boy was fairly well camouflaged, but he knew that he had to be on his guard. The signs and the fifteen-foot-high fence entwined with rusted barbed wire were enough to keep most people away, but there were the men as well. The estate workers. A couple of times he'd spotted a pair of them walking the perimeter, shotguns cradled in their elbows, and although it was a few days since he'd seen anyone up here, he knew that they were never far away.

At the moment, however, apart from the sad corpses of the animals, he was alone.

The afternoon light was fading into evening, taking all the detail from the land with it. Here, on this side of the fence, among the thick gorse and juniper and low rowan trees, he was well hidden, but soon ... soon he was going under the wire, and on the other side the tree cover quickly fell away. He could just see the scrubby grassland, dotted with small rocks, which sloped down towards the peaty brown waters of the loch.

Soon he'd be fishing those waters for the first time.

The trek up here had taken nearly an hour. School had finished at four o'clock and he'd had nothing to eat since lunchtime. He knew that once he was inside the fence there would be no time to eat, so he slipped his knapsack from his shoulders and took out his ham sandwiches and a crisp apple. He ate them quickly, gazing up at the mountain that stood watch over the loch. It looked cold and barren and unfeeling. It had stood here for millions of years, and would stand for millions more. The boy felt small and alone, and when the wind vibrated the wires in the fence, making them moan, he shivered.

Before the new laird had come there had been no fence. The land had been open for miles around. The loch had been a good fishing spot then, and the old laird hadn't been bothered by those few hardy folk who braved the long haul up from the village. What did he care if one or two of his trout went missing each year? There were always plenty more.

But that had all changed when the new fellow had taken over, five years ago. Everything had changed. The land was fenced off. The locals were kept away.

But not this evening.

The boy chucked his crusts and apple core into the bushes, then crawled over to the fence and pulled away the pieces of turf that covered the hole he'd dug.

The turfs rested on a grid of strong sticks, which he quickly removed. The ground up here was rock hard and full of stones, so it had taken the boy several days to hack this narrow tunnel under the fence, scrabbling in the dirt with his mother's gardening tools. Last night he'd finally finished the work, but it had been too late to do anything more so he'd reluctantly gone home.

Today he'd been too excited to concentrate at school, all he could think about was coming up here, ducking through the hole, going down to the loch and taking some fish from under the new laird's nose.

He smiled as he made his way into the hole and pushed aside the old piece of sacking that he'd used to cover the entrance at the other end. His tackle bag and knapsack he easily pulled through the tunnel behind him, but his father's rod, even when broken down into three sections, was too long to fit through, so he went back, took it out of its case and slotted the pieces one by one through the fence.

Five minutes later, his rod in one hand, his tackle bag in the other, he was darting between the rocks down towards the water.

Before he'd died, his father had described Loch Silverfin to him many times. He'd often come up here as a lad to fish, and it was his stories that had inspired the boy. His father had loved fishing, but he had been wounded by a shell blast in the Great War of 1914 and the pieces of shrapnel buried in his flesh had slowly ruined his health, so that by the end he could barely walk, let alone hold a fishing rod.

The boy was excited; he was the man of the house now. He pictured the look on his mother's face when he brought home a fine fresh trout, but there was more to it than that. Fishing is a challenge – and this was the biggest challenge of all.

Loch Silverfin was shaped like a huge fish, long and narrow and fanning out into a rough tail at this end. It was named after a giant salmon from Scottish folklore – *It'Airgid*, which in Gaelic meant Silverfin. Silverfin was a fearsome salmon who was bigger and stronger than all the other salmon in Scotland. The giant Cachruadh had tried to catch him, and after an epic battle lasting twenty days the fish had at last swallowed the giant, and kept him in his belly for a year before spitting him out in Ireland.

Legend had it that Silverfin still lived in the loch, deep in its dark waters. The boy didn't quite believe that, but he did believe that there were some mighty fish here.

The loch looked wilder than he'd imagined it; steep, sheer rocks bordered most of the shore beneath the mountain, and a few stunted rushes were all that grew. Way down at the other end, partially shrouded in the mist rising off the water, he could just make out the square grey shape of the castle, sitting on the little island that formed the eye of the fish. But it was too far away, and the light was too bad, for anyone to see him from there.

He scouted along the shingle for a good place to cast, but it wasn't very encouraging. The shoreline was too exposed. If any of the estate workers came anywhere near, they'd be bound to spot him.

The thought of the estate workers made him glance around uneasily and he realized how scared he was. They weren't local men and they didn't mix with the folk in the village. They lived up here in a group of low, ugly, concrete sheds the laird had built near the gatehouse. He'd turned his castle into a fortress and these men were his private army. The boy had no desire to bump into any of them this evening.

He was just thinking that he might have to chuck it in and go home when he saw the perfect spot. At the tip of the fish's tail there was a fold in the edge of the loch where a stream entered. The water here was almost completely hidden from view by the high cliffs all round. He knew that the trout would wait here for food to wash down the stream.

Twenty feet or so out in the lake there stood a single, huge granite rock. If he could get there and shelter behind it, he could easily cast towards the stream without being seen by either man or fish.

He sat in the grass to pull his waterproof waders on. It had been a real slog, lugging them up here, but he needed them now. They slipped over his clothes like a huge pair of trousers attached to a pair of boots, coming right up to his chest, where they were supported by shoulder straps. They smelt of damp and old rubber.

He fastened his reel to his cane rod and quickly threaded the line through the loops. He'd already tied on his fly line, so he took out his favourite fly, a silver doctor, and knotted it to the end.

He skirted round the water's edge until he was level with the big rock, and then waded out into the water towards it. It took him a few minutes to pick his way across, feeling with his feet for safe places to step. The bottom of the loch was slippery and uneven and at one point he had to make a long detour round a particularly deep area, but once he neared the rock it became shallower again and he grew more confident.

He found a good solid place to stand and from here he had a clear cast over towards the stream. He checked his fly, played out his line, then, with a quick backwards jerk of his arm, he whipped it up into a big loop behind him, before flicking it forward, where it snaked out across the water and landed expertly at the edge of the loch.

That part had gone very well, but it turned out to be the only part that did. He didn't get a single touch. Try as he might, he couldn't attract any fish on to his hook. He cast and recast, he changed his fly, he tried nearer and further – nothing.

It was getting darker by the minute and he would have to head for home soon, so, in desperation, he decided to try a worm. He'd brought a box of them with him just in case. He dug it out of his pocket, chose a nice fat lobworm and speared it on a hook, where it wriggled enticingly. What fish could resist that?

He had to be more careful casting the worm and he flicked it gently, underarm, away from him. Then he got his first bite so quickly it took him completely by surprise; the worm had scarcely landed in the water before he felt a strong tug. He tugged back to get a good hold in the fish's mouth, then prepared for a fight.

Whatever it was on the end of his line, it was tough. It pulled this way and that, furiously, and he watched his rod bow and dip towards the water. He let the fish run for a few moments to tire it, then slowly reeled it in. Still it zigzagged about in the water in a frantic attempt to get free. The boy grinned from ear to ear – it was a big one and wasn't going to give up easily.

Maybe he'd caught the awesome Silverfin himself!

For some time he played it, gradually reeling in as much line as he dared, praying that the hook wouldn't slip or the line snap . . . This was a very delicate business, he had to feel the fish, had to try and predict its wild movements. Then, at last, he had it near, he could see something moving in the water on the end of his line; he took a deep breath, hauled it up and his heart sank . . .

It wasn't Silverfin, it was an eel, and, even as he realized it, something brushed against his legs, nearly knocking him off balance. He looked down and saw a second eel darting away through the water.

Well, there was nothing else to do: he had to land the thing to retrieve his hook and line. He hoisted it out of the water and tried to grab hold of it, but it was thrashing about in the air, twisting itself into knots, snarling itself round the line, and, as he reached for it, it tangled round his arm. It was a monstrous thing; it must have been at least two feet long, streaked with slime, cold and sleek and brownish grey.

He hated eels.

He tried to pull it off his arm, but it was tremendously powerful and single-minded, like one big, writhing muscle, and it simply twisted itself round his other arm. He swore and shook it, nearly losing his footing. He told himself to keep calm and he carefully moved closer to the rock, which he managed to slap the eel against and pin it down. Still it squirmed and writhed like a mad thing, even though its face showed nothing. It was a cold, dead mask, flattened and wide, with small, dark eyes.

Finally he was able to hold its head still enough to get a grip on the deeply embedded hook, and he began to twist and wrench it free. It was hard work. He'd used a big hook and the end of it was barbed to stop it from slipping out once it had stuck into a fish's mouth.

'Come on,' he muttered, grunting with the effort, and then – he wasn't sure how it happened, it went too fast – all at the same time, the hook came loose, the eel gave a frantic jerk and, the next thing he knew, the hook was in his thumb.

The pain was awful, like a freezing bolt shooting all the way up his arm. He gasped and clamped his teeth together and managed not to shout – it was a still evening and any sound up here would travel for miles, bouncing off the high rocks and water.

The eel slithered away and plopped back into the water. A wave of sickness passed over the boy and he swayed, nearly fainting. For a long while he couldn't bring himself to look at his hand, but at last he forced his eyes down. The hook had gone in by his palm and right through the fleshy base of his thumb, where it stuck out on the other side. There was a horrible gash and flap of skin where the barb had broken through on its way out. Blood was already oozing from the wound and dripping into the icy water.

He was lucky that the point had come out and not stayed sunk deep inside his flesh, but he knew that he couldn't just pull the hook free; it had the curved barb on one end and a ring on the other where the line was attached.

There was only one thing to do.

He rested his rod against the rock and with his other hand he reached into his tackle bag and got out his cutters.

He took a deep breath, clamped the cutters on the end of the hook where the line was knotted, pressed them together and – *SNAK* – the end broke off. Then, quickly, so that he didn't have time to think about it, he pulled the hook out by the barb. A fresh pain hit him and he leant against the rock to stop his knees from giving way.

He knew he wouldn't do any more fishing today. He started to cry. All that effort for this: a lousy eel and a wounded thumb. It just wasn't fair. Then he pulled himself together. He had to do something about his situation. Blood was flowing freely from the wound. He washed his hand in the loch, the blood turning black and oily in the cold water, then he took a handkerchief from his shirt pocket and wrapped it tightly round his thumb. He was shaking badly now and felt very light-headed. As carefully as he could, he secured all his gear and set off back to the shore, wading through the dark slick in the water that his blood had made.

And then he felt it.

A jolt against his legs.

And then another.

More eels. But what were they doing? Eels never attacked people. They ate scraps and frogs and small fish . . .

He pressed on; maybe he'd imagined it.

No. There it came again. A definite bump.

He peered down into the water and in the dim light he saw them . . . hundreds of them, a seething mass in the water, balled up and tangled together like the writhing hair of some underwater Medusa. Eels. All round him. Eels of all sizes, from tiny black slivers to huge brutes twice the length of the one he'd caught. The water was alive with them, wriggling, twisting, turning over and over . . . They surged against his legs and he stumbled. His wounded hand splashed down into the water and he felt hungry mouths tug the bloodied handkerchief from his hand and drag it away into the murky depths.

He panicked, tried to run for the shore, but slipped and, as his feet scrabbled to get a hold, he stumbled into the deep part of the loch. For a moment his head went under and he was aware of eels brushing against his face. One wrapped itself round his neck and he pulled it away with his good hand. Then his feet touched the bottom and he pushed himself up to the surface. He gulped in a mouthful of air, but his waders were filled with water now . . . water and eels, he could feel them down his legs, trapped by the rubber.

He knew that if he could get his feet up he might float, but in his terror and panic his body wasn't doing what he wanted it to do.

'Help,' he screamed, 'help me!' Then he was under again, and this time the water seemed even thicker with eels. The head of one probed his mouth and clamped its jaws on to his lip. He tore it away, and his anger gave him fresh strength. He forced his feet downwards, found a solid piece of ground, and then he was up out of the water again. All about him the surface of the lake was seething with frenzied eels.

'Help, help . . . Please, somebody, help me . . .' His mouth hurt and blood was dripping from where the eel had bitten his lip. He thrashed at the water, but nothing would scare the beasts away.

And then out of the corner of his eye he saw some- one . . . a man running along the far shore. He waved crazily and yelled for help again. He didn't care any more if it was an estate worker ... anything was better than being trapped here with these terrible fish.

The man ran closer and dived into the loch.

No, the boy wanted to shout. Not in the water. Not in with the eels. But then he saw a head bob to the surface. It was all right. He was going to be rescued.

The man swam towards him with strong, crude strokes. Thank God. Thank God. He was going to be saved. For a while he almost forgot about the eels and just concentrated on the man's steady progress towards him, but then a fresh surge knocked him off balance and he was once more in the snaking embrace of a hundred frenzied coils of cold flesh.

No. No, he would not let them beat him. He whirled his arms, kicked his legs and he was out again, gasping and spluttering for breath.

But where was the man? He had disappeared.

The boy looked round desperately. Had the eels got him?

It was quiet; the movement in the water seemed to have stopped, almost as if none of this had ever happened ...

And then he saw him, under the water, a big, dark shape among the fish, and suddenly, with a great splash, he rose out of the loch and the boy screamed.

The last thing he saw before he sank back into the black depths of the water was the man's face; only it wasn't a man's face ... It was an eel's face, a nightmare face; chinless, with smooth, grey, utterly hairless skin pulled tight across it, and fat, blubbery lips that stretched almost all the way back to where the ears should be. The front of the face was deformed, pushed forward, so that the nose was hideously flattened, with splayed nostrils, and the bulging eyes were forced so wide apart that they didn't look in any way human.

The ghastly thick lips parted and a wet belching hiss erupted.

Then the waters closed over the boy and he knew nothing more.